I Am So

I Am Sophia

A Novel

By
J. F. ALEXANDER

RESOURCE *Publications* · Eugene, Oregon

Resource Publications
An Imprint of Wipf and Stock Publishers
199 W. 8th Ave., Suite 3
Eugene, OR 97401

www.wipfandstock.com

PAPERBACK ISBN: 978-1-7252-9186-7
HARDCOVER ISBN: 978-1-7252-9185-0
EBOOK ISBN: 978-1-7252-9187-4

03/17/21

For my son.
May your soul have deep roots and strong wings.

Contents

Acknowledgments

A good teacher is a great blessing. Among the ancient and modern seekers, seers, and saints who have influenced this theologically engaged novel, I would like to acknowledge three whose work led to especially important inflection points in my spiritual journey to date: the mythologist Joseph Campbell, the theologian Elizabeth A. Johnson, and the ecumenical Franciscan teacher Richard Rohr. Readers familiar with Rohr's work will readily perceive its influence on the novel, which reveals itself most plainly in the first part of Chapter 18.

Without necessarily endorsing the novel's contents, theological or otherwise, several friends and acquaintances provided criticism on early versions or other much appreciated assistance. Thanks are due especially to David Bird, Claudia Fischer, Audrey Greathouse, Katherine A. Helm, Eric K. Hinds, Lakshmi Karan, Julia McCray-Goldsmith, Shannon Mullen O'Keefe, Scot Sherman, Susan Van Norman, and Andreas Wendlberger and to past and present members of the Bay Area Stanford alumni fiction writers' group, including Nancy Baker, Brianna Griffin, Joann McEntire, Crystal Tindell Seiler, Tracy Turner, Jennifer Wang, and JoAnne Wetzel. Any and all errors are mine alone.

I appreciate the creative, capable, and reliable staff of Wipf & Stock Publishers and Resource Publications, including but not limited to Shannon Carter, Ian Creeger, Zechariah Mickel, and Matthew Wimer.

It would be impossible to express the depth of my love and appreciation for my wife and son, who suffered gracefully through all of this; for my parents, Jim Sr. and Jane, who first incarnated love to me; for Alice and Herb, Ethel Jane, Mary and Bryan, Steven and Bobbi, my wonderful in-laws, and the rest of my family, who have encouraged me through the decades; and for the vibrant, diverse, welcoming faith community at Trinity Episcopal Cathedral in downtown San José, California.

And then there is the dancing, demanding, laughing One who so filled me with thoughts and longings that I had no choice but to write. Regardless how wavering and compromised an artist's faith may be, a sincere desire for wisdom and beauty may unlock ethereal vaults filled with ideas, motifs, and unanticipated connections. When this happens, one may feel oneself to be as much a simple conduit as a creator: the work's virtues mysteriously outstrip the sum of the artist's meager gifts.

J. F. Alexander
Season of Epiphany 2021

PART ONE

What now are all these churches but tombs and sepulchers for God?

—Friedrich Nietzsche

1

The Last Bishop

"See that crisscross up there? The cultists' magical hero was murdered when his enemies nailed him to crisscrossed planks of wood."

A little girl gasps.

"Oh, but don't you worry." The graying tour guide winks at the girl. "You see, he got resuscitated and flew up to a land in the sky."

Momentarily the center of the adults' attention, she brightens and claps her hands together. "Was it Meres? My aunt and uncle live there."

"No, my dear. The G-Zeus story comes from before people lived off-earth. The cultists believed he went to a place up in the clouds where there were shiny people who had wings like birds."

"Ooh," says the girl. She looks up at the scrap of blue sky visible between the summits of the towers surrounding the cathedral. "That's silly!" The girl's mother puts a hand on her shoulder.

The cathedral is the sixth attraction on the guide's "Oldtime Sanef" walking tour. Like other earthside nations, Sanef has suffered through its portion of perpetual crisis—rising heat, rising sea, rising costs. Yet it never ceases to attract affluent tourists, refugees from parched inland nations, and investments by the international cartels. Gleaming two-hundred-story towers dominate central Sanef's skyline from Yerba Buena halfway to the Golden Gate.

Wedged among the towers, the old cathedral property fills a city block, punching a deep hole in the crowded cityscape. Much as the surrounding towers dwarf the cathedral, so the cathedral's sculpted concrete walls dwarf the dozen tourists and their guide. They stand clustered together near the building's main entrance: a weathered portico framing a pair of heavy, locked doors. Brittle gothic façades practically ooze ancient nightmare.

A young man wearing a *Sanef National University* tee shirt tentatively raises a hand. "People used to come here to perform bizarre ritual sacrifices, didn't they?"

"Excellent question. They not only 'used to' come here, I'm afraid." The guide meets the eyes of his listeners one by one. This is the moment that makes this attraction worth the stop. "There are still a few cultists who gather inside there every week and pretend to drink blood."

"Ugh," blurts a middle-aged woman. She covers her mouth.

"Gross!" squeals the little girl.

"Intriguing," pronounces the student. He purses his lips. "I once accessed on the net that this cult had a special class of shamans who led their metafiz rituals."

"As I understand it," the guide says, "the fellow in charge here is the very last G-Zeus shaman in the entire System. His title is 'bishop,' which means 'overseer.' In ancient Europe, the G-Zeus cult's overseers basically ruled everything."

A balding man harrumphs. "Thank good the System has outgrown metafiz. What stupid inefficiency." Heads bob in unanimous agreement.

The student raises his hand again. "How can it be that they're still—" A distant but powerful burst of noise interrupts him. It thunders among the towers for several seconds before gradually fading to a low, tinkling rumble. The tourists and their guide crane their necks to scan their surroundings.

"Sounds like the explosion was high up in one of the towers," mutters the balding man.

"From down here, it's impossible to tell where it was," says the guide. He wipes perspiration from his neck. "To be safe, let's get under the little roof here for a few minutes, just in case any debris comes down from above."

The tourists huddle together under the cathedral's portico as the guide cranes his neck again. "Batshit nuns," he mutters.

The explosion kills dozens in an upper tower restaurant a few blocks from the cathedral. Surprisingly, a week passes with no follow-on bombings in central Sanef—the copycats are lying low. *Perhaps the summer heat is making it too uncomfortable for mass murder*, thinks Peter Halabi bitterly.

Peter should be comfortable enough. He's tucked away in the cool, dark grotto that is the cathedral's tiny side chapel—"the Chapel of the Nativity," as attested by a tarnished plaque. But his jaw aches. He's been grinding his teeth at night again. He's twenty-nine and has a flexible work schedule, so he wouldn't strike one as a likely candidate for a stress-related condition. But he doesn't feel twenty-nine. In his bones, he feels millennia old.

Probably going to have to get one of those mouthguard things.

More negative thoughts dance through Peter's mind until he catches himself. He realizes he hasn't been praying for several minutes, at least. With a sigh, he lifts his knees from his padded kneeler and sits back onto the antique wooden chair behind him. Its grumpy creaking momentarily echoes through the cathedral, then silence returns. At almost any moment, these thick walls enclose the closest thing to complete silence in all of bustling central Sanef.

Wax candles—Peter insists on "real" ones, with actual fire—project shimmying light imps along the chapel's altar. They wordlessly cavort against the side of the gold-colored box resting on the altar. This box is the tabernacle: the center of the Christworshippers' universe.

To Peter's left, the cathedral's cavernous nave broods in pitch-black stillness. It feels to him as if it's been years since anyone has turned on the lights in there. For all one can tell, a thousand silent saints or bloodthirsty bandits might be lurking within. Had any visitor ever dropped by the chapel, he might be excused for nervously glancing over his shoulder into the darkness from time to time. Peter doesn't glance, though. He's spent his whole life in this place.

Instead, he looks up at the Virgin Mary. As she has done since long before his birth, she stands motionless on her hillside. A silvery stream flows past her and the infant in her arms, widening until it reaches the bottom of the mural. If paint could miraculously transfigure itself into water, the stream would gush down onto the gold-painted tabernacle and chapel altar. Darkness looms over Mary's shoulders, but it's a darkness which differs from the nave's. It's a pregnant darkness: pregnant with stars. Alas, in that eternal moment the starry heavens painted overhead appear to escape the notice of Mary and the baby Jesus. Both stare forward, fixing earnest gazes on a distant point above and behind Peter.

If only God would, just once, cause her to look down and flash me a smile of encouragement, Peter thinks to himself. *Just something to strengthen my faith. How much would a little trick like that cost the Almighty One? It would be enough of a miracle for me—if there ever was such a thing as miracles.*

He stares at Mary's unmoving face for a minute, sighs, and looks away. He holds up his hands and begins naming digits out loud. "Dorcas, Martin, Phoebe and Junia, Nastya. Lupe and Marco, Bede and Felipe, Thad."

Peter turns his palms toward the mural and addresses Jesus: "Now I can count our entire flock on just two hands." Add one bishop, and that makes eleven.

But there had been *twelve* tribes of Israel.

There had been *twelve* apostles.

When they were still twelve, Peter felt that they were still *the Church—* that a seed of hope remained. But now, even that low threshold has been crossed.

Mother would have reminded Peter that the loss of a human life is worthier of contemplation than the issue of how many Christworshippers are left in the System, as important as that may be. He guiltily turns his thoughts back to the late Matthias Jian: grandfather, lifelong Christworshipper, and random victim of yet another radical Isnotist suicide bombing.

Peter kneels and resumes his prayers, now offering thanksgivings for Matthias's life. In the candlelight, Peter's gangly frame casts a long, wavering shadow. His dark, wavy hair and brown eyes complement a fairer-than-average complexion. Although he grew up in Sanef, his fair skin tone occasionally leads people to assume he's a refugee from one of the inland nations. Peter is unpartnered, but he has taken no vow of celibacy: the bishops of Grace Cathedral have always followed the rules in the dusty canon-book of the cathedral's founding denomination, which permit clergy to marry. A ro-male, Peter simply has not met a desirable ro-feme his age who could respect or even understand his strange vocation. More than one love interest concluded, without saying it in so many words, that his attachment to metafiz indicated a mental imbalance.

Enough other people did say so in words, however. After Peter's schoolmates learned about his mother's job, he had to absorb every name in the book. *Cultist. Nutjob. Metafizzler. Throwback.*

Even as an adult, Peter must occasionally deal with shock or hostility when people learn of his vocation. It isn't that Sanefers are especially closed-minded, Peter knows. Sanef has long maintained its famous "anything goes" culture—well, anything except poverty and metafiz. In any event, Peter blames only himself. If his faith were stronger, none of it would matter to him. If only God would give him a sign, an answer beyond bleak and stubborn silence!

It wasn't like this for Mother, Peter thinks. Bishop Priscilla believed that the Lord would, somehow, save His Church, even as her congregation dwindled through natural attrition: The faithful aged went to meet Jesus, but no one ever came to replace them. Then, not long after Peter's twenty-fifth birthday, Priscilla went to meet Jesus at far too young an age—but not before she, with the consent of her geriatric congregants, consecrated her son bishop: the bishop who would most assuredly shepherd the Church into its extinction. As she laid her frail hands on him, a rueful thought inserted itself into his grief. *I'll be more like an undertaker than an overseer.*

As it has turned out, the job of bishop feels a lot like what he imagines managing a home for the elderly would be like. The routine nature of it, at least, suits him. Peter expects to use up the best years of his life ministering to his remaining congregation: presiding over Sunday services, praying with them, visiting them in the hospital, visiting them in hospice, and finally conducting their funerals. And, then, the Church will officially die . . . just another cosmic failure . . . just another tradition, like worship of the Greek and Roman gods, swept from living religion into dead mythology.

I'm sorry, Mother, Peter says inside his head. *I'm sorry I can't do more. But I'm still here. I haven't left, even though He seems to have abandoned me. That should count for something.*

Peter looks up at Mary. "God sent you an angel," he whispers. "I'm not asking Him for some big miracle like that. Just something to let me know He's really up there." He directs his next words to the babe in her arms.

"Lord, I believe; help my unbelief!"

The plaintive words spill out of the chapel and reverberate through the gloomy cathedral. Unmoved, the flickering images of Mary and Jesus stare stubbornly ahead into an eternity Peter cannot see.

That evening, Sunday, June 25th, Peter sits through a meeting with the Church Council. They've gathered at one end of the ancient wooden table in the cathedral's vesting room. A few deteriorating tapestries and framed icons add color to the room's dark paneling.

"I don't understand," Martin is saying, "why we can't just do it all at once."

Peter sighs. "It's not that simple. The north rose window has seven sections, each with a luminor. Each removal legally requires a separate 'Historical Impact Assessment.' The fees are tied to these assessments, so we have to pay the fee seven times to get the entire window done."

Martin taps an arthritic knuckle against his forehead. "I can't believe even Nation Hall can be such knuckleheads!"

The other two elderly Church Council members, Dorcas and Phoebe, exchange a look.

"I remember the day," Martin continues, "when even 'cultists' had rights. And when the ninnies in the nation bureaucracy had a little decency and common sense—"

Peter holds up a hand, and Martin draws a breath. "I know the Sanef government can be crazy," Peter says, "but we wouldn't still be in this place if they hadn't given us reservation status."

"Well," Martin says. "Respectfully, Bishop, I'm not sure—"

A rap on the room's stout wooden door interrupts him. It opens, and Martin's son Dan peeks his head in. "Sorry to interrupt, folks. Pop, how's it looking?"

"We got maybe ten more minutes."

"I'll be outside."

"Please come in, Dan," Peter says. "There's no reason you can't sit with us while we wrap up."

Dan shrugs and steps into the room. He closes the door and sits down at the far end of the long wooden table. Behind him hangs a dusty, threadbare tapestry depicting mounted knights who bear shields emblazoned with crosses. With a sour glance at the tapestry, Dan places an index finger to his nose to forestall a sneeze.

Peter and Dan have known one another since they played together on the cathedral's front steps as children, but Dan has not attended a service since he was fifteen. In fact, Dan usually avoids the cathedral—his current partner is thoroughly embarrassed that Dan's father is a "cultist." But Dan has realized Martin won't live forever, and he's making an effort to spend more time with the old man. Martin is making his own effort as well, having feigned enthusiasm for watching the Virtual Combat Quarterly Championships to spend time with his son.

Peter addresses the three Church Council members, mustering as much eloquence as he can. "I know our work on the luminor issue has been slow and frustrating. But let's not forget the progress we've made. It's true, we don't have enough funds to complete the entire north rose window at once, but I think we'll have enough to get started with two sections now and then start on a new one every couple of months. When the entire window is done, it'll be a lovely sight."

"You're right, Bishop," Dorcas says. "We've discussed this long enough. Let's move forward with this window."

Martin grudgingly nods his agreement. Phoebe does, too. A consensus among Dorcas and Peter usually carries the day.

Dorcas Williams comes from a long tradition of Christworshippers. Various lines of her family tree produced Presbyterian, Roman Catholic, Baptist, and Episcopal clergy, and her paternal grandfather was a bishop at this very cathedral. The portraits of prior bishops which hang in the cathedral crypt include one of Bishop Williams, a wiry, stooped, silver-haired patriarch with a serious gaze. In Dorcas's case, the apple has not fallen far from the proverbial tree.

"Good, it's decided," Peter says. "Okay, 'luminor remediation' was our last agenda item. Let's wrap up the meeting with our bible reading. Let's see, this month's reading is the fourteenth chapter of the Gospel According to

John. Phoebe, I believe it's your turn." He slides an oldtime codex across the table. At the other end of the table, Dan shifts uncomfortably in his seat.

Phoebe grimaces as she touches the codex's delicate pages. She takes a breath and begins reciting the passage. As usual, her words are barely audible. "Do not let your hearts be troubled. Believe in God, believe also in me. In my Father's house are many drawing—no, sorry—many *dwelling* places . . ."

Out of the corner of his eye, Peter notices Dan glance at the time.

". . . No one comes to the Father except through me. . . ."

A deepening frown creases Dan's face.

" . . . But the Advocate, the Holy Spirit, whom the Father will send in my name, will teach you everything, and remind you of all that I have said to you . . ."

Distracted by the task of ignoring Dan, Peter barely hears the words of the bible reading.

Phoebe concludes: ". . . may know that I love the Father. Rise, let us be on our way. . . . Here ends the reading. Amen." The other Christworshippers respond with an "Amen," and she closes the codex. As they stand and prepare to leave, Dan saunters over to Peter.

"You amaze me, Petey," he says.

"Pardon?"

"How much longer are you going to go on with this?"

"Go on with . . . ?"

"All this 'church' stuff."

"I'm sure I don't know what you mean."

The others are now standing by the vesting room door, where they are speaking in quiet voices. Martin says, "Son, are you ready to go?"

Dan holds up a hand. "Give us a second." He leans in closer to Peter.

"Listen, I know how important your mom was to you. All the Christworshippers adored her. But she's gone, and you have to live your life—you can't just keep hiding away in this place. I keep telling Pop that your group should liquidate all this. The land itself must be worth a fortune. Sell it and divide up the proceeds, or give it all away to the lowcontribs if that's the sort of thing you still do. But as it is, this is all just an inefficient waste."

Peter fails to keep his voice from trembling. "My job is to teach the Gospel, not to sell off God's Church."

"Come on, what 'good news' are you teaching?" asks Dan. "You would have people believe the System is so chock full of evil because some dude and his wife ate a piece of fruit in a garden. And this one act of disobedience was so terrible that your supposedly loving God would have thrown everyone into flames to *burn forever* if his divine son hadn't come to take our sins upon himself."

"Well, that's sort of the basic idea, but there's more to it, of course—"

"It's garbage, Peter." Dan shakes his head. He clearly did not intend to say all of this, but he seems unable to stop himself. "Forgive me, but the 'God' you worship is an asshole."

"Danny!" cries Dorcas as Martin stares at the ceiling.

Dan turns to face the elderly Christworshippers, raising his hands in a calming gesture. "I'm sorry. I'm sorry. I don't mean to hurt anyone's feelings. But somebody has got to try to talk some sense into . . ." He points a thumb at Peter. ". . . *His Holiness* here."

Dan's gaze travels from face to face. "I'm worried about all of you. You've been brainwashed into believing in a supernatural being—sorry, *three* supernatural beings who are somehow also *one*." He rolls his eyes. "And the father in heaven is supposedly good and loving, yet he would send his son to be brutally murdered to satisfy his own wrath. It's just horrible. It's not loving at all, and I've never understood why you insisted on teaching children such things. There's a reason your children and grandchildren won't set foot in this place, except for poor Felipe. There's a reason this cult died."

Phoebe flushes.

Martin groans.

Dorcas gives Dan a hard stare but visibly restrains herself from speaking. She turns instead to young Bishop Peter and waits for him to defend the Faith.

Peter clears his throat and faces Dan without quite meeting his eyes. Quietly, he says, "The Church is not dead as long as we are still here. If what we believe doesn't make sense to you, it's because it's a mystery."

"A mystery? Uh huh. Here's what's not a mystery. I would never torture my children, no matter how badly they were acting, to satisfy some ideal of honor or justice. I know that's true for the rest of you, too. So how could a God be truly good and all-powerful and all-knowing but be a worse parent than I am? I'm sorry, but it's nonsense. And it breaks my heart to see people here in this giant tomb dedicating their final years to an ancient lie."

"You just," Peter stammers, "you just have to have some faith. You—"

"In other words, you have to believe things that don't make sense."

Peter opens his mouth. After several pregnant seconds pass, he closes it. *There must be a good response—I know there must be.* He's still trying to call it forth, as all eyes in the room bore into him, when Martin rescues him.

"Danny," Martin says to his son in an unusually calm voice. "We're going to miss the first quarter if we don't get going."

After a few moments, Dan unlocks his gaze from Peter's and nods at Martin. "I'm sorry, Pop. I've said what I needed to say." He gives Peter a quick squeeze on the shoulder. "Sorry to harsh your meeting, bud. I'm sure you're doing the best you can with what you've got."

Peter can only nod numbly.

The others leave the vesting room in awkward silence, first Martin with Dan and then a frowning Dorcas with a wide-eyed Phoebe. Motionless, Peter listens to them exit the cathedral into the darkening evening. Only when he hears the door in the north transept clang shut does he exhale.

He turns out the lights in the vesting room and shuts the door. Walking with a stiff gait, he passes through the shadowed passageway paralleling the choir and crosses the north transept, his shoes occasionally squeaking on worn tiles. Peter stops to bow toward the tabernacle in the Chapel of the Nativity before leaving through the cathedral's north exit. Locking the door behind him, he sighs as he looks up at the cold, metallic luminors that cover almost every window.

Peter crosses the cathedral grounds and takes a right onto an empty street where he picks up a few pieces of litter on his walk home. Only pedestrians are permitted to use the oldtime streets found at ground level. Peter does not encounter anyone else—most people navigate the city center using transitubes or the enclosed pedestrian bridges which connect the towers at various levels. But it's a convenient walk for Peter since The Bishop's Residence is only a block away.

The Bishop's Residence. That's what the Christworshippers insist on calling Peter's studio apartment—the least expensive floor plan in the Sacramento Tower. It's wedged into a corner of the ground level between two of the tower's primary support columns, and his front door opens directly onto the street.

When Peter arrives at his apartment, he spends a few minutes distracting himself from his thoughts by accessing current netstories:

Meres terraforming is falling short of internationally agreed benchmarks. Average temperature has risen only two point one degrees in the past ten years, a small but significant departure from the one-quarter degree per year goal set forth in . . .

The Independent Nation of Artamst sentenced thirteen political criminals to death. In a closely watched decision, the magistrate determined that the criminals were fit to stand trial despite having undergone involuntary neurpro treatments . . .

Undersea treasure hunters discovered a trove of precious jewels lost decades ago. They made their find in what was once the oldtime city of Palm Beach, a part of the former US-American region of Florida . . .

In the outer System, cartel alliance Beta's Ganymede mining facility has begun operation. Markets reacted positively to Beta's continuing commitment to developing the Jovian moons, lifting the stock prices of nine of its eleven member cartels an average of three percent . . .

The Independent Nations of New Maharashtra and Greater Kerala have announced a fourth cease-fire, but tensions remain high on the subcontinent . . .

Peter closes his eyes and yawns. It's a good night to go to bed early.

He changes into his pajamas, brushes his teeth, stretches, and climbs into bed. Once he settles in, he manages to doze off quickly . . .

. . . and begins to experience an especially vivid dream.

Peter is standing in the cathedral's vast nave, at the high altar that holds the great altar table. The pews and columns have gone missing, leaving the nave empty. Also missing is the worn stone labyrinth that was inset into the floor farther back in the nave. The entire floor has been transformed from limestone tiles into hard, ash-colored asphalt. In place of intricately patterned stonework, the walls appear to be windowless bulwarks of dull gray metal. The vaulted ceiling has simply disappeared, leaving the cathedral as nothing more than a cold industrial box, open to a gray sky.

Peter leans over the altar table. Priscilla lies there with tubes protruding from her dying arms. Her skin is leathery, and her gaze is distant. She slowly lifts her head from her pillow and whispers: "There used to be so many groups of Christworshippers. There used to be pastors and patriarchs and ministers and popes. You're all that's left now. Peter, promise me the gates of hell will not prevail against Christ's Church."

"I promise, Mother."

And then it's a table again. A chalice has tipped over and spilled its contents onto Peter's white liturgical vestments. Warm, thick blood covers his chest and runs down his legs like crimson syrup. He wants to wipe it off, but his hands are frozen in place. When he looks back up at the table, two enormous crows are eating the Eucharistic wafers. They snap at one another with hard, black beaks, fighting for the best morsels of the body of Christ. Still paralyzed, Peter gags as one of the crows pushes a cold beak down his throat and pulls out the contents of his stomach. Satisfied, it flies into the sky.

Tracking the bird's ascent, Peter notices a giant leg the size of one of central Sanef's towers just past the church's farthest gray wall. He can finally gasp out a word.

"Lord!"

As soon as Peter speaks, the leg lifts itself up and begins to move through the sky. Its monstrous foot wears a massive brown sandal which descends earthward, quickly accelerating toward Peter. Its shadow plunges him into darkness.

"Lord?"

He hears the nauseating sound of his own bones splintering beneath an unbearable weight. Panic jolts him awake to sweat-drenched sheets.

~

A block away, a homeless person climbs the forty steps leading up to the cathedral's main entrance. At the top, the vagrant sets down some gear and begins assembling a low-tech canvas tent on the concrete in front of the locked doors. Practiced hands click tent poles into place by the light of a portable electric lamp.

A fashionably dressed young couple—a male and a feme—look down on the transient's efforts from one of the balcony bars in the neighboring Huntington-Union Tower. Glasses tinkle above the din of conversation. The feme sips her appetizer drink and carelessly fans herself. She points toward the cathedral. "As if looking at that run-down old monstrosity weren't bad enough, now it's going to be a squatters' village. What in the System *is* that, anyway?"

The male shrugs. "Some kind of museum. I'm sure they police their property. They'll kick him out as soon as they notice him."

"What people have been saying is right. This neighborhood really isn't what it used to be."

"Sorry, darling. Next time, let's go to the Sunset district and try one of the ultrabars."

She smiles.

The male peers down at the homeless person. "*That* is exactly why we need a stronger neurpro law. Sanef is just flooded with these lowcontribs. Human garbage everywhere."

The feme nods and takes another sip from her drink.

Below, the lowcontrib deftly connects canvas to tent poles, giving shape to a makeshift dwelling.

2

The Lowcontrib

Peter spends Monday on the net trying to navigate Nation Hall's permit system, so he fails to notice the tent until Tuesday.

That morning, after he has his breakfast, he tells Trinity his plan for the day. "A clinic in one of the towers is offering a course on cardiopulmonary resuscitation, sweetie." Peter's mind briefly flashes to a memory of Matthias Jian's funeral. "Life is fragile, and I should know how to help someone in distress. Yes, I should, sweetie. Yes, I should." He often baby-talks to Trinity.

Her long ears perk up when Peter speaks. She has white fur with black spots and a curious and active disposition. Peter sets out fresh hay and rabbit pellets, and Trinity dashes back into her cage for a meal.

He departs The Bishop's Residence and strolls a block before turning left to cut through the cathedral grounds, descending a set of thoroughly cracked steps to enter a large concrete courtyard. To his left, the former cathedral school and parish hall stand on the north side of the courtyard. These mostly three-story sculpted concrete buildings have not been used for decades, and the flaccid morning sunlight reveals the deterioration of their pillared façades. The cathedral proper looms to Peter's right, while the Huntington-Union Tower fills the sky ahead of him.

Passing by the front of the cathedral, Peter glances to his right and sees that someone has pitched a primitive canvas tent next to what is technically the cathedral's main entrance. The tent stands directly in front of the tarnished copper and gold-colored Ghiberti Doors—an oldtime copy of a set of Renaissance-era doors depicting various scenes from the Christian Old Testament. Detailed panels include images of Adam, Eve, Noah, Abraham, and others: figures now known to but a very few. For decades, the heavy, locked Ghiberti Doors have stood as quiet sentries, unopened.

He stops and blinks at the tent. The eyesore obstructs Moses and his tablets as well as David and Goliath. *A lowcontrib camping here?* His nose wrinkles. *Hopefully he's found the public restroom across the street.*

Peter carefully approaches the tent. The translucent white canvas is opaque enough to frustrate Peter's efforts to see whether someone is inside. The tent looks just large enough for two adults to sleep in, and its apex stands level with Peter's chest. For a few moments, he glances around as if someone might come along and tell him what he should do. Finally, he takes a nervous breath and addresses the tent.

"Hello, is someone in there?"

"Come in," immediately answers a feminine voice.

He instinctively takes a step back and then rolls his eyes at his own timidity. He steps forward again, but he has no intention of climbing into a lowcontrib's tent. "Um, sorry, perhaps you could come out?"

"Come in," she repeats breezily.

Peter blinks and thinks. After some moments, he slowly leans down, pulls back a flap, and peers into the tent.

Surprisingly, its interior looks clean and uncluttered. It has a green canvas floor that covers the concrete beneath. A rolled-up mat and a blanket rest in a corner of the tent next to a clapboard footlocker. The lowcontrib sits straight-backed and cross-legged on the ground as if she had been meditating.

She appears to be about Peter's age. In other times and places, one might have puzzled over her ethnicity: perhaps she's a mix of African and European lineages; perhaps her family comes from somewhere in East Asia or South Asia; perhaps she's descended from an indigenous group. If Peter were to think about it, he might decide she somehow has a face that could fit into any family portrait. But Peter's concerns are more practical. He notes that the lowcontrib's eyes are clear, not bloodshot in the way that signals stim addiction. She does not seem agitated by his presence. Her clothes are clean and cheap, probably bought second-hand. He does not detect the foul odor he expects from a lowcontrib camping on the streets.

That said, life clearly hasn't been easy on her. Peter tries not to stare at the jagged, three-centimeter scar that intersects the lowcontrib's left jaw-bone, running from the bottom of her cheek down toward her neck. It's an old scar that appears to have healed without any cosmetic repair.

Notwithstanding the scar, her face is neither repulsive nor especially beautiful. *All things considered, this situation could be a lot worse,* he decides, and he relaxes an iota.

The lowcontrib seems to be taking her measure of Peter, as well. "Welcome, guest. Please sit." She gestures toward the space in front of her.

Peter quickly takes stock of the tent's canvas floor. After several moments, he enters the tent and sits down gingerly, crossing his legs. "Thank you," he says. "Although, actually, you're my guest."

"Am I?"

"My name is Peter. Among other things, I'm in charge of this property."

She glances up and around as if surveying the cathedral grounds through the fabric of her tent. "It's seen better days," she says.

Peter grimaces. *So have you,* he thinks. Then he chides himself: *Do not return insult for insult.*

She turns her gaze toward him. "So, you're the owner of this building?"

"Not exactly."

"Ah. Perhaps, rather, you have been charged by the true owner to maintain custody over it until the time comes for him to reclaim it for his own purposes?"

The strangely specific phrasing of her question puzzles Peter, who has not entirely ruled out the possibility that the woman is a stim addict. After all, many lowcontribs fall victim to that pernicious form of addiction, spending whatever little money they have on it. He speaks slowly and clearly. "This building is called a 'church.' It is a place of worship. I am the leader of the group that worships here. You have probably been taught to call groups like ours 'cults,' but we call ourselves 'Christworshippers.' We follow the Christian religion, a very ancient form of 'metafiz.'"

Her eyes never waiver from his. She whispers, "What does a member of the Christian religion do when a stranger takes refuge on his front porch?"

Peter would be well within his rights to have her removed from the property. *Why did she decide to set up camp here, of all places?* He takes a few moments to consider his options and his duties before finally responding. "This is God's 'front porch,' not mine. All of His children are welcome here." He pauses, uncertain if she understands the word "God" or, for that matter, the other words he's saying. "In other words, you may stay here for a while."

Her mouth turns up in a warm, unselfconscious smile.

Peter checks the time and realizes he's going to be late for his CPR class. He lifts himself up and quickly steps out of the tent. Peeking his head back inside, he says, "I'm afraid I have to go. Are there any necessities you need right now, toiletries or anything?"

"No, thank you."

He nods and hurries off.

Only later in the morning does he realize, chagrined, that he thought-lessly failed to ask the lowcontrib for her name. He stops by the tent that afternoon on his way back to The Bishop's Residence, but she's not at "home."

Peter spends some time the following Saturday checking the net for resources to help lowcontribs. After several minutes, he leans back and sighs. He assumed there would be some public services, but the options in prosperous Sanef are remarkably limited.

Officially, Sanef is called "The Independent Nation of Sanef Bay," but it depends a lot on the neighboring La Nación Independiente de San Joaquin for agricultural products and on the System-spanning cartels for jobs and investments. Despite this dependence, few nations can boast as many generations of relative affluence. After pioneering nettech, Sanef established itself as a major center for the ecotech that continues to wrestle Earth's remaining biome through the various ecocrises. The genengineering, carbon sequestration, and managed extinction cartels each maintain a sizeable footprint in Sanef. The nation has also recently attracted substantial investments from the offearth settlement industry.

Long a bastion of cosmopolitan secularism, Sanef would have been considered an unlikely place to harbor the last Christian church. Dorcas and some of the others like to tell themselves that their group's exceptional faithfulness saved Grace Cathedral while other church buildings across Earth were closed and then demolished or repurposed into museums, offices, homes, or nightclubs. But the truth is more complicated, Peter knows. Money, politics, and chance all played important roles.

As the cathedral's original denomination shriveled alongside the others, a large endowment and canny investments carried its small congregation through decades of decline. By the time the money was gone, so few Christian churches remained that the capricious Sanef Parliament decided to declare the Grace Cathedral grounds a "Protected Multicultural Reservation." PMR status still entitles the church to assert protection from eminent domain and to receive a property-tax exemption and a tiny annual maintenance grant.

Just enough to hold the bug in its amber. Just enough to be a museum piece on a dusty shelf.

Peter's mind is wandering.

I haven't finished my sermon for tomorrow, he recalls with a start. He shakes his head. The last bishop loathes writing sermons.

3

I Am

The cathedral's nave is simply too cavernous—its echoing emptiness too depressing—for only a dozen souls. So, for many years, the Christworshippers have held their services in the Chapel of the Nativity. Beneath its stone ceiling, they pray their prayers and sing their hymns as the ghosts of the centuries whisper from the darkness beyond.

It is Sunday morning, and Peter rises from his ornate wooden bishop's chair to stand at the lectern in front of the chapel's stone altar. As Mary and Jesus gaze fixedly ahead from their starry scene above, Peter surveys his congregation. They sit in two short rows of wooden chairs divided by a center aisle.

To Peter's left, Lupe and Marco sit in the front row, rosaries in hand. After the last church in Mexico City fell apart, they uprooted themselves and moved to Sanef to "morir entre otros cristianos": die among other Christworshippers. Nastya sits next to Lupe, and she's whispering something into Lupe's ear that makes her smile. Years earlier, Nastya had a career with an international organization that aids megahurricane victims.

Bede and his grandson Felipe sit in the row behind them. Chronologically, Felipe has a year on Peter, but he's like a child. He was born with a rare and untreatable genetic condition causing several severe learning disabilities. He can speak, but he can't read. He can hum along with hymns, but he can't put words together with music to sing them. With both of Felipe's parents dead, the aging Bede and his grandson look after one another with the support of the Christworshippers.

To Peter's right, Dorcas sits in the front row next to the center aisle, quietly praying. Martin sits next to her. Earlier, Peter noticed him staring at the luminor-covered rose window near the chapel, no doubt still pondering the knuckleheadedness of the Sanef bureaucracy. Next to Martin, Thad vigorously digs a pinky into an ear canal. Good, stolid Thad isn't the brightest candle on the altar, but he's been a reliable Christworshipper throughout his long years of life.

Junia and Phoebe sit in the back row on Peter's right, rounding out the congregation. Gregarious Junia keeps up with gossip as zealously as her introverted sister keeps silent. After decades in the congregation, Phoebe finally consented to serve a term on the Church Council. Given the dearth of words that escape Phoebe's lips, people tend to listen closely when she does speak.

With the entire congregation present and accounted for, Peter begins the liturgy. Together, he and the Christworshippers recite:

> *Almighty God, to you all hearts are open, all desires known, and from you no secrets are hid: Cleanse the thoughts of our hearts by the inspiration of your Holy Spirit . . .*

Peter and Felipe are far younger than the rest of the Christworshippers, whose average age exceeds retirement age by a decade or two. Peter still feels it would have made more sense for Dorcas to succeed Priscilla as bishop—she has always had the strongest faith. But Dorcas insisted she was too old and that younger blood was needed. Peter was the only young blood left that could be tapped, so here he now stands, Holy Father to people old enough to be his grandparents.

> *. . . For you alone are the Holy One, you alone are the Lord, you alone are the Most High . . .*

Presiding over Sunday services does gratify Peter, despite the requirement to come up with sermon ideas. And he does love these sometimes difficult old people, almost all of whom he's known his entire life. *Sure, we may be quarrelsome at times*, he ruminates. *But this last remnant holds tightly to one another and to our faith. Even though we won't be able to pass the faith on to another generation, at least we—*

Peter loses his train of thought when the heavy wooden door at the cathedral's north entrance cracks open and light pours in. Heads turn and eyes squint as the lowcontrib walks in and quietly closes the door behind her. Peter is both delighted—*An outsider interested in our service!*—and embarrassed. *The first time in years I've had someone to try to evangelize, and I don't even know her name yet, even though she's been camped out here for nearly a week.*

He was about to begin the first reading for the morning, from the Christian Old Testament book of Deuteronomy, as prescribed by the lectionary. He beckons to her to come join them, and she approaches, ascending the few steps leading up to the raised chapel floor. A part of Peter's mind notices how gracefully she walks, as if she was trained as a dancer. This thought lingers as she continues forward until she stands right in front of Peter's lectern.

The Christworshippers stare awkwardly at the lowcontrib for a few heartbeats. Peter, assuming she's standing directly in front of him because she's confused, clears his throat and softly says, "It's very nice that you've joined us this morning. If you'd care to take a seat, this is the time in our worship service when I am going to read—"

She shakes her head and says, "I am."

Gently but decisively edging Peter aside, the lowcontrib faces the congregation and turns the pages of the oldtime codex on the lectern. Peter stares at her with wide eyes as she recites:

> *The hand of the Lord came upon me, and he brought me out by the spirit of the Lord and set me down in the middle of a valley; it was full of bones. He led me all around them; there were very many lying in the valley, and they were very dry. He said to me, "Mortal, can these bones live?" I answered, "O Lord God, you know." Then he said to me, "Prophesy to these bones, and say to them: O dry bones, hear the word of the Lord. Thus says the Lord God to these bones: I will cause breath to enter you, and you shall live. I will lay sinews on you, and will cause flesh to come upon you, and cover you with skin, and put breath in you, and you shall live; and you shall know that I am the Lord. . . ."*

There's something about the cadence of her voice. Peter can't quite put his finger on it, but he's never heard anyone read scripture with so much, so much . . .

> *. . . So I prophesied as I had been commanded; and as I prophesied, suddenly there was a noise, a rattling, and the bones came together, bone to its bone. I looked, and there were sinews on them, and flesh had come upon them, and skin had covered them; but there was no breath in them. Then he said to me, "Prophesy to the breath, prophesy, mortal, and say to the breath: Thus says the Lord God: Come from the four winds, O breath, and breathe upon these slain, that they may live." I prophesied as he commanded me, and the breath came into them, and they lived, and stood on their feet, a vast multitude.*

Instead of concluding with the traditional "Here ends the reading" or "The Word of the Lord," she says, "Mark my words" and closes the bible.

Dorcas scowls while the other Christworshippers glance at one another in confusion. The lowcontrib steps away from the lectern and takes the empty chair next to Phoebe where Matthias Jian used to sit. Phoebe nervously eyeballs the lowcontrib, who quietly folds her hands and looks attentively at Peter. He takes a deep breath, allows several seconds to pass in silence, and then simply picks back up on the liturgy, leading the recitation of Psalm 15 as prescribed by the lectionary:

> O Lord, who may abide in your tent? Who may dwell on your holy hill? Those who walk blamelessly, and do what is right, and speak the truth from their heart . . .

The lowcontrib stays for the rest of the service and appears to listen intently to Peter's sermon, which he has titled *The Delicate Balance Between God's Loving Mercy and His Just Wrath*. She does not join the Christworshippers in receiving the bread and wine. After the dismissal, they warily turn to speak with the stranger. She converses amiably with both the women and the men, asking their names and inquiring about their experiences. Peter changes in the vesting room and then comes over to talk with the lowcontrib as the Christworshippers begin to file outdoors to the courtyard to share refreshments. Junia is speaking with her.

"—so tragic," Junia says. "He retired just last year. He used to joke that he was such a youngster compared to the rest of us."

"You're telling her about Matthias," Peter says.

Junia nods and says to the lowcontrib, "I need to go put these muffins out on the table for our fellowship time. You'll be joining us?"

"I am. At least for a while, if your bishop doesn't mind."

"Of course, I don't mind," Peter says.

Junia nods and heads out to the courtyard, leaving Peter with the lowcontrib.

"Your reading was powerful, albeit—unexpected," Peter says. "In any event, I'm embarrassed that I didn't ask for your name when we spoke a few days ago. That was rude of me."

"I forgive you, Bishop Peter. I have told the others my name, but they did not understand."

She gazes at him steadily. In the silence, Peter begins to feel the throbbing of his own pulse.

She lifts her chin slightly and says, "I am Sophia."

Peter's eyes widen as the pieces click together in his mind: her earlier question about the property, her reading, the archaic name she's given him. Despite its obscurity, Peter recognizes *sophia* as the Greek word for "wisdom"—but also more than that. "Sophia" is a name that was used for millennia to denote God's presence. Ancient books such as the Wisdom of Solomon and Ecclesiasticus portray "Sophia" as a feminine image of God's Holy Wisdom, as a name for the Divine manifest in the here and now. According to the gospels, Jesus Himself referred to her.

Peter has realized, in other words, that this lowcontrib thinks she's . . . God.

Holy hell, he thinks to himself.

"Sophia" gazes calmly at Peter as he works this out. After several moments, he says, "Sophia. That is an—an evocative name. Where does it come from?"

"The Father gave it to me."

Not "my father." The Father.

Felipe is the only one still inside, and he's following Bede through the exit to the courtyard—out of earshot, fortunately. Peter's eyes cautiously meet the woman's once more. "I take it you, uh, have some familiarity with the Christian religion. Can you tell me more about yourself?"

After a few heartbeats, she says, "Before Abraham was, I Am." Her smile radiates the iron assurance of a disturbed mind.

～

Socrates Darius Jefferson—"Jeff" to his friends and "Uncle Jeff" to Peter—is a polymath. As Priscilla once said, to Jeff's delight, he's also a "real character." He worked on some of the most important energy efficiency projects of his time. Now retired from engineering, Jeff teaches a course in history—his true passion—at Sanef National University, where he ranks as a minor celebrity on campus. Handsome and distinguished, he has penetrating eyes that frequently attract the admiration of his ro-feme and q-male students even though he technically could be their grandfather. But at this time in his life, his interests lie in exploring ideas, not seducing undergrads.

His corner condo is located on the two-hundred third floor of the Hopkins Tower, which stands just a couple of towers southeast of the cathedral. It's a clear day, and from Peter's seat at the dining room table, he can easily make out the gray line of Sanef's western dike, frozen in its eternal embrace of the Pacific.

"Ho ho!" Jeff says, pulling his chair closer. "A messianic quote from G-Zeus himself! I'll bet that puckered your sphincter."

"Jesus," Peter says. He rubs his temples.

"So your G-Zeu—sorry, *Jesus*—gets a heavenly sex change operation and decides to return from the beyond and camp out, in a tent, in front of the church. Makes perfect sense!" Jeff grins. "You know, back in the day when there were something like a billion Christworshippers and a billion Muslims and such, mentally ill people used to turn up all the time thinking they were the savior or a prophet or what have you."

"I know," Peter says. "I accessed some articles about it. It's hard to imagine what it must have been like when people took religion so seriously." He shakes his head. "But this lowcontrib doesn't live in an age like that. How did she even learn about the Christian religion? And what kind of awful trauma must she have suffered to start believing she's divine? I don't know, maybe the best thing would be to just call the Central Psych Administration."

"As one who's seen where that road leads, I would strongly advise against it." Jeff stares out his picture window. "Unless it's something a little psychological counseling will help with, the CPA just pushes neurpro, neurpro, and more neurpro. Let me tell you, it's nasty stuff."

"Nation Hall is always saying neural reprogramming is 'safe and prosocial,' you know."

"Yeah, sure it is. The truth is that scientists still don't understand the human brain at its deepest levels. Neurpro seems to be the only way they know how to deal with criminals and with mentally ill people like my dear sister—and it's like using a hammer to kill a mosquito. It's barbaric, really."

"I hear you," Peter says.

Jeff brings his eyes back to Peter's. "Obviously, this 'Sophia' hasn't already been committed to neurpro treatments, or she wouldn't be living on your front step. That means the nation bureaucrats really can't do anything with her unless and until she endangers herself or someone else—at least as the law stands today, although that may soon change." Slipping into lecture mode comes naturally to Jeff. "Public disgust with lowcontribs was already creating a push for tighter neurpro laws, which would make it easier to commit people so that they can be 'reprogrammed' to be 'efficiently contributing' citizens. And the recent uptick in nun attacks like the one that got your poor Matthias is adding fuel to the flame. The pundits are saying the Sanef Parliament is on the verge of following the neighboring nations' example and increasing government powers to compel neurpro."

Peter shakes his head. "It doesn't seem right."

"It's not, though I admit I can understand why they're taking a hard line against the nuns. So-called 'Isnotism' is not a philosophy, you know. The oldtime word for it was 'nihilism,' related to the word 'annihilate.' It's simply the pessimistic view that life lacks any meaning or purpose. Dressing up murder-suicides with slogans doesn't make them any saner." Jeff strokes his chin and squints. "Hell, what's the catchphrase again?"

Peter closes his eyes, recalling the words an authentic Isnotist Denunciator is supposed to yell before setting off an explosive. "Man sees everywhere the absurdity of existence—"

Jeff nods to himself and joins in: "—and loathing seizes him. I denounce all values. That which you think is, *is not*." Jeff sighs. "'Isnotism' is nothing but a manifestation of social and psychological illness."

"No disagreement here," Peter says. He lifts a finger into the air. "You know, the word 'nun' once meant something almost the opposite. Maybe the Denunciators and their nihilism can be traced back to the loss of religious faith."

"Oh, please. Anyway, that's one debate we're not going to resolve today. Back to your charity case." Jeff thumps the dining room table as if he were a judge pounding a gavel. "Let's see, legally speaking, she would be trespassing if you told her to leave and she refused. So you *could* just give her a fair warning and then have her removed from the property and make her someone else's problem."

"You know I'm not going to do that."

"Didn't think so. Doesn't seem like what G-Zeus would do. And . . ."

"Jesus."

". . . that being the case, all you can do is keep an eye on her and hope she doesn't do anything dangerously nutty. I'm pretty sure that thinking she's a dead messiah doesn't rise to that level."

"Okay, I must point out, theologically—"

"I know, I know, it is written that He is not dead but lives. I read your mother's propaganda materials. Maybe He would like to descend from His heaven and straighten your new friend out?"

Sarcasm constitutes the ever-present foam on the root beer of Jeff's personality, as Peter knows all too well. Jeff and Peter's father grew up together. Having studiously avoided partnering, Jeff was free to step in and partially fill the void left when his friend died. Peter was five years old at the time.

Priscilla and Jeff's relationship remained platonic as far as Peter knows—but Peter always maintained a policy of willful ignorance on that score. Priscilla and Jeff sometimes sparred about what Jeff, when in a sour mood, referred to as Priscilla's "obsolete superstitions." As a "modern scientific" person, Jeff has always found Christianity to be silly, albeit basically harmless. As a historian, he finds the arc of its rise and fall fascinating. As a natural-born debater, he has never been able to resist challenging Priscilla and now Peter on matters of faith. Notwithstanding which, Peter admires Jeff's deep learning and values his mentorship and affection.

Peter responds deadpan to Jeff's jibe: "Well, it is also written that Jesus will appear and give us one wish if we sacrifice a virgin pig during each week of the Lenten season."

Jeff's eyes widen. "Is that really written?"

"Ha! And you have the gall to call me credulous."

"Very nice, you got me. But you must admit it sounds like something that could be in there, given all the . . ."

"Ancient claptrap," Peter drones in parallel with Jeff.

". . . in the Christian scriptures," Jeff concludes. Before Peter can rebuke him, he changes the subject. "Speaking of virginity, how's your love life?"

"Speaking of—? Uncle Jeff!"

"All right, just tweaking you. Keep in mind, though, since I don't have any kids—as far as I know—you having kids would be the closest *I'll* come to having grandkids to spoil. So I hope you're not just hanging out in your bell tower every night waiting for your Lord's return instead of going out to meet some nice young ro-feme. And stop moaning every time I mention the female gender! That's not the kind of moaning that's called for here."

"We seem to have gotten off track. Way off track."

"Fair enough." Jeff straightens and assumes a scholarly mien. "Back to the subject at hand. As I was going to say, since your job description is to 'save souls' and this lowcontrib is clearly a lost one, you could start by trying to get through to her. I mean, if she thinks she's *the messiah*, use this as your angle of attack. Start asking her questions and see if she starts to realize she doesn't really know things that G-Zeus—"

"Jesus."

"That *Jesus* should know. Maybe she's lucid enough that she'll realize she can't answer them."

Peter rubs his temples again. "So your brilliant advice is, essentially, to reason with a crazy person. Great, thanks so much."

Jeff grins. "Why the hell not? You've been trying to reason with me for years."

⁓

The following afternoon, Peter decides he might as well give Jeff's advice a try. He doesn't have any better ideas, and at worst he wastes some time. He wants to be able to tell himself that he made a reasonable effort to get through to the lowcontrib. He researches some points of Christian theology and heads over to the cathedral grounds.

"Um, doop deep," he says when he reaches the tent. He's mimicking the ubiquitous automated sound signaling that someone wants to enter a private room. The lowcontrib's primitive tent has no dooper, of course.

After a moment, her voice emerges. "Come in, Bishop."

This time, Peter girds his loins and does not hesitate, much, to enter the tent and sit down on the canvas floor. Once more, she is sitting cross-legged and looks as if she has been meditating or praying, and he begins to wonder if that's all she does. A slight breeze ruffles the canvas, and he's surprised to feel a sort of peaceful airiness. He relaxes a little and manages to give the lowcontrib his most sincere-looking, pastoral smile. He notices an old codex resting on top of her footlocker.

Of course.

It's a bible—a beat-up, oldtime one with thin pages and a leather cover. He wonders what translation it is. One time Peter spent an entire day in the cathedral crypt comparing different bible translations of the sixth chapter of John's gospel.

"Good morning, *Sophia*. Thank you for inviting me in. I thought maybe we could talk if you're not, um, busy."

"It is kind of you to visit me," she says. "You come with questions?"

"Why, yes. Yes, I do." Naturally she assumes he has questions for *the messiah.*

"I hope you can hear the answers."

"Sophia, I heard what you said about being the 'I Am,' and I'm hoping you can answer some questions for me."

She smiles at his rehearsed and redundant statement. "You only pretend to seek answers. But your pretending is motivated by compassion, so I will listen to your questions."

He nods toward the codex. "It seems as if you've read our scriptures."

"I know something about Christian scriptures and traditions."

"Okay, well, in that case, here is my question." He clears his throat. "In the year 451, the ecumenical council of Chalcedon declared that Jesus was both fully human and fully divine without confusion, change, separation, or division." Peter speaks like a professor giving an exam question. He rehearsed this a few times on his way over. "What does that mean in terms of subjective experience? How can one person be both a finite creature and Almighty God without feeling like He is suffering from multiple personality disorder? If you really were who you say you are, you would have to know the answer."

"My." She slowly lifts a palm to her cheek. "What an esoteric question."

"But do you know the answer?"

"I do."

"Okay. What is it?"

She smiles. "I'm afraid you're not ready for it yet." She reaches out and momentarily puts a finger to his chest. "That question is not what's in your heart, anyway."

He scoots back a few centimeters and glances at the canvas flap that leads outside. *She's just going to avoid answering my questions. Uncle Jeff's idea was actually pretty terrible—trying to reason with someone who's living in a fantasy world.*

"If I were you," she says, "I would want to know why God allowed my friend to die in a suicide attack."

Peter's eyes widen, and he sits up straight. "Are you suggesting I don't want to know that? You bet I do. Matthias, of all people! He was a good person and a faithful Christworshipper. If he hadn't gone out for lunch that day, he would still be alive. Sure, I'd like to understand why that happened. There are so few of God's people left—why would He just stand back and allow one of us to be killed by random chance? Why would He ignore us all the time?"

"It sounds," Sophia says softly, "as if God has felt distant to you."

"Yeah, distant. Obviously, we've displeased Him." Peter looks down at his hands. *Oh Lord. I didn't mean to say all of that to this woman.*

"How do you think you've displeased God?"

"I. I couldn't say. I mean, well, sometimes I think He just may be hard to please. The other day, a person who grew up in the Church told me that my God is an assho—that He doesn't sound like a loving God."

"Why does this person think that?"

"He doesn't think it makes sense that God the Father would require His Son to be nailed to a tree just because some people ate a fruit in a garden a long time ago. And he thinks threatening to send people to hell for eternity also shows that the Father, as we conceive Him, is a cruel parent to His children."

"And what do *you* think?"

Peter's eyes narrow as he realizes the woman has somehow managed to make the conversation about *him*.

"I think *I'm* not the one who needs psychiatric help." As soon as the words come out, Peter begins to blush. *This person needs my help, and now I'm hurling insults at her. I'm the worst damn pastor ever.* "I—I'm sorry, I shouldn't have said that."

"You feel as though I'm trying to psychoanalyze you," she says. "But I just want to know how you're feeling. It's nice to talk with someone about these things."

This makes Peter feel a little better. It occurs to him that opening up might help him get through to the woman. "Some of the things we Christ-worshippers were taught about God can seem bizarre or even cruel," he says, "but I accept them as a mystery. I mean, why do terrible things happen at all? If God is truly good and all-powerful, why does He let so much unjust suffering happen?

"You might think the leader of the Christworshippers would have some good answer to that question—what oldtime theologians called a 'theodicy.'" Peter shrugs. "Some used to say that evil is a necessary byproduct of free will, that you cannot have one without the other. But the 'free will' explanation doesn't seem to offer a complete answer. Surely God could have created a universe that includes free will but is better than what we have.

"Anyway, when it comes down to it, my job is to teach this Gospel as best I can, not to figure it all out. I suppose I just have to accept the mystery."

"Bishop, it is good and right to take a humble approach to ultimate questions. And yet, if you cannot say anything more than this, how can you draw people to your faith? How can you move people in their hearts when you are unable to address their most basic questions?"

In fact, Peter has never brought anyone new to the faith. These days, that would take a miracle. He says, "Okay, just how would *you* explain the existence of evil and suffering?"

"You're not ready for the answer to that question, either—not yet."

"What a surprise."

"Rather than an answer, let me offer you more questions," she says. "Let's say we lived in a universe with no unjust suffering. No wars. No poverty. No ignorance. No separation from our loved ones through death or otherwise. No hatred or abuse or addiction. How different would that existence be?"

"Very different."

"Would Matthias have been the same person?"

Peter considers the question. Matthias suffered abuse as a child and struggled with addiction as an adult. Yet he somehow felt himself grow closer to God through his long struggle. The grace Matthias said he felt "lift" him "out of the prison of addiction" seemed to provide a path to peace that Peter did not really understand but saw in the man. *Would Matthias have been the same person if he lived in an existence without any of that?*

"No," Peter says aloud. "He wouldn't have been the same person. I suppose he would have been a better person."

"Perhaps. Perhaps not, in the course of eternity. But let's set 'better' and 'worse' aside for now. In the magnificent existence I've described, Matthias wouldn't have been the person you knew?"

"No, he wouldn't have been the same person," Peter says. "His unique character—his soul, I guess you could say—was molded by suffering and struggle."

"And if you and I lived in an existence without suffering, would we be the people we are?"

"I certainly wouldn't be."

"So, if God granted your wish for *that* universe in place of this one, wouldn't you be wishing us—the actual, specific people we are—out of existence?"

Peter stares at the woman in silence. He's never thought of it like that.

4

Tomb

"Bishop Peter!" cries Dorcas with a rap on the vesting-room door. "Yes, what, what is it?" He's in the middle of donning his liturgical vestments. Not for the first time in the past few days, he was thinking about his conversation with Sophia. He realizes he's pulled his faded green chasuble on backwards.

"Bishop, the tabernacle!" The door partially muffles Dorcas's voice. "The keys are missing. I was setting out the vessels for the Holy Eucharist, and I can't find the keys *anywhere*."

Peter pulls open the door and ushers her into the room while he wrestles with his vestments. "Dorcas, you know I always put them in the same place."

"I know, but they're not there. I've scoured the chapel." She stands behind him and helps him straighten his chasuble. "There. Now come help me look again."

The ornate, gold-painted tabernacle houses extra bread and wine that has been blessed as the body and blood of Christ. While the remaining Christworshippers vary in their views, Dorcas and some of the others feel that He is truly present in the bread and wine, and hence the tabernacle, in a special way. Only the bishop handles the timeworn metal keys that open the tabernacle. Near the end of each service, he can be seen ritually locking its oldtime mechanical lock and placing the keys on a small ledge which protrudes from the chapel wall.

Now fully vested in his clerical garb, Peter walks with Dorcas the twenty or so steps from the vesting room to the chapel. The keys are not on the ledge, nor have they been left on the altar or fallen behind the cushion on the bishop's chair. Peter scowls as he finishes scanning the chapel's floor. "You're right, they're not here."

"You know who must have taken them," Dorcas says as if she's reading Peter's mind. "There's only one outsider who has been to a service recently."

Peter frowns at the way Dorcas enunciates the word "outsider." He gives the tabernacle doors a tug to confirm they're locked.

"She would have seen you put them on the ledge," Dorcas continues.

"I think Soph—the homeless woman has enough problems without us accusing her of stealing. She's probably never even seen oldtime keys and wouldn't know what they're for. And if she were going to steal something, I don't think it would be two old metal keys. There are certainly more valuable things one could take from the cathedral."

Dorcas crosses her arms. "Peter, don't be naive. Someone like that— who won't get *help* and who lives in a tent!—someone like that will steal anything they can get their hands on. Who knows how many stims she's on? You can't assume she's rational."

"Well, I've spoken to her, and I don't think she's irrational." *Okay, that was a ridiculous statement—she thinks she's God!—but Dorcas is going to stroke out if she doesn't calm down.* "She's just a poor person who has probably struggled a lot and is trying to put her life back together. The last thing someone like that needs is a bunch of unsubstantiated accusations."

"That may well be, but what about the tabernacle? We're just going to leave the body and blood of Christ locked in there forever? Or break the doors open with a crowbar?" Dorcas's breath catches in her throat, and it takes her a moment to regain her composure. "For heaven's sake, I'm not demanding you burn her at the stake, but can't you at least *ask her* if she did something with the keys?"

"All right, sure. Of course." He doesn't want to admit that Dorcas is probably right. Sophia behaves erratically, and no one else would have moved the keys. Peter is confident he put them in their normal spot the prior Sunday, as always.

Peter checks the time and then exits the cathedral through the north entrance and walks around toward the front of the building. Dorcas follows. As they march along the outside of the cathedral, they both glance up at the luminors that sadly disfigure it. Peter shakes his head and mutters words of Jesus: "Woe unto you, lawyers."

Many decades earlier, the natural sunlight reaching the cathedral started to diminish as the mighty corporate towers sprang up on Nob Hill. The bishop at that time decided that the stained glass windows must continue to shine on his congregation with undimmed brightness. His solution to the problem required installing durable luminous panels—"luminors"—which fully covered the exterior of every stained glass window in the cathedral. Each luminor radiated bright, heavenly light into the interior, safeguarding the glory of the windows and, thereby, the cathedral itself—or so he thought.

Over the succeeding decades, austerity measures slashed spending on luminor maintenance, eventually abandoning them to a state of disrepair. None of the luminors functioned by the time Priscilla was bishop. By then, they did nothing but block all exterior light, making the solution *much* worse than the original problem.

A couple of the oldest parishioners claim they can remember seeing several of the windows lit up in their youth, including the rose window high above the Ghiberti Doors, which must have dominated the east side of the cathedral. The window is named "The Canticle of the Sun" after a poem by Saint Francis of Assisi.

"It was magnificent," Thad recalls rather too frequently. "It really was like the sun, but with lots of different colors."

Arranging the specialty repair of the long-obsolete luminor system would be expensive, and simply removing the panels also poses problems. A permit is required before a building owner may remove any "exterior fixture" from a building falling into the cathedral's historic classification, and the process for getting the permits is a legal and bureaucratic nightmare. Peter first waded into the nightmare six years ago, while Priscilla was still bishop. To date, he has succeeded in scraping together the funding, arranging the permits, and hiring the skilled labor to uncover three stained glass windows in the Chapel of the Nativity and the adjacent north transept. Among various intricate patterns, those windows depict angels, figures from the Christian Old Testament, and a startling image of the Milky Way galaxy outlined by the shape of a woman. Each of the small victories has intensified Peter's thirst to resurrect the other gems of glory hidden in the cathedral's many dozens of darkened windows.

Peter and Dorcas reach Sophia's tent, and Peter's thoughts turn to the confrontation at hand. He glances at Dorcas, takes a deep breath, and says, "Doop deep."

A rustling noise comes from inside the tent.

"Excuse us, young lady, you in the tent," Dorcas says. "The bishop needs to talk with you."

Sophia emerges and blinks at them, her calm face the picture of composure. Peter notices she has her hair pulled back that morning.

"Good morning!" he says. "I do hope you will be joining us again today for worship."

"I am. And you need not worry." She smiles. "I don't plan to read aloud today."

Peter smiles back. "Great. I mean, that's proper. Although, of course, if you continue to join us, you could certainly serve as an official lector for the, for the readings prescribed for a given Sunday when you read."

Dorcas stares at Peter with wide eyes as he trips over his polite words.

"Also, I wanted to ask you about something else." Peter unconsciously runs a finger between his neck and collar. "You may have noticed the little pieces of metal I use to lock and unlock the gold-colored box at the front of the chapel."

"The keys, yes."

"You haven't, by chance, seen them, have you? I'm—" He clears his throat. "I'm asking everyone, really."

Her eyes continue to meet his, and she says matter-of-factly, "I took them."

His eyes widen. "You say you—*took*—the keys to—"

"To the tabernacle, yes. It is right for me to have them, for now."

"Well, actually, they belong to the Church, and we need them to open the tabernacle and remove what's inside."

She says nothing to this, and he feels the heat rise in his face. "The body and blood of Christ are in there—we eat and drink them, we don't just leave them in there!"

Peter shuts his mouth, realizing how openly he's speaking. Sophia has plainly read some scripture, and now she's been to a service, but who knows what she really understands? He normally describes the Holy Eucharist to "outsiders" only in highly circumspect terms. Even in famously tolerant Sanef, a rite that resembles cannibalism could easily be labeled as the most antisocial sort of metafiz.

Sophia's face betrays neither surprise nor revulsion. She simply glances from Peter to Dorcas and says, "The fast precedes the feast." Then she turns from them and reenters her tent, abruptly ending the exchange.

Peter stares at the tent, perplexed.

Dorcas clenches her jaw in poisonous silence.

Sophia attends the service that morning as promised. Creating no disruption apart from drawing distracted glances from the curious Christworshippers, she remains serenely quiet, listening as the group moves through the liturgy. Like Felipe, Sophia merely hums along with the hymns. She appears to listen as Peter gives his sermon, titled *The Almighty Sovereign Power of Our Invulnerable Lord*. She does not join in the spoken prayers, nor does she come forward to receive the bread and wine, which Peter brought out from his supplies in the vesting room to be blessed.

Dorcas stares at Sophia occasionally and at Peter frequently, chastening him with her eyes for not forbidding an admitted thief to join the assembly. Peter tries to ignore Dorcas's stare, but he knows what it will come to. He'll have no choice but to tell Sophia to remove her tent from the Church's property.

When the service ends, Marco heads outside to set up the rickety table they use to serve refreshments in the courtyard after each service. As the Christworshippers slowly move through the chapel to follow Marco, Junia and her four-year-old grandson join Peter and several of the adults. This is the second or third time Junia has been able to bring the boy. His parents are not Christworshippers, but they are tolerant, and they sometimes read to him from an old codex of bible stories.

Peter kneels down to the boy's level. "I was so happy to see you in church today. Are your parents away on a trip?"

The boy nods.

"What a good chance for you and your grandma to spend some fun time together, huh?"

The boy nods again, and Junia ruffles his hair. His eyes are focused on the sparkling silver pectoral cross hanging on Peter's chest. As Peter begins to stand up, the boy says, "I, I have a question."

"Oh, sure." Peter kneels once more.

The boy begins to reach toward Peter's cross and then pulls his hand back. He lifts his eyes and asks, "What's God made out of?"

The adults grin. Martin raises an eyebrow and strokes his chin. "Indeed, Bishop, what *is* God made out of?"

Peter keeps a smile pasted on his lips and looks into the boy's earnest brown eyes. How to answer the question in a way a small child can understand? Recondite theological terms like *ousia* and *hypostasis* flit through Peter's brain. He glances up and notices Sophia. She's talking with Lupe, Bede, and Felipe, none of whom yet know about her thievery. Peter hears himself say, "God is made out of love."

"Ooh," says the boy. He nods vigorously and wraps himself around Junia's leg.

Peter stands, and Martin leans in toward him. "Brilliant answer, Bishop."

Peter pulls his gaze away from Sophia. "You know, I didn't just invent the idea that 'God is love.'"

∽

The following morning, Peter finds Sophia reclining on the cathedral's front steps, her arms spread out to catch the sun's rays. The July day is particularly warm—*too warm to sit outside for long*, Peter thinks. The prior summer was a real "grumbler," and the current one is shaping up to become another one. While grumbling against the geoengineering cartel never seems to result in cooler weather, it does give people a convenient scapegoat for their wrath.

Sophia regards Peter as he approaches. "Where have you been?" she asks. "It's nearly eleven."

"Um, I didn't realize I was expected to be here at all, much less at an appointed time."

"Are you not the guardian of this cathedral?" Still reclining, Sophia raises an arm with a flourish. "It's been over twenty-four hours since you learned of a crime. What if the thief hid the stolen goods in the meantime? What kind of overseer are you, anyway?"

"This is hardly an appropriate situation for mockery. I should tell you that I've considered whether to report this to the authorities." His solemn declaration elicits no visible reaction from her. He sighs and says, "But they would never be able to see the theft of two slivers of metal for the serious crime it is."

"Hmm. I suppose you don't burn criminals and heretics anymore? And this church doesn't appear to have a dungeon. That just leaves you with excommunication. But, as you know, I haven't been communicating that much anyway."

He stares in perplexed silence as she stands up from the steps.

"I know you don't want me here," she says, softly now. "And I will respect your wishes. I never force anything." She nods toward her tent. "But before I disband my empire and move along, would you do me one favor?"

Peter feels relieved that he won't have to order her to leave. To his surprise, a pang of emptiness immediately follows, as if something important is about to end prematurely. "Well, I—I suppose you're right that it would probably be best for you to, to go somewhere better for you—"

"The favor?"

"I'd be happy to." He furrows his brow. "Provided it's within reason."

"Naturally," she says. "The cathedral has a lower level where you keep Christian artifacts."

"Yes, we call it the 'crypt.'"

"I'd like you to show me what's in your crypt. Will you give me a tour?"

Peter considers her proposal. On the one hand, she might try to steal something else. On the other, it sounds as if a brief visit will smooth her transition off the cathedral grounds. And Peter will watch her with a Trinity-to-carrot-like focus.

"We have a deal, Sophia."

They enter the cathedral through its north entrance. A narrow stairwell near the cathedral's locked-down main doors links the nave level to the crypt below, which long ago housed Sunday School classrooms, a gift shop, and a café, among other things. Most of those rooms have been shuttered for decades.

The two of them descend the flight of stairs and step into the crypt. Down the hall to their left, there was once a separate entrance via steps leading up to the street level. The doors fell apart some time ago, and someone, at some point, filled the entrance with a translucent polymer to keep the elements at bay. In the dull light that enters, the corridor looks dingy, Peter's eyes now register. Every corner has a cobweb, and a subtle moldy stench exudes from God-knows-where. Down there, the old cathedral feels even more like a great tomb.

They turn right, and Peter leads Sophia thirty steps down a corridor to a heavy door. She aims her light while he punches a four-digit code into a worn keypad, causing locks to unbolt with two loud clangs. He pushes open the door, and ceiling lights automatically flare on, bathing a large, utilitarian room in stark white light.

Sophia follows Peter into the room, where they encounter a rambling, tightly-packed jungle of archaic Christian objects strewn across tables, shelves, and the floor and hanging from the walls: icons, altarpieces, prayer beads . . . dalmatics, chasubles, mantellettas, miters, and other vestments . . . shelves of bibles, hymnals, lectionaries, commentaries, systematic theologies, and other fading codices . . . sculptures of Jesus Christ, the Virgin Mary, and various saints . . . framed paintings by Renaissance masters stacked up against one another like decks of playing cards . . . chalices, ciboria, thuribles . . . and a variety of other objects whose significance most Sanefers would be at a loss even to guess. If added together, the collective age of all the artifacts would be measured in the hundreds of millennia. Some of them had once been world-famous.

Peter has played tour guide to curious scholars on a few occasions, so he's prepared. "Welcome to the largest single collection of Christian objects in the System. We attracted many generous donations through the years from churches that were closing down. So we are the heirs not only to the history of this cathedral or a single denom—group of Christworshippers—but to the Church as a whole."

Sophia stares in silence, slowly turning three-hundred sixty degrees to scan the entire room. Peter is surprised, and then a little amused, to see her nonplussed expression. After some moments, she whispers, "Such abundance. Why do you bury your treasures?"

Peter's eyes widen. "No, no, we haven't 'buried' them! We bring out different holy artifacts on different feast days for veneration and reflection. I switch out the painting in the north transept's alcove every month. And anyone can make an appointment to come see these things."

Still panning her eyes across the packed room, Sophia asks, "How old are you?"

"Twenty-nine. About the same as you, right?"

"Thirty. Sometimes you sound like you're ninety."

He stiffens and then forces a smile. "I spend a lot of time with older people. In my experience, age brings wisdom, so I'll take that as a compliment."

"In cases of doubt, assume a charitable spirit," she murmurs as she turns to examine a stained glass window held in a wooden frame. The window's central pattern comprises three rabbits chasing one another inside a circle, as if they're running in an oversized zero-gravity hamster wheel. Each rabbit is symmetrically spaced from the other two. The rabbits' long ears converge in the center in such a way that each ear connects to two rabbits. Even though there are only three ears in total, forming a central triangle, each of the three rabbits looks complete if viewed by itself.

"That's delightful," Sophia says, smiling.

"I rather like it myself," Peter says. The rabbit window inspired Trinity's name, but Peter doesn't feel like mentioning he has a pet bunny. "It's from one of the German nations. It was one of my mother's favorite pieces."

"Priscilla. Such a beautiful person."

Peter stiffens again. He opens his mouth and then closes it without uttering a sound.

Meanwhile, Sophia approaches a small table reserved for a single, tiny statue carved from bright green stone. An exquisitely detailed, voluptuous woman wearing an intricately flowing dress holds out her arms. Sophia points at it. "Where did you get this?"

Peter swallows and takes a breath. In a flat voice, he says, "It's a rare and valuable piece we received from a former cathedral in Africa. She is the Virgin Mary, the mother of Jesus, carved in African jade."

Sophia picks up the statuette and cradles it in her hand.

"If you could please refrain from touch—"

"Who are the people in that painting?" interrupts Sophia. In one fluid gesture, she sets down the jade statuette and points at a painting tucked away in the nearest corner of the room.

Peter approaches the painting and squints at it. It's a fictional group portrait of several women from different eras in history: two in medieval nuns' habits, one wearing a plain white dress, and a pale one with an oldtime-style pearl necklace and broach. Peter furrows his brow and reads the tarnished plaque at the bottom of the frame: *Daughters of the Spirit: Hildegard of Bingen (1098–1179), Teresa of Ávila (1515–1582), Rebecca Cox Jackson (1795–1871), and Evelyn Underhill (1875–1941).*

"They're, um, 'Daughters of the Spirit,' it says."

Sophia smiles. "Do you know about any of these people?"

"Well, the painting has been here as long as I can remember."

"But do you know who they were?"

"Uh, no, not really. I guess they must have been important since someone painted them."

She frowns and shakes her head. Then she turns and points at a towering, oldtime-modernist stone statue of a man with outstretched arms. "Who is this?"

This time, Peter speaks with confidence. "That's Saint Francis of Assisi."

"Do you know of him?"

"He was a well-known saint."

"Why?"

"He was the patron saint of animals."

"Animals—he loved animals?"

"Yes."

"Why did he love animals?"

"Why?"

"Yes, why."

Peter shrugs. "Why does anyone love animals?"

Sophia frowns and shakes her head again. She walks over to a large shelf containing a collection of oldtime codices and begins scanning the titles on the books' spines. "Do you read much?" she asks.

"I often access writings about Christian history and doctrine archived on the net. I just finished a biography of Saint Leo the Great." He gestures at the shelves. "I don't like to read these codices, though, because it might damage them."

Sophia continues to scan the books, and she pulls one from its shelf. A thin comet's tail of dust trails the book.

"Those are delicate antiques. If you must look at them, please take out only one at a time."

She pulls three or four more books from sections of the bookshelf marked with peeling yellow labels—*Theology, Theopoetics, Wisdom Literature*—as Peter watches nervously. She hands him the stack and says, "Start with these."

"Pardon me?"

"Start with these."

Peter pulls his shoulders back, raising himself to his full height. "I happen to be the leader of the Christian Church. It's my job to teach its theology, you know."

"And an absolutely dynamite job you've done," she says.

"Now, just a damn—"

"Your first duty is to open your heart to God. And to open your heart, you must open your mind."

"I—you—"

As Peter stammers, Sophia turns from the bookshelf and approaches an ostentatiously calligraphed yellowing parchment hanging in a wooden frame. "What's this?" she asks.

"That? That? It's nothing. Uh, it's—it's a list."

Peter chews a thumbnail as Sophia scans the parchment. Beginning with a giant, flowery "P," the text reads:

> *Prompted by a reverent desire to reunify the Christian Church, and authorized by the authorities now representing its historic branches, the Right Reverend Timothy Feng, Episcopal Bishop of the See of Sanef and Other Territories of Oldtime California, on behalf of himself and his apostolic successors, has assumed the authority and responsibilities of the following ecclesiastical offices:*
>
> *Bishop of Rome (in absentia) and Supreme Pontiff*
>
> *Ecumenical Patriarch and Eastern Orthodox Primate*
>
> *Archbishop of Canterbury (in absentia) and Anglican Primate*
>
> *Presiding Bishop of the Sol System Evangelical Lutheran Churches*
>
> *Moderator-Designee of the Unified System-wide Presbyterian/ Reformed Church*
>
> *Secretary General and CEO of the Worlds Evangelical Alliance*
>
> *Chairman-Designee of the Pentecostal System-wide Fellowship*
>
> *President-Designee of the Conservative Baptist-Methodist-Congregationalist Convention*
>
> *President-Designee of the Progressive Methodist-Congregationalist-Baptist Alliance*
>
> *Primate of the Church of the Lord (Aladura) Systemwide*
>
> *Pope of the Coptic Orthodox Church of Alexandria (in absentia)*
>
> *Catholicos of the Assyrian Church of the East . . .*

More titles spill down the parchment.

"Intriguing," Sophia says. "These titles now belong to you, don't they?"

"I inherited them from the prior bishops at this cathedral, but I don't know what they all mean." He sighs. "It's not like any of it matters now, anyway."

Peter doesn't feel like telling her the whole story. Tim Feng, an earlier bishop at Grace Cathedral, secured the grand, meaningless titles for himself and his unfortunate successors. By the time Tim became bishop, the ancient denominations, including his own, had bled out. Even the once Earth-straddling Roman church had collapsed as an ordered institution following a series of scandals, the loss of Vatican City, and what one sociologist labeled "a shift in the *zeitgeist* away from theistic cultic patterns." Not the hatchet-blow of oppression but rather the seeping, saturating poison of indifference had ravaged, root and branch, Eternal Rome and the other churches.

Bishop Tim had been blessed with modest success as an entrepreneur prior to his consecration as bishop. He felt the Holy Spirit had called him to reunify the "one, holy, catholic, and apostolic Church," so he traveled to places such as Old New York, Canterbury, Lagos, Hannover, Rome, Istanbul, Alexandria, and New Seoul to hunt down aging bishops and former church leaders: men and women who no longer had congregations, much less cathedrals or churches. In all cases, Tim's persuasion—and generosity—carried the day. His efforts culminated in a press release announcing the Christian Church's "Grand Reunification," which ranked as a top netstory for an hour and twenty minutes on a Thursday. The ecclesiastical titles eventually passed from the finally penniless Bishop Tim to Bishop Priscilla and then to Peter—the latest Great Patriarch of Nothing Left.

Sophia walks over to a display case. "What's in here?"

"Look, I think we've spent more than enough time down here—"

"Oh, 'Fragments of the True Cross,'" she reads from a rusting plaque. She gazes at five ancient slivers of wood housed in a reliquary. After a moment, she says, "None of them."

"Sorry?"

"It's clear that none of them were actually part of the True Cross."

"Oh, for God's sake, you think you know—?" He stops and takes a breath. "Really, this has gone far enough. I think it's time you told me your *real* name and where you come from."

"I've told you my name. I come from Bethlehem."

He closes his eyes and groans. "Now, look—"

"Let me ask you a question," she interjects. "You have wishes for this place, for these people who worship here. You don't understand what you've been entrusted with, but you do have a desire to save the Church and to help the System. Many of the objects in this room are quite valuable. Why don't you sell some of these things and use the money to help you work for your goals?"

Peter's eyes bulge. "You must be joking."

"No."

He furiously shakes his head from side to side. "If you really were who you think you are, you wouldn't need to ask that. You'd understand that *these things* are our sacred history. You'd know that people bled and died to protect them, that they're our heritage, who we are. There's so little of this heritage left in our hands. Do you think I have the right to sell our holy artifacts on the net as if they were bars of soap or embroidered socks?" His voice trembles, and he grabs a codex to keep it from sliding off the stack in his arms.

"No, I suppose not," she concedes.

At that moment, a chorus of loud but serene baritone voices suddenly begins to chant:

> *. . . imple superna gratia*
> *quae tu creasti pectora . . .*

Both Peter and Sophia remain motionless for several moments following the music's abrupt commencement.

> *Qui diceris Paraclitus,*
> *altissimi donum Dei . . .*

Peter unfreezes. "Um, sorry."

> *fons vivus, ignis, caritas,*
> *et spiritalis unctio—*

He moves to a table near the door and presses a button on a tiny device. As suddenly as the chant began, it disappears into silence.

"The trigger that turns on the room's lights also turns on the outlets, and sometimes this thing turns itself on after it gets some juice. It dates from back when people carried around devices like this to listen to music."

Before Sophia can comment, Peter begins to usher her toward the exit. "Anyway, this has been a real load of fun, but I have a lot to do today, so I'm taking this as a sign that we should wrap up here."

She silently complies, taking a last look around the room as they exit.

Peter leads the way through the dreary hallway and back up the stairs, feeling as if he's just taken part in a long wrestling match. They emerge onto the nave level near the main entrance. Darkness blankets the cavernous space beyond, where past generations of Christworshippers gathered. Peter can't see the rows of timeworn wooden pews he knows stretch back in their direction from the high altar. He can make out part of the worn stone labyrinth inset into the floor between the pews and the spot where he and Sophia stand. A vast, aching emptiness surrounds Peter.

"The chant was beautiful," Sophia says softly. She sighs. "How lovely it is to ponder all the centuries of Christian people seeking and loving God. So many souls. So many hopes and dreams." She turns toward him. "Thank you for the tour."

"You're welcome," he says, still staring ahead.

"I suppose we now say goodbye."

Sophia gazes at Peter, but he's still looking in the direction of the altar. Beyond the penumbra from the small light Sophia holds, the darkness stretches before Peter like an infinite void, and he cannot pull his eyes away from it. In the deep silence, the voices of long-dead monks echo in the last bishop's ears louder than they did in the crypt.

There must have been dozens of voices on the recording—more than we have left in the entire Church. What would those oldtime monks say if they could see us now?

It strikes Peter just how odd it is that every city block around them hosts thousands of people at any given time, while this one presently has only a population of two—a population that will be halved as soon as Sophia moves on. Indeed, when Peter goes home to his apartment, it will have a population of zero. Zero living people, billions of ghosts.

All the centuries, she said. So many hopes and dreams. Peter thinks of martyrs facing lions' jaws . . . of stoneworkers spending their lives building cathedrals they would never see completed . . . of civil rights marchers stoned and shot for the Kingdom of God. *How much blood was shed for this faith? How many generations worshipped at this very spot and at so many others like it?* And there he stands: the last lonesome shepherd tending the dying remnant, swaddled in the superficialities of his worldly city living. An unworthy undertaker.

Peter shivers.

Sophia raises her hand to lightly touch his cheek, bringing him back into time. To him, she looks strangely enfleshed, abnormally concrete, compared to the spirits inhabiting his imagination.

"I'm, I'm sorry," he whispers.

"You love deeply," she whispers back.

She withdraws her hand, and, after some moments, he clears his throat. "Since you were kind enough to give me *reading recommendations*," he says, "I suppose the least I can do is give you another week to find a place to stay."

She nods.

The sun's brightness temporarily blinds Peter when they finally emerge from the building.

~

Unlike Grace Cathedral's interior, its front steps rarely enjoy complete darkness or silence. At night, a babbling brook of light and sound dribbles down from the Huntington-Union Tower's balcony bars. Occasional bursts of raucous laughter identify patrons intoxicated from alcohol or hopped up from stimming.

An elderly lowcontrib shuffles down the street pushing a rusted metal cart filled with her worldly possessions. Her clothing hangs off her wrinkled, wiry frame. She softly sings to herself.

> *A timeworn gigolo, a son of the West,*
> *Got no home or credit, can't get any rest . . .*

With a yawn, she decides to sit down on the cathedral steps for a moment, temporarily halting the squeaking of her cart's wheels. The elderly lowcontrib's ears are still good, and she can hear how the youngsters up in the bars sound like they're having fun. Not her thing, though. At least not since many years ago.

Her ears detect soft human sounds coming from behind her. She turns and cranes her neck, and she sees a canvas tent in front of the doors to the old building. Light from electric lamps shines through the tent fabric.

Goofy place to camp.

The urgency and volume of the sounds increase, and the elderly lowcontrib can now make out a young woman's voice. She's repeating words like some kind of mantra.

"Give me the strength to abstain. Give me the strength."

Poor girl, thinks the elderly lowcontrib. *Another wretch fighting her addiction day and night.* The old woman knows what it's like and sympathizes, but she also knows she should move on. She's learned the hard way that street folks looking to fund their next stim aren't above robbing even a poor old lady with nothing but a couple of ragged blankets. She begins to squeak her way down the street once more.

As she passes out of view, the young woman emerges from her tent. She looks around quizzically. Seeing no one there, she turns her attention back to the object she holds in her hand. Ever so gently, she caresses Mary's hair. The priceless African jade glows in the sheen of the electric lamps.

5

Russ

A boy named Russ pants as he sprints down a dirt road, kicking up dust. In his part of the former US-American meganation—a couple thousand kilometers from Sanef—there's little that can be done about the weather other than sweat. But Russ doesn't bother to gripe about the heat, and he isn't going to let something as far away as the sun slow him down. "I'm not a little kid anymore," he's told everyone in the valley. "I'm double-digits now."

He'll be the shortest one in fifth grade just like he was in fourth, but he's used to that—he's been the shortest ever since Billy Reeves moved away in second grade. What Russ lacks in some departments, he makes up for with speed and energy. He didn't advance to the finals of the spelling bee, but by good, he got the letters out faster than anyone else.

He runs into his yard and toward the house, leaping over cracked planters growing nothing but dirt. The paint on their oldtime wooden-frame, three-bedroom ranch house used to be light blue, but it has gradually faded to a peeling gray in the years since his daddy last painted. The roof is missing several shingles, an unnecessary luxury in a valley where it never rains. Russ's favorite part of the house is the front porch, which is big enough to seat more people than ever visit. The overhanging roof shades it just about all day long. Russ often sits with his daddy on the porch swing, which is where Russ now finds him.

"Hi, Daddy!"

"Hey, son."

"Veronica's not back yet?"

"No."

"That's good. But, Daddy, guess what I saw! You're never gonna guess!"

"Calm down, now. Wha'd you see?"

Russ hops up on the porch, and warped boards creak beneath his feet. "Old Clark's is closed. All boarded up. Sign on the store says he's headed north. He just up and left. Did you know?"

"Yeah, he gave me a couple days warning. Can't say I blame him for going."

Russ stares at his father with wide eyes. "Whaddya mean?"

Spence smiles, but it isn't a happy smile. With a calloused hand, he pats the spot next to him on the porch swing. "Sit down," he tells his son.

Russ obeys. He stares into his father's pale blue-gray irises.

Spence gestures toward the valley. "There used to be a river here, you know," he says. "When I was your age, I used to could see farmland from our house as far as the eye would go. All that yellow down there in the valley and up on the hillsides was green. But now the water's gone. So the agriculture has gone, and there's nothing here for the cartels. Which means there's no jobs, no money, no nothing but empty land and a hot sun. You see, son, the valley's dying."

Russ pulls his eyes away from his father's somber face and scrutinizes the landscape, staring at it as if he hasn't looked out at the valley every day of his life. Stillness reigns. Deprived of any breeze, any living thing big enough to make a noise is hiding from the summer sun. As Russ surveys the yellow hills and fields with new eyes, he echoes its silence for a minute. But he can never stay quiet for long.

"Daddy?"

"Yeah."

"Remember when Aunt Alma looked up our gene—gene-ology—"

"Genealogy."

"—our genealogy on the net."

"Yeah." Spence snorts. "Another one of Alma's big projects."

"Well, she said that we come from pioneers. They moved through a bunch of different nations: Apachea, Arkansaw, Texoma—"

"It's Appalachia. And they weren't different nations back then."

"Well, what I mean is, if things are bad here, why don't we just pioneer our way somewhere else?"

Russ waits expectantly for his father's judgment, but Spence just stares into the distance. Russ takes off his shoes and folds his feet underneath himself on the porch swing. His favorite gray tomcat drops by for a visit, and Russ meows at him. The skinny cat leaps onto the swing and allows Russ to pet him, purring with pleasure at the boy's affectionate touch.

It isn't long before Veronica appears, kicking a rock ahead of her. Her blond hair and flowery, hand-me-down summer dress shimmer in the heat haze. Spence puts a hand to his forehead to shield his eyes. He says to Russ, "If you want to know what your mama looked like when she was a teenager, take a good look at your sister. She's almost the spitting image."

Mama was beautiful, Russ thinks. *Weirdo Veronica doesn't look like her at all.* As Veronica comes into earshot, he says out loud, "But Mama was so pretty."

Veronica eyes Russ as she steps onto the porch. "What are you saying about Mama?" She falls heavily into a faded plastic lawn chair. Her sweat-soaked dress clings to her thin frame.

"Nothing," Russ says. "Guess you got turned down again."

"Shut up, bubbie." Veronica addresses Spence. "No luck, Dad. Thirty people show up for every opening. The one they ended up hiring had gone to a university a couple years."

"I know you did the best you could, Precious," Spence says. "Good knows I've gone from one end of this valley to the other without finding work. Ever since the agro-cartel pulled out, there just isn't near enough to go around."

"The government or somebody should do something," Veronica says.

Spence's gaze travels back and forth between his children's faces. "That'd be real nice, but you know that's not gonna happen. Remember, children, life is a fight—everybody against everybody else. I wish it wasn't true, but anybody who says different you can be sure is trying to sell you something. Except for your family, nobody owes anybody anything." He nods at the stray cat in Russ's lap. "Every creature in this System, including us, is just here to eat what it can, and to take care of its own—"

"Skip the sermon, Dad," Veronica says.

"Fine. But my point is that we've got a problem no one is going to solve for us. It's that we're at the bottom of the food chain here in this valley."

"Now, that's the truth," huffs Veronica.

Russ looks back and forth at his father and sister. He hasn't seen any chains of food at all—*I would have remembered that*, he thinks. So he doesn't understand what they mean, exactly. But he can tell they're both sad.

I know what we need to do. He gently scoops the cat from his lap, stands up from the swing, puts a hand on his hip, and points toward the horizon. "That way! I claim that direction for our family. Let's go pioneer that way until we find a new valley with a big, wide river and lots of food chains!"

Veronica snickers and rubs the top of his head. "Bubbie, honey, you can't be pioneers where there's no frontier."

Spence furrows his brow and slowly tilts his chin upward.

6

Face-to-Face

Peter smooths his vestments as he walks around to the cathedral's front entrance. Sophia's weeklong extension ends tomorrow, and Peter has been avoiding her, trying to think his way into a good solution to the situation. But the service is going to start in fifteen minutes. *I have a duty to get advanced warning of any shenanigans she might be planning,* he rationalizes. Thankfully, a fire-breathing Dorcas does not ride his heels that Sunday morning.

As Peter rounds the corner of the building, he sees Sophia emerge from her tent. Instead of plain, simple clothing, she wears an outfit which could only be described as remarkably fashionable. Peter stops in surprise, wondering where she could have gotten the money to buy herself nice new clothes. Sophia notices him and gives him a smile that seems uncharacteristically nervous. Or is he just imagining it?

The morning sun peeks through the surrounding towers. Sophia's hair reflects its rays, and Peter can't help but notice the sculpting of her neck and collarbones. Her smooth, almond skin is almost lustrous, and she moves with graceful self-possession.

She's actually rather . . . beautiful. Huh.

He shakes his head and clears his throat. "Good morning, Sophia. I just wanted to welcome you to join us at this morning's service. Um, one of the scripture passages I'll be reading is an interesting one, about the prophet Hosea. God orders him to marry a prostitute, and the marriage symbolizes the relationship between God and His unfaithful people, um—" He tapers off as she shakes her head.

"I can't join you today."

"Oh. I'm sorry to hear that," he says, relieved and disappointed. He fleetingly considers complimenting her on how nice she looks. But the thought of the bishop, clad in his vestments and pectoral cross, remarking on a feme's appearance feels . . . inappropriate.

"I hope my brothers and sisters have been kind to you?" he asks.

"Yes, very kind."

"I'm glad to hear it."

They stand in silence for a few moments as Peter tries to think of what to say next.

"I'm sorry, Bishop," Sophia says, "but I cannot tarry here right now."

"Oh, right. It looks like you're going off to take care of some important business?"

"I am. I must be about the Father's work."

A quarter of an hour later, Peter is still reproaching himself as he stands in the chapel and recites the call to worship. *My Lord, I'm an idiot. I keep forgetting that feme is nuts.*

He notices Junia lean forward and whisper something into Dorcas's ear. Dorcas frowns as she glances back toward the empty chair next to Phoebe.

Felipe stares at the empty chair, in his wooden way, for a long time.

~

Early Monday afternoon, Dorcas comes over to the cathedral and walks up to the tent. Birds chirp from their perches on the niches and finials in the stone portal surrounding the main entrance, but the sounds do not register with Dorcas. She takes a deep breath and pulls herself up as straight as she can. She hates the way old people hunch, especially the wrinkled wreck who stares back at her from the mirror every morning.

She speaks toward the tent. "Excuse me, Miz. Young lady, excuse me." Receiving no response, Dorcas begins to slowly pull aside a tent flap with one finger, eyeballing the interior.

"Hello!" comes the homeless person's voice from behind Dorcas.

Dorcas steps back from the tent. She turns and sees the homeless person squatting down on the large patio overlooking the cathedral steps. This patio stands several meters north of the Ghiberti Doors, adjacent to a shuttered two-story building and to the large courtyard where the Christworshippers gather after Sunday services. Unlike the bare concrete courtyard, the patio is covered by washed-out, light green artificial turf. For reasons Dorcas is sure she cannot comprehend, the homeless person was apparently inspecting the turf. She stands up and approaches Dorcas.

With distaste, Dorcas notices an oily stain on the homeless person's lightweight summer blouse. Also, she's showing a little too much leg to be considered modest, in Dorcas's opinion. *Perhaps a feme with a scarred face—and who knows how she managed to get that!—has to resort to immodest clothes to attract attention from males.*

Dorcas focuses on the homeless person's expectant face and says, "Young lady, I wanted to come talk to you about what you've done."

"Of course, I'd be happy to talk with you." The homeless person gestures toward the steps—an invitation to sit down together.

Dorcas ignores the gesture. "You aren't one of us, I know," she says. "So you cannot realize what you've done. I understand that, and I did not come here to scold or blame you. I assume you have some real problems to have been brought to this, this state." She vaguely motions at the tent. "As a Christworshipper, I want to help you, I do. But I also want you to understand what those keys mean.

"That tabernacle, that is our center, the center of our lives. Our savior, Jesus, He died for us. We believe He died for us and was raised from the dead. And before He was killed, He told His disciples to eat His body and drink His blood to remember Him always."

The homeless person listens silently.

"I, I know this must not make any sense to you. But when Bishop Peter says his blessing over the bread and the wine—remember? Some of us believe that when he says that blessing, it becomes the body and blood of our savior. In a mysterious way that can't be explained, it becomes the body and blood of Jesus. And this sacrament is *not* cannibalistic 'metafiz'—it's an ancient and revered practice that has been passed down for many, many centuries.

"We keep some of this bread and wine in our tabernacle, the only one left in the System. That makes it the most sacred place there is for us, so we would never break it open or damage it. Some in the congregation might say that you trapped the very body and blood of our God in the tabernacle when you took the keys." Dorcas stares at the homeless person.

She remains silent.

Dorcas puts her hands on her hips. "Young lady, I know we must just seem like a bunch of cranks or weirdos to you. Nowadays, everyone is taught that all 'metafiz' is a sickness. But to us, this place is our center. It's family and tradition and who we are and who we're supposed to be." Her voice cracks. "You're a child of God, so you're welcome here, yes, yes you are. But please don't try to steal what's important to us."

Dorcas feels a tear roll down her cheek, giving her cause for surprise and embarrassment. *That's not supposed to happen. Now I'll look weak in front of this young person.*

Presumptuously, the young person touches Dorcas's cheek to wipe away the tear. Her hand is warm to the touch, but Dorcas flinches.

"Mother," the young person whispers, "you are dear to God. Why do you fear?"

"What—what do you know about our God?"

"This I know: your God 'is love.' Tell me, what is the adversary of love?"

"The adver—oh, hatred, I suppose."

"No. In the same moment, one can love one thing and hate another. Strong love and hatred may exist side by side, at least for a time. No, the opposite of love is *fear*. Each drop of fear in one's heart displaces ten drops of love. We must soften in order to love, but fear makes us rigid. This is why the command Jesus gave most frequently was 'Fear not.'" The woman raises her hand to Dorcas's cheek again. Dorcas does not flinch this time.

"Dorcas, nurture your love for your God and your Church. Have faith and do not fear anything. Your seed will be broken to sprout a field of wheat."

Dorcas was prepared for another incoherent conversation or even an agitated rant, but not for this. No one has ever spoken to her like this before.

"I'm—not sure you—I'm not sure you understand. I'm an old lady. All I want is to die soon, before the Church does."

"Then I have come to bring you bad news. You will not die soon. Nor will your Church."

"Oh—oh! What fluff-brained nonsense! I mean—look, who do you think you are? You obviously know something about us, but how? Are you trying to tell me you think you're some kind of prophet or that you can see into the future?"

Slowly, in a deliberate tone, Sophia says, "Who do you say that I am?"

Dorcas recognizes the quotation from Jesus. "Oh! Oh, my—you think—you believe—oh, you poor girl!"

Sophia smiles. "I am poor. But, despite what your bishop may think, I'm not insane."

Dorcas just stares. Sophia touches the old woman's arm. "Come with me for a stroll. We need to talk more."

Dorcas does not move.

Sophia tilts her head in the direction of the courtyard. "Fear not. As an 'old lady' with nothing better to do than die, you can spare a few more minutes to talk. Come."

Dorcas gapes at Sophia, at her effrontery, but she does not turn away. She thinks Sophia might be mad, yet she's not afraid. After several breaths, Dorcas makes her decision.

As Dorcas follows Sophia, she suddenly notices the playful birdsong overhead.

~

The following day, Peter opens the door to The Bishop's Residence to find that it's Sophia who dooped. Rays of late-afternoon sunlight reflect down to the street in front of the Sacramento Tower. Sophia wears a relaxed smile and plain, second-hand apparel that looks baggy on her—even so, she looks nice. A warm breeze caresses Peter's face as his eyes meet hers. The moment stretches out as they regard one another.

"Sophia. Hello."

"Hello, Bishop Peter. I'm sorry I had to leave you abruptly the other day. I really hate to rush."

Peter considers and quickly rejects the idea of inviting her into The Bishop's Residence. "Dressed as you were," he says, "I'm guessing you were going to a job interview. If there's anything I can do to help, please ask. Even the Almighty has to make a living, right?" He can feel himself blush involuntarily at the silliness of his quip.

"Thank you. With your sense of humor, it's shocking the pews aren't overflowing."

"Touché." He lifts his hands to the sky in mock resignation.

She laughs. "Seriously, thank you for your offer. But, you see, I've come here not to ask you for something, but rather to give you something. And I think you will enjoy what I have to give you."

Peter feels the heat rise in his cheeks again. "How, um, mysterious. I'm not sure there's anything I really need."

"You don't need what I want to give you. But I'm certain you will like it."

It suddenly feels to Peter as though they are standing very close to one another. "I'm not sure if I should ask . . ."

She steps away from the door and motions for him to follow her outside. "Come and see."

"Oh. Okay."

Peter follows Sophia the short distance to the cathedral grounds, where she leads him to the concrete patio overlooking the front steps. For as long as Peter can remember, the patio has been covered by a faded green carpet of outdoor flooring material worn down in a few places to the rubber matting beneath. At some point in time, the church used this area as a children's playground and covered it with these materials to protect the children from falls. The play structures later fell into disrepair and were removed. If there were even one or two children in Peter's congregation, it might make sense to invest in refurbishing the playground in some way. But, as it is, the space is unneeded and has been untouched for many years.

Peter finds the patio overlaid with several cheap plastic coverings. "Oh my," he says. There's nothing of value here she could harm, so he's not especially worried. *Still.*

"I can't wait to see what you've done now," he says.

"More like what I've undone." She pulls back one of the coverings from the edge of the patio, revealing a concrete surface.

Peter realizes that Sophia must have pulled up the tattered artificial turf and ossified rubber, exposing what lies beneath. Darker lines arc across the lighter-colored cement. At first glance, it looks to Peter like there are narrow lanes, as if little people once ran footraces on a tiny track.

"Help me," she says.

Sophia and Peter silently work their way around the patio, pulling off the pieces of plastic to reveal additional parts of the design. Peter can see it is a circular shape about twelve meters in diameter that contains a narrow, winding path. The particular shape of the path's twists and turns gives rise to a cruciform pattern which visually breaks the circle into four quadrants.

"A labyrinth!" he cries.

He walks over and pulls the last covering off the center, revealing what looks like a six-petaled blossom a couple of meters in diameter. Then he steps back to view the entire pattern.

"It's a labyrinth—the same pattern as the labyrinth inside," he says. "I never knew there was another one out here. Wow. Marvelous. The pattern is based on a labyrinth that used to exist in a place called Chartres in one of the French nations. Seekers would prayerfully walk the path as a sort of mini-pilgrimage." He points at a darkened window in the shuttered building that stands near the edge of the patio. "And that used to be the bishop's office. He could look out and see the people walking the labyrinth, and bless them." Peter smiles.

He turns toward Sophia. "How did you know?"

"Presence."

"Presents? I—well, look." He strides over to where she stands and takes her hand. He feels a sudden tingle along his spine. "Let's walk it," he says. "We'll be the first people to walk this path in a long time."

She nods.

He gestures toward the entrance into the pattern. "You found it. You should go first."

"Come, follow me," she says.

They take several steps in silence, then she murmurs, "Empty your heart of fear and grasping desire as you walk your path. Find the love in its center, then look out at all creation with new eyes."

"Okay," he says uncertainly, wondering whether she's quoting something.

The path winds to and fro, in and out, through the four quadrants of the circle. The sky is turning dusky, and the city air tastes oddly sweet on Peter's lips. Sophia walks with a slow, graceful deliberateness, and Peter follows two or three meters behind her. He tries to empty his mind: he just breathes and takes a step, breathes and takes a step. At one point, surprised by a joyful feeling, he begins to sing the first verse of an old hymn that pops into his head:

> Holy, holy, holy! Lord God Almighty . . .

He must be singing louder than he intends, because a few people in one of the lowest balcony bars crane their necks to look down at him. A couple of them smile and shake their heads. "Those cultists must be do-ing some sort of metafiz ritual!" one of them bawls to another. Despite the distraction, Peter finishes the verse.

> . . . God in three Persons, blessed Trinity!

When Peter finishes his impromptu hymnody, Sophia claps and he blushes. He didn't plan to sing—it just happened.

He refocuses his attention on his footsteps. The labyrinth's narrow path continuously doubles back on itself, repeatedly bringing the two face-to-face as they walk past one another. Peter isn't sure if he should look up at her. Most of the time, he keeps his head bowed in prayer. He feels his arm lightly brush against hers several times as they walk the winding path.

"Peter," she says after a while.

He looks up, and they stop a meter and a half apart.

"Has God ever spoken to you?"

Now we're getting somewhere, he thinks. *She's heard voices, and she thinks it was God talking to her.*

"Sophia, do you recognize my authority as the leader of the Christworshippers?"

She tilts her head in apparent assent.

"I'm telling you with all the authority I have that God doesn't talk to people like voices in their head. That's not, that's not God. It's important for you to understand that that's not how God comes to us."

"I see. How does God come to us?"

"I. Well. He." Peter has overreached. The bitter truth is that he's never felt like God has come to him. "Well, I read somewhere that God comes to us as our life itself—in other words, as our whole path, as everything that happens to us and among us. The point is, if you—if one hears a voice in one's head, I can promise you it is not God."

"And has God come to you as your life itself?"

"I—I guess God must be there, I think, whenever I feel love or friendship."

"Ah. So, do you think God is here now?"

"In *that* sense, in the sense I just talked about—yes. Yes, I admit that I do."

"So even though I'm nuts, we're friends?"

"I never said you were n—"

She cuts him off with a hard stare.

He clears his throat. "Yes, Sophia, you are my friend."

She smiles, and they resume walking, patiently following the path as it weaves from the labyrinth's interior to its edge and back again. The darkening sky signals that evening is nearly upon them. After a couple of minutes of companionable silence, she says, "God doesn't push a person beyond what he can handle."

Peter scrunches his eyebrows, cocks his head, and recites a bible verse: "God is faithful, who will not suffer you to be tempted above that ye are able."

"Indeed."

After several more paces, she says, "What if you did meet God face-to-face and God had a plan for you?"

"Sophia. My friend. I do not believe you are—"

"I'm asking you a hypothetical question." She stops and turns toward him. "*If* God appeared to you face-to-face and had a plan for you, what do you think you would do?"

"I would do as He asked, of course."

"Of course? Of course? What makes you say 'of course'? Many would run off to Tarshish."

"Ah, the prophet Jonah."

"A real heartbreaker, that one," she says as she resumes her walking. "But hardly the only person to flee from the will of God."

Her pace slackens, and Peter soon walks just two steps behind her. He is gazing at the back of her head when she turns and takes a step toward him. He glances down and realizes they've reached the center of the labyrinth. The pattern at the center reminds him of a flower. Or a stump. Or perhaps a clearing in a dense forest.

A mountaintop! That's where it feels like I am.

There he stands, completely surrounded by two-hundred story towers, and he feels as if he's on a mountaintop!

Sophia stands close enough that Peter can smell the soap on her skin. His eyes roam across her face, briefly lingering on the scar. The breeze tousles her hair, and the corners of her lips turn up in the hint of a smile. He draws in a breath and glances in the direction of a seagull which is busily cawing at the setting sun.

Goose bumps raise up on his neck as she slides her hand around the back of his head. He feels her fingertips in his hair, and his pulse throbs in his ears.

"Sophia—"

"Shh." Pulling him closer, she whispers, "When you're used to the edges, the center can be a shock."

His heart pounds as they simply gaze at one another, face-to-face.

∿

A few days later, Peter contentedly leans back from Uncle Jeff's dinner table. Peter dramatically pats his stomach—cooking counts among Jeff's many talents. "I didn't think I was hungry when I got here, but your couscous seduced me. I'm stuffed, Unc."

Jeff grabs a few dishes from the table and takes them into the kitchen. "Glad you liked it. You may remember it was one of your ma's favorites, too."

As Jeff putters around in the kitchen, Peter thinks. He says, "Can I ask you a question?"

Jeff peers into the dining room. "Hmm, the sort of question you have to ask if you can ask? Well, go on."

"Did you love my mother?"

"You mean, did I—?"

"Did you *love* her?"

Jeff walks back to the table and sits down. "What do you think?"

"I think *yes.*"

Jeff's mouth draws itself into a tight smile. "The question is: Did she *love* me?"

"Didn't she?"

"Oh, she loved me, sure. But was I the love of her life?" He looks down at the table.

"Are you saying—"

"Peter, let's let the past lie for tonight. The bottom line is that your mother meant the System to me. And you mean the System to me. So, humor an old man, and tell me about your life."

In the face of Jeff's gentle words, what else can Peter do? He begins to tell Jeff the latest news from the cathedral, such as it is, and finds himself describing his recent encounters with Sophia. ". . . and, to be fair, I think I have to say, at a minimum, she is quite perceptive in her own way. I mean, well, she's got some philosophical chops. I'm still trying to draw out the implications of her question about wishing myself into non-existence by demanding a reality without suffering . . . ."

When Peter pauses to take a breath, Jeff arches an eyebrow and says, "You're excited by her 'chops,' huh? What did you say she looks like?"

"Uh—just, uh, she's got very—hey, this isn't about her looks. You're not listening to me."

"Oh, I'm listening. Look, Peter, it's perfectly normal for a healthy young ro-male to become fascinated by a pretty feme who camps on his doorstep. She's vulnerable, she's available—"

"Now, wait a minute. You really don't know the situation. Why must you always leap to something sexual?"

"All right, maybe I do that. But let me tell you what the situation looks like to me. It *looks* like you're fascinated with a feme who we both know has a serious psychological problem if not a diagnosable mental illness." Jeff leans forward. "That path leads nowhere good, son."

Peter considers the best way to defend his innocence. "I think we've gotten off track here," he says. "Do you know that over the centuries there was practically a whole genre of literature and vids about the idea that Jesus and his disciple Mary Magdalene were lovers or were married?"

"Okay."

"Do you know why?"

Jeff shrugs.

"Because in our culture we've idolized sexual love for a long time. We've come to believe that it is the highest love there can be. But there can be a higher eroticism, a soul-to-soul love, with others and with God. At least, that's what I read in a book I got from So—someone."

"So you have a *soul-to-soul love* with this feme?"

"No! That's, that's not what I'm saying. I'm just saying that you don't have to try to turn it into something sexual."

"Fine, but it just seems like you're getting a little too wrapped up with someone who's mentally unbalanced."

"First, I'm not getting 'wrapped up' with her. *You're* the one who's constantly trying to get me partnered—"

"I don't know about *partnered* necessarily, but at least get you some—"

"Second, I'm not sure she's mentally unbalanced. Yes, she sometimes says odd things, and I think she's heard voices . . . ." Jeff's eyes widen, and Peter hastily continues, "But she doesn't *seem* mentally ill to me. She doesn't seem agitated or tortured or sedated. If anything, she seems more vibrant and at peace than anyone I've ever met!" Peter stops abruptly, surprising himself with his own words. He rubs his chin in thought.

Jeff leans back. "I've always been proud of your open heart. But I would advise you to limit your interest in this particular feme to her philosophical insights." He stands and starts back toward the kitchen. "And that's all I'll say—you know all the reasons as well as I do. Come help me clean up."

Peter sighs. *Of course I do.*

First thing the next morning, Peter walks over to the tent. Although it's still early, the breeze is already warm. As usual, the surrounding city hums with activity.

"Sophia? Doop deep."

"Just a minute."

Peter hears a rustling noise. It sounds as though she might be changing her clothes. As he waits, a thought occurs to him: if she joins the Church, they will be *twelve* once more—like the apostles, like the tribes of Israel—at least until the next funeral.

She emerges from the tent with a yawn and stretches her arms.

Peter has been feeling progressively worse about Sophia sleeping outside in a tent. The days are long gone when Sanef could count on sea fog to cool the summer nights. "Good morning," he says. "Rough night?"

"Just a late one."

Peter cocks his head inquisitively, but she does not elaborate.

"What would you like to ask me today, Bishop?"

What kept you up late into the night? He pictures Sophia out dancing at some Friday-night party. *She's young and physically healthy, and it's not as if she has anything else to occupy her time, after all. Why had I assumed she would just hang around the cathedral grounds every night?*

"You know," he says, "not every conversation I have involves religious questions."

"Thank God for that. But I suspect this one will."

"Well, yes."

She gestures toward the steps, and they sit down side by side. "Aren't you about ready to banish me?" she asks. "It has been longer than a week, you know."

He looks into her eyes, and he feels only warmth. Whatever else she is or is not, he now knows that she's his friend.

"You know I'm not going to do that." Oddly, Dorcas hasn't complained to Peter about the stolen keys all week.

Sophia gazes out toward the Huntington-Union Tower. "What's your question?"

"Sophia, you know I don't believe you are who you think you are. But you know something about us, and . . . I do believe you have a certain wisdom."

Her lips part in a thin smile. She continues to gaze out at the densely towering web of civilization surrounding the cathedral grounds.

"So maybe you can help me with my question. It's a really important one to me." He takes a breath. "If God exists and Christ is His Son, why would God let Christ's Church fall into decline? That's it. Do you happen to have an answer to that one?"

"Yes."

Surprised by her unhesitating response, he waits for her to elaborate, but she says nothing further. Finally, he says, "Let me guess, I'm 'not ready' for it."

"Oh no, you're ready for the answer to your question, but first you need to take me to the redwoods."

"Sorry?"

"You. Need to take me. To the redwoods. I'm new here, and I've read about the famous redwood forests, but I've never actually walked in one."

Peter recalls that he still has no idea where Sophia actually comes from—presumably *not* Bethlehem. It doesn't seem like the right time to mine her for that sort of information, though. "You're saying I need to *take you to a forest*, and then you'll answer my—unanswerable—question?"

"Have I ever lied to you?" she asks with a guileless grin.

A little while later, they stroll onto a dirt trail that meanders through one of the Sanef Peninsula's nature preserves. Douglas firs tower overhead while sunlight and shadow dance across the trail. Peter and Sophia step gingerly to avoid crushing the long, shiny yellow slugs luxuriating every few meters along the path. She actually giggles when he tells her locals call them "banana slugs."

He spots a sign showing the distance to Purisima Creek. The Pacific Ocean will slide into view in another hundred meters down the trail. On a clear day such as this one, the view will be gorgeous.

She's wearing shorts and a lightweight button-up blouse, a comfortable hiking outfit in the summer heat. He can't help but notice her figure. She's thinner than he had realized, a little thinner than he prefers in a feme, but not unattractively skinny.

Jesus, Peter. Stop thinking stupid, adolescent thoughts.

They encounter a grove of soaring redwoods. Peter points out the way the higher branches glisten, which means the fog machines were on earlier in the day. Sophia smiles broadly as she walks over to a tree and gazes at it. She circles several of the redwoods, staring up at them as if she has no other thought or concern. He stands back to observe her delighted exploration of the grove.

Ten minutes pass, and Sophia is still admiring the trees.

"This is nice," Peter says, "but if we walk just a little farther this way, we'll be able to see the ocean."

She touches a large redwood stump. The tree must have been many centuries old when it was logged some time ago. The stump could serve as a table big enough to seat a dozen people around its circumference. "See this," she says.

He's seen a stump before. "It's, uh, a dead tree," he says.

"Really? Did you know that cutting down a coast redwood often doesn't kill it? I accessed that if the roots are healthy, they can spring a circle of new trunks around the old stump." She pats it. "And here we can see it."

He surveys the stump and its surroundings more closely. Several thin trunks grow around this one, and he realizes one even emerges from the other side of it. These aren't saplings that happened to sprout near the stump. These are new trunks growing from the root system of the logged tree.

"I actually didn't know that—which is embarrassing since I've spent my whole life in a nation that prides itself on its redwood groves." A thought strikes him. "A tree that *resurrects!*"

"Yes. A blessing of God's vast abundance." She points at another circle of redwoods. "Look over there. See those four tall ones? They share a root system. They all grew out of the same stump, cut down long ago to build houses and furniture for people in the city."

"It's a shame," he says. It seems like the most sensitive thing to say.

"What's a shame?"

"To cut away at something so grand just to make a chair."

"Some of the wood from these forests was used to build hospitals, schools, and baby cribs. Was that shameful?"

"I—well, no, I suppose not."

With utmost gentleness, she lovingly caresses one trunk's soft, coarse, red bark. "The wood from a tree can be used to create beautiful and useful things. It can also be used to create clubs for people to beat one another over the head with."

"It can be used for good or for ill."

She nods. "Either way, once the wood is cut from the tree, it no longer lives, however good or useful it may become."

Peter stares at Sophia. *She's no longer speaking only of trees.*

"The living tree was given to you to use," she says. "From it, you could cut the furniture of identities and moral codes. You could cut philosophies and ideologies. These can be valuable, but they are not the living tree. Unlike these things, the living tree is filled with the sap of growth and novelty."

She turns to him. "Your problem was that you cut and cut and cut the branches, mostly to make clubs to hit one another over the head with. Then you used the clubs to smash all of your furniture. And then you used the smashed pieces of furniture to make more clubs. You cut the tree down to a stump, and you started to confuse the deadwood you held in your hands with the living tree."

Sophia keeps using the word "you," and it feels to Peter as if she's addressing him as a representative of something larger—of the Church's leaders throughout the ages, perhaps.

"After a while, you no longer knew the difference," Sophia says. "You mistook the deadwood—idols of order, empire, self-justification, wealth, false certitude—you mistook them for the living tree: the sublime good news of God's life-giving cosmic story and intimate presence. Even though this good news was always there, in your scriptures, in your traditions, you no longer had the eyes to see it, the heart to believe it. Why, Peter?"

"Wh—why?"

"Because you lost the keys."

"The keys!?"

She nods and takes a step closer. "You are the guardian of a great treasure. This treasure is neither gold nor silver nor the things that moths can eat. It is your tradition, and it has incredible spiritual value, an almost miraculous capacity to change lives for the better. But you misplaced the keys to the treasure chest. This happened long ago, when scripture and religion became primarily about trying to determine who was right and who was wrong. For so long, you could see only the minutiae and not the great message, because focusing on the little things made it easier to assure yourself you were *right*. You have to find the keys again."

"What are these keys you, you say we misplaced?"

"The keys are the deep understandings of your symbols—the eternal meanings underlying your scriptures and forms of worship. When you lost them, it became ever harder to draw nourishment from your tradition's roots."

Peter realizes he's holding his breath, and he exhales. He knows rationally that he shouldn't give any weight to her ideas and mixed metaphors, yet something about what she said hits him hard. He gazes at the stump and furrows his brow in thought.

"Fear not," she says. "It is God who decides when the tree wanes and when it flourishes. Never forget that 'a thousand years is a day in God's sight,' as scripture says. The Holy One is very, very patient. Remember that, and everything that comes next will make more sense."

Comes next? A part of Peter wants to ask what she means, but he can't seem to pull his attention away from the stump.

Sophia squints at him. After a moment, she leans over and gives him a chaste kiss on the cheek. Roused from his thoughts, he swivels his head and stares at her in surprise.

"Come on, Peter. Let's see the ocean." She takes him by the hand and guides him toward the path.

7

Hunger

Russ and Veronica sit at their kitchen table. Russ keeps leaning his chair back on two legs and letting it fall forward with a clunk.

Clunk.

Clunk.

"You're gonna bust your tiny head one of these days," Veronica murmurs without lifting her eyes from the moldy codex in her hands. She dug it out of the attic the last time they looked up there for something to sell.

Russ clunks his chair down again. He sighs elaborately. It's been two days since the family's net access was cut off for non-payment, and he's *bored*. He peers at the codex's faded cover. "Why isn't that man wearing a shirt?" he asks.

"None of your beeswax. Grown-up stuff."

"You're not a grown-up!"

"More grown-up than you, short stack."

Russ clutches his stomach. "Stop! You're making me think of pancakes."

Veronica slowly lifts her eyes from the codex and grins, showing her teeth. "A stack of thick, fluffy flapjacks covered in butter and syrup?"

"Stop it!" Russ is really hungry, but if he says too much, Veronica will call him "whiny baby" for the rest of the day. *Teenagers are gross*, he thinks. *I don't ever want to have to be one.*

Veronica pantomimes eating pancakes. "Mmm. Mmm. So good. So scrumptious." She closes her eyes in mock ecstasy.

Russ retaliates by grabbing the romance novel out of his sister's hands.

"Bubbie! Give me that back, you little wank!"

Russ bounds toward the door, and Veronica jumps to her feet to give chase. In Russ's haste to escape the kitchen with the book, he almost careens into Spence.

"Daddy!"

"In a hurry, son?"

"Uh—"

"What'd you bring?" asks Veronica.

Spence holds up a greasy sack. Russ tosses the codex down on the table, and the three of them sit down. Spence sets the sack down and tears it open, exposing four glazed donuts. "They're from the Schuetzes," he says. "Two each. I ate mine on the way back."

Russ shoves a donut into his mouth, and his consciousness briefly implodes into a heady world of bready sweetness. Before he knows what's happened, both of his prizes have met their fate. He looks up and sees Veronica still holding half a donut.

"Thank you, Dad. These are so good," she says. She languidly chews her remaining portion while staring at her little brother. "Mmm, so good."

"Also," Spence says, "while I was out, I think I found what we're looking for. Look at this." Spence pulls out a creased page covered with advertisements.

Veronica takes it from his hand and stares it. "You want to join the 'International Christian Capitalist Club'?" she asks, focusing on the first ad she sees.

"Don't be silly. That's for rich people. This is the one I mean."

Veronica peers at the advertisement, and Russ leans over her shoulder to get a glimpse, too.

EXOTIC AMAZONIS BECKONS!

Fast-growing Merian economy needs workers of all education and skill levels. Take refuge from crowded, dirty Earth: A new life on a new frontier! Free passage for individuals and families, with work commitment. Room and board. Learn cutting-edge technologies. Make the System a better place! Contact @0807131–TVRM-PROC–GORDII, Indep. Nat. of Amazonis, Meres.

"Meres!" cries Veronica. "You never even leave the valley, and you wanna take us offearth? What about following Aunt Alma to the West Coast?"

"Alma hasn't exactly struck gold out there," Spence replies. "She always thinks the grass is gonna be greener, but she hasn't been able to find work. And they don't give public assistance until you've lived there a long time."

"At least their nation believes in public assistance."

"They can afford it. My point is that if we went there, we'd just be city-poor instead of country-poor—'lowcontribs' camping on the streets." Spence looks at Russ, and his scowl morphs into a broad smile. "What we need is a *new frontier.*"

Russ's eyes bulge, and he nods excitedly. "Yes, like I was saying! Let's go! Meres or bust! A new frontier!"

Veronica sits back and crosses her arms until the boys are done nodding at one another.

Spence locks eyes with his daughter. "I know going so far would be hard, but there's nothing left for us here. We've gotta go somewhere where we can start again." He gestures at the advertisement. "I'm not naive like my sister Alma. I don't expect something like this will be a paradise. But steady work with 'room and board' sounds pretty good right now. . . . Precious, we're running out of options."

Veronica gazes at the empty chair across the table. Spence and Russ's eyes follow Veronica's. She says, "I wish—"

"I wish your mama was here, too," Spence says. "If there was some way she could see you now, she would be so proud of both of you."

They sit in silence for several minutes. Russ stares out the window and wonders what it would be like to live in a place where the landscape isn't always yellow.

Veronica sighs. "Is it cooler on Meres?" she asks.

~

It's the fourth Sunday morning since Sophia pitched her tent in front of the cathedral, and she has once again joined the Christworshippers for their weekly service. To Peter, she looks fetching even in her simple, modest attire. He avoids her gaze as he presides over the service, to keep from becoming distracted.

In any event, he's busy worrying about Bede—Felipe's cheeks have been wet during most of the service. If Felipe is falling apart, it could only mean that his grandfather got bad news at his biotech appointment on Friday. Bede looks fine, but that hardly means everything really is fine, especially at his age.

After the service, Peter changes out of his vestments and joins the others in the courtyard for refreshments. The Christworshippers are loosely clustered into a few conversations around the folding table where Martin pours lemonade. Peter sees Felipe standing with Sophia near the edge of the courtyard. To Peter's surprise, Felipe reaches out for her hand and kisses it several times. Sophia gently wipes a tear from the disabled man's cheek, and Peter realizes that Bede's health is not the issue. Outrage rapidly overtakes relief.

She must have told Felipe who she thinks she is. He doesn't know any better, and he believes her. Peter feels as if his feet have been pulled out from under him. *How could she do it? How could she take advantage of someone like him?* As these thoughts swirl, someone touches Peter's arm from behind.

"Bishop, thank you for another excellent sermon today." Before Peter can respond, Thad continues, "I have a question about what you were saying regarding the Holy Trinity. You said that God being 'three persons in one substance' is like water, which can be a solid, a liquid, or a gas. It reminded me of a conversation I had with Bishop Tim many years ago after he got back from a trip to Europe . . ."

Peter nods vigorously as Thad continues to speak, seeking to move him along to his point. Peter leans down so that he towers less over the hunched old man.

". . . so, I mean, water isn't ice and liquid and vapor all at the same time. I mean, I guess it could be, in some sort of weird space environment or something." Thad scratches the crown of his head, ruffling his white hair. "But usually it's just one at a time. So isn't the Holy Trinity different because God is the Father, the Son, and the Holy Spirit all at the same time?"

Peter tries to hide his displeasure. *Ugh, he's right. Did I preach a heretical analogy?* Peter knows he would hardly be the first preacher in Christian history to bungle a sermon on the Holy Trinity, but that's no excuse. He would never admit it to any of the Christworshippers, but trinitarian theology makes his head hurt. He's poured over several old treatises and doctrinal documents, but he's never really succeeded in grasping what it means for one God to be three different "Persons." *And why exactly three? If not simply one, why not four or twelve or some other number?* Nevertheless, Peter feels duty-bound to remind his flock once or twice a year about the Doctrine of the Trinity so prized by the ancients.

Aloud, Peter says, "It's a good point, Thad. My analogy was imperfect, because God is not limited to being just one at a time. I'll clarify that at the start of next week's sermon." He sighs.

Thad scrunches his eyes. "Bishop, are you all right? You seem a little stressed."

"I'm all right, thank you. I was just surprised by something someone did." Peter carefully avoids looking in Sophia's direction.

"Yeah, people'll surprise you. Anyway, how about that new girl? Think she's going to join us permanently? I know she must be going through a rough time, living in a tent and all, but it would be a joy to have another young person here." The light of curiosity shines in Thad's eyes.

Thad's not quite as oblivious as he lets people believe, Peter reminds himself. "I think we'll just have to see," Peter says softly. "Please excuse me for a moment."

As Peter turns from Thad, Sophia claps her hands, eliciting silence from the Christworshippers. Felipe has a rare, childlike grin on his face, and Bede gives him a "thumbs up" signal. Peter stands rigidly and stares.

"My friends," Sophia says, "you have welcomed me into your midst as warmly as I would hope and expect from Christians. In appreciation for your generous welcome, I am pleased to offer you a hymn."

The Christians nod and smile—all except Peter.

"This version is a duet, so I'll have some help," says Sophia. She glances at Felipe. "Ready?" she whispers.

Felipe nods solemnly.

Slowly at first, the two of them begin to sing:

> *Immortal, invisible, God only wise,*
> *In light inaccessible hid from our eyes,*
> *Most blessed, most glorious, the Ancient of Days,*
> *Almighty, victorious, thy great Name we praise . . .*

Peter realizes his mouth is hanging open. Poor Felipe has never before been able to sing the words along with a hymn. No wonder he's so emotional! Sophia taught him how to do something he and everyone else thought impossible. *Thank God it wasn't because she filled his head with nonsense about being the Second Coming!* Peter smiles and feels himself start to relax. *Thank God.*

As they sing, Bede grins encouragement to Felipe. Junia holds a hand to her mouth, eyes wide. Peter thinks he sees moisture in Nastya's eyes. Felipe's voice strengthens, driving the melody as Sophia harmonizes.

> *. . . To all, life thou givest, to both great and small;*
> *In all life thou livest, the true life of all;*
> *We blossom and flourish, like leaves on the tree,*
> *Then wither and perish; but naught endeth thee!*

Those are the two verses Felipe memorized, but he doesn't want to stop, so they repeat them. When they finish, the courtyard resounds with shouts of "Amen!" and thunderous applause. Each of the Christians hugs a blushing Felipe and tells him how proud of him they are. He keeps looking over at Sophia, whom the Christians also hug and thank.

The fellowship breaks up later than usual that day. Peter waits as the last of the Christians depart so that he can speak to Sophia in private. "That was amazing, Sophia. I didn't think Felipe was capable of it. I always thought his brain just wouldn't let him put words together with music." He touches her arm. "How did you do it?"

"Faith is a powerful thing."

Peter's eyes widen, and he withdraws his hand. "'Faith'? What do you mean 'faith'?"

"I mean Felipe has a living faith that God is present here, in his life. In his unique and beloved way, Felipe has been inspired."

"You didn't say to him that . . ."

"I told him the truth."

Peter steps back and stares at her with wide eyes. "Don't you see you're, you're just going to confuse him?" He rubs his forehead, suddenly realizing how deeply in denial he's been about her mental illness. "No, I suppose you really can't see."

Sophia sighs. She looks uncharacteristically tired. "Peter, dear Felipe is the least confused among us."

∾

That Wednesday night is especially warm, and even Trinity is restless. As Peter lies in darkness, he can hear her scratching on the small carpet in her cage. She stops for a moment, and Peter hears a transitube's distant whine. Then the scratching resumes.

He sighs and rolls over onto his back, stretching his arms straight out and pressing his palms against the sides of his bed. Peter is nearly thirty, and he's never owned a double bed—he's never had need of one. He rolls onto his side as the bunny scratches continue.

It's no use. I can't sleep. He sits up and begins to pray silently. *Almighty God, Heavenly Father, my head and heart are at war. Give me certitude about what is happening. Help me to be free from doubt. Please tell me what to do!* He beseeches the Almighty for guidance until he feels he can pray no more. Then he sits still and waits. As usual, he feels nothing—no sense that God above is pointing His pontiff in any specific direction. "Maybe I'm just the last and biggest fool," he mutters to himself.

Hungry for a diversion, he gets up from his bed and accesses the latest netstories:

> *With earthside demand reliably outstripping supply, freshwater shares continue to outperform gold, processed tovramium, and*

many cartel bonds as an investment asset promising robust quar-
ter-over-quarter growth . . .

More naval skirmishes in the Arctic today . . .

A massive human trafficking ring in Edinburgh . . .

The International Christian Capitalist Club announced its acqui-
sition of the storied La`aumake Resort and Spa. The influential
private society plans to offer advanced business courses to cartel
executives at the luxury facility . . .

The Independent Nations of New Maharashtra and Greater Kera-
la have announced a fifth cease-fire, but . . .

One item catches his attention:

The popular netcast "Raw Expanses" will record its upcoming
season on location on Meres. Contestants will scale the Tharsis
Mountains, navigate the maze-like Noctis Labyrinthus, and sur-
vive a night on the frigid Australe Plains. The winner and a guest
will spend three months on an all-expense-paid grand tour of the
System.

Peter shakes his head. *There are people out there who get to climb mountains*
on other planets and jet around the System. Talk about living! Have I ever
really lived? I spend all my time in what's basically a museum, looking toward
the past. That's all we who are left in the Church seem to do these days. But
how can we really live if we never look to the future?

He imagines himself jetting off to Meres or the Stroids. *I bet I could get*
enough money for a first-class ticket by selling just one of the paintings in the
crypt. The thought makes him feel doubly ashamed—both that he would
entertain such a despicable idea and that he would never have the courage
to do anything like it.

He decides to get dressed and go for a nighttime walk. He has no
particular destination in mind as he departs The Bishop's Residence. Five
minutes later, he finds himself just a few meters from the tent.

It seems she's also up late: a small, portable electric light burns brightly
in each of the tent's four corners, hazily visible through the opaquely translucent canvas. Peter stands beyond the penumbra they create. He remains
there in silence for several minutes, neither moving toward the tent nor
stepping away from it. A few tinkles and murmurs float down from the balcony bars.

Peter takes a deep breath and approaches the tent's entrance, trembling
slightly. "Doop deep."

"Huh?" comes her soft reply, thick with sleep.

Oh no. She must have fallen asleep with her lights on.

As he's about to walk away, her voice comes again. "Peter?"

"Uh. Yes, it's me. I'm, I'm sorry to bother you. I could see you have lights on, so I thought you were still awake."

A rustling noise emerges from the tent, then Sophia says, "Come in."

"It's okay, I should go."

"Why did you wake me if you don't have anything to say?"

"I—well, okay. I'm coming in."

He pushes back the flap covering the entrance and stoops to enter the tent. Sophia has rolled her thin mattress over to one side. She sits cross-legged, leaving him room to sit down. She looks pale and sleepy.

"I'll just stay for a minute," he says as he sits. "I wouldn't have dooped if I knew you were asleep. Again, I'm sorry."

She waves away the apology and yawns. "If I didn't want you here, I wouldn't have chosen to invite you in."

He glances at one of the electric lights. It's a common type of cheap, high-efficiency, solar-charged lamp guaranteed not to waste any energy producing heat. Yet Peter feels so warm. He asks, "Do you normally sleep with the lights on?"

She blinks. "It's a long story."

"Well, I won't ask you to tell me a long story at this time of night."

They sit in silence. A soft snippet of laughter wafts down from above. Peter has no idea what to say. He hasn't come to ask a theological question or to scold Sophia about Felipe or even to "help" Sophia. If he's honest with himself, he came because he's, because he's . . .

"I've been reading," he says, "through a couple of the books you handed me. Maybe we could discuss them sometime."

She nods and yawns again. "I'm sorry, I guess I am a little tired." As she covers her mouth, the sleeve of her nightshirt slides a couple of centimeters down her upper arm. The flesh over the front of her shoulder looks sunken in. He takes a closer look at her. Her eyes are sunken, too. She looks very thin—emaciated, really.

I hadn't noticed how skinny she seems to have gotten. He asks, "Sophia, are you ill?"

She shakes her head.

"Are you getting enough to eat?"

"Please don't worry. I'm doing what I need to do. And this is the place where I need to do it."

"What you . . . 'need to do'? Hold on, are you getting enough to eat or not?"

"I have had to eat a bit at some intervals. Forty days is a long time, and I am, after all, human, too." She smiles ruefully.

"What? Are you telling me you're on a forty-day fast?" His eyes grow wide. "Because Jesus fasted for forty days in the desert? Dammit, Sophia, forty is a symbolic number. That's too long!"

"As I said, I've had a bit. But you see, this is the fast time."

"No." He shakes his head. "No, not here. This is my place. I say what happens here."

"God's place."

"Fine, it's God's place. And the Christian God doesn't ask people to starve themselves until they waste away. The Christian God doesn't extract pain from His creatures. He doesn't ask for that kind of sacrifice."

"You're right, in this instance. And you're good. You have a lot to learn, but you're a good bishop." She takes a deep breath. "God does not sacrifice God's creatures. God sacrifices Godself for God's creatures."

Peter feels he'll be hard-pressed to defeat her if the conversation turns into some sort of theological debate. Seeking a different footing, he says, "I could call the Central Psych Administration, you know. You're endangering yourself."

"I would be gone before they got here."

"I'm willing to give it a try rather than watch you starve yourself to death!"

"I already *told you*—!" She stops, swallows, and takes a breath. Calmly now, she says, "I already told you that I've eaten a bit. This is not my time to die. That's not why I am in Sanef. Have faith in me." She puts a hand on his.

He lifts his gaze from where her hand touches his and stares into her eyes. They silently judge one another's resolve.

He glances away first. "How far along are you?"

"I've got a week and a half to go."

He looks her over again, bows his head in thought, and nods to himself. "I'll be checking on you daily. You're young and healthy, but your body has limits—don't push yourself beyond them. And I don't care if you've been on a water fast. I want you drinking fruit juices. When you break the fast, you can't gorge yourself. Start with small amounts, or you'll get sick."

"You know something about fasting."

"Many times, I've begged Almighty God for guidance, and sometimes I fasted. . . . It didn't help." He shakes his head. "But I've never tried to fast for forty days. That's nuts."

She shrugs. "You already thought I was nuts."

8

Collapse

It's Martin's turn to lead the congregation through the intercessory prayers. Peter and Felipe kneel while the elderly congregants spare their knees by standing. Phoebe and Sophia's chairs are empty this Sunday, because Sophia felt too weak to join them and Phoebe insisted on staying with her.

Peter's head is bowed, but he isn't actually praying. He's just too anxious and angry. He rubs his jaw—he must have ground his teeth again last night. *As the one who's supposed to be in charge here, I shouldn't be allowing Sophia's fast to continue.* But, for reasons he can't explain even to himself, he *is* allowing it despite his anxiety. And the congregation is supporting the fast. Peter doesn't know all the things she's told them, but she seems to have convinced them that there is some sane rationale behind what she's doing.

After reciting the standard prayers for the Church and the System, Martin takes it upon himself to add a new one: "Gracious Lord, bless your unblemished treasure, your beloved one, that she may without undue suffering complete the forty-day fast . . ."

Peter's head lifts abruptly.

". . . which you, in your powerful and holy wisdom, have laid before her—"

Peter's on his feet. "Stop!"

Martin breaks off the prayer mid-sentence and looks up at his bishop with wide eyes.

"You know. You know what she thinks she is!" Peter is practically yelling. He sees the slow nodding of heads and some sideways glances.

"You believe her."

Several heads continue to nod.

"And you're letting her do this. You're supporting her, encouraging this, this delusional self-abuse!" Peter is shaking with adrenaline. His friends look at him with sympathetic eyes.

"Don't you see? You're so desperate for God to reach down and save us, to save *this*—" Peter thrusts his hands outward. "—that you're clinging to insanity. Can't you see that she's sick in her mind? Can't you see that we're letting her put herself in danger? That we're hurting her?"

Now he *is* yelling.

"No, you don't care! You just want a messiah. You'll do anything for one! You don't care that she's a person, a sick and sad person!"

Peter turns from them and storms out of the chapel. He marches into the vesting room and slams the door. Still shaking, he throws himself into the nearest chair and sits with his head in his hands.

Only then does he realize what he has done. He, the celebrant, staged a sudden walk-out in the middle of the divine liturgy. He has effectively cancelled the Holy Eucharist. But he can't go back out there and face them now.

Mother . . . she would never, ever have thrown a tantrum in the middle of a service. She would have held it together. She would have been a leader. Peter feels more shame than he's ever felt. *The last bishop. I'm the last one—and the worst one.*

He cries. He cries for beautiful, deranged Sophia. He cries for his people, abandoned by their God. He cries for all the credulous generations who trusted that God in vain. But mostly, he cries for himself and his utter failure to bear the mantle of leadership that was thrust upon him. What could have ever made him believe he was worthy to fill Priscilla's shoes?

After perhaps ten minutes, he hears a rap on the door. For a moment, he seriously considers pretending he's not there. As if they didn't see where he went. As if he could just disappear into nothingness.

"Peter. Petey, sweetheart." It's Dorcas. She called him that when he was a child.

"I—I just, I just can't—"

The door creaks open, and Dorcas enters the room. He doesn't look at her. She softly closes the door and sits down in the chair next to him. After a minute, he slowly leans toward her, and she puts an arm around his shoulder.

"I disrupted the service. I shouted down the Church. My friends. I'm, I'm supposed to do better!" He shakes his head. "Dorcas, I can't do this. I can't *be* this anymore."

"Shh, shh, it's okay. It's all okay." She pulls him closer. "We're in love with her, too."

~

It's Monday afternoon, and Peter is sitting alone on the floor of The Bishop's Residence. He has no desire to pray. Trinity lies on his lap enjoying his absentminded petting. She yawns a demure bunny yawn.

Peter hasn't visited Sophia yet today, but he knows that others from the congregation—maybe all of them—are looking after her. When he checked on her the previous afternoon, she looked so frail. It hurt him to look at her.

Peter has never heard a word from the Father or received a vision from Jesus. The great Patriarch of the Church cannot truthfully say he's certain they exist. But Sophia exists. And, for good or ill, she means something to him.

He leans back in his chair and looks out the window of The Bishop's Residence. *Is it possible? Could she be Who she thinks she is? Didn't most of Jesus' contemporaries doubt Him? Didn't the religious authorities of His time simply see Him as a peasant rabble rouser? Here was God, Yahweh, the Lord of the Universe, walking right in front of them, and they never saw it. They thought He was nuts.*

Is Peter any different from the Pharisees and the Sadducees? Is it possible he's been blind to the truth after all? Is it possible she is an embodiment of the Divine, maybe in a way beyond his current understanding? Could it be that his people are right and he's wrong? *Am I so obsessed with duty that I can't see and do what's right for my people? Is the leader of the faith actually the least faithful one?*

Peter stands up, lifting the rabbit in his arms, and moves to put her back into her cage. After a moment's reflection, he thinks better of it. He sets her down on the floor, and she begins to roam freely around The Bishop's Residence.

He walks over to his mirror. "Five minutes," he says to himself. He will allow himself to believe—believe in *her*, all the way—for just five minutes. He'll let himself see what it feels like, as a sort-of experiment, he tells himself.

He sets an alarm.

Then he begins to hum an ancient chant. He adds words, visualizing Sophia's face as he speaks to God of holy love.

After chanting for a time, his imagination places him inside a maze. Not a labyrinth like the ones at the cathedral, which have no dead ends. No, it's a maze, filled with dead ends. Obsidian walls tower above Peter's head and block his vision. He cannot remember a time when he didn't stumble around inside this maze, when it didn't hold him captive. And then he realizes:

I make these walls.

And with that, the walls momentarily fall, and the maze becomes an open field drenched in sunlight. At least that's how he'll later try to describe the sensation in his personal journal.

Even after the sensation ebbs, he holds onto his surprising new insight: *I'm hemmed in by walls of my own making.* He works this phrase into his chant and then continues to alternate between chanting and spoken prayer. As he visualizes Sophia's face, the words he says feel like something different—have a different heft—than Peter's usual dry, brittle prayers. They emerge moist with love's longing.

More than an hour after the alarm sounded, he finally stops. Tearful and exhausted, he lies down for a nap.

Hours pass before Peter is pulled back into wakefulness.

Doop deep.

Doop deep.

Doop deep.

It's dark now, and his time display reads: MONDAY 21:09.

"Coming! Just a minute!"

When he opens his door, he finds Nastya waiting on the doorstep. A cool breeze wafts through the doorway. Peter hasn't yet apologized to her for his shameful outburst yesterday morning. Every single one of his flock deserves an apology.

"I'm so sorry about yesterday. I—"

She waves her hands. "No, no, Bishop Peter, you were right. You were right!"

His heart starts thumping. "What's happened?"

Nastya motions in the direction of the cathedral. "She collapsed. She was unconscious. We called emergency services." Peter now recognizes that Nastya, no spring chicken, is pale and breathing hard herself.

"They've taken her to the hospital," she says.

I was right, yesterday. She's just a sick and sad person.

Without another word, Peter grabs a sweatshirt from a peg on the wall behind him, and they head into the darkness.

∽

Two days later, Peter stands in the hallway outside Jasmine Chandevi's hospital room. He finds himself accessing Uncle Jeff's note from the prior evening, yet again. Ever-clever Jeff took it upon himself to uncover the sad and terrible truth: Jasmine is mentally disturbed because of childhood abuse and trauma. Jeff's hurried, colloquial writing style allows neither obfuscation nor any platitude to soften the hard facts.

From: Socrates Jefferson
To: Peter Halabi
Date: Tuesday, August 1 22:52
Subject: JASMINE CHANDEVI, aka "SOPHIA"
Attachments: 5

P – quick summary/details re my call to you earlier this evening. once I engaged the private investigator it took her only a few days to ID "Sophia."

born in town of Belén, Indep. Nat. of Tennissippi, a couple hundred km north of the hurricane exclusion zone. horrific case of child abuse and prostitution by the bio father—a trafficker and pimp. the mom was a prostitute trafficked from the Indep. Nat. of Manipur. she died when Jasmine was a young girl.

according to police records, Jasmine spent most of her childhood locked in a room with nothing but a little shelf of old codices, no surprise including a bible and other christian metafiz works. unknown who taught her to read.

records of mental health counseling in Memphis after escape from bio dad (now deceased). she has a fear of the dark. 2 misdemeanors on her record. current age: 30. see attached records for details

I'm sorry for prying, son. for your sake, I had to find out the truth.

Peter rubs his eyes as Lupe and Marco emerge from Jasmine's room, where she lies unconscious. "I'm sure it's going to be okay," Lupe says as she gives Peter a long, maternal hug.

It's not okay, Peter thinks as they embrace. *When I yelled at my friends, I was accusing myself. I'm the one who was so desperate for God's guidance that I started to believe this poor, abused woman might be* the messiah. *Oh God. Instead of saving Jasmine, I may have let her kill herself. Instead of being a healer and a leader, I played along with her delusions.*

Lupe breaks off the hug, and Marco warmly shakes Peter's hand, cradling it in both of his. As they begin to walk away, something occurs to Peter. He calls after them, "Lupe? Marco?" They stop and turn.

"The word 'Belén'—it's a Spanish word, right?"

"Bee—ee—el—ee with an accent—en?" asks Marco.

"Sí."

"Yes, Bishop. 'Belén' is where Jesus was born—you know, 'Bethlehem.'"

～

"Bishop Peter. Peter!"

He doesn't know why Bede barged into The Bishop's Residence to wake him up. It's not like him not to doop.

Oh, right.

Painfully, Peter sits up. He must have dozed off for a minute slouched over the nightstand next to Soph—Jasmine's hospital bed. A needle connected to a tube still penetrates the clammy skin of her arm. A biotech is standing next to her bed, once more checking her vital signs. The muscles in Peter's lower back ache.

"What's up, Bede?"

"They're saying we have to leave."

"What time is it?"

"It's twenty-two. She's got a roommate now." Bede points at the next bed, where an unconscious older woman now lies. "They say you've got to respect visiting hours tonight."

"What night is it?"

"It's Friday, Bishop. When was the last time you slept?"

"Just now, apparently."

"I mean before this ten-minute catnap."

"Tuesday. Mm, Monday?"

"That's it. Go home."

Peter looks up at the biotech. "Is she responding?"

The biotech shakes his head. "Not yet, not as expected. It's bizarre, to be honest. For simple malnourishment, she should have responded quickly. But she's still unconscious, and I'm afraid it remains a dangerous situation."

"She was, she was abused as a child," Peter says. "Badly." But that has nothing to do with why she's there in the hospital, at least not directly. Peter tries to clarify, "So, I mean, she has suffered a lot. Maybe suffering weakened her."

"Maybe it strengthened her," Bede murmurs.

"All I can tell you, Mister Halabi," the biotech says, "is that she's in the best hospital in Sanef. We are doing everything we can."

Peter stares vacantly at Jasmine. "Tell you what, I'll just sleep on the floor. I won't bother—"

"Dammit Peter, *go home!*" says Bede, now standing. "You're making a mess of yourself, and you're not helping the girl." Just then, Dorcas enters the room carrying snacks. Bede turns to her. "Dorcas, we've got to clear out. My God, I just realized you look almost as bad as he does, but can you make sure he gets home? He needs some sleep."

"Yes, you old charmer, I'll take him home. *I did* get some sleep last night, I'll thank you very much." Dorcas takes Peter's arm as he mumbles incoherently about how he could just sleep on the hospital-room floor. She steers him toward the door, looking back over her shoulder to give Bede the evil eye.

The biotech audibly exhales after they leave the room. "Thanks," he says.

"Sure thing. Just keep a close eye on her." With an old-man groan, Bede leans down and places a goodbye kiss on Jasmine's forehead.

～

The last day has come.

The wind is blowing, and dust devils spiral through the dried-up fields. But Russ has no time to chase them. *Time to pioneer!* He runs along the road home, singing the song he made up:

> *Gonna fly on a spaceship*
> *Gonna fly like a star*
> *To a whole other planet*
> *So far, so far, so far, so far*

He holds nails in each fist. *There's a lot laying around towards town if you've got good eyes to look*, he thinks.

As he enters the yard, he imagines the captain of the spaceship saying, in a terrified voice, "Emergency! We need someone with real good eyes to fly the ship." *And I'll stand up and take the controls and save everybody. And when they interview me on the net, I'll tell them it's just another day's work for a space hero.* He smiles and pumps his fists.

"Russ. You gonna bring those to me, or what?"

And Russ's heroic interview, like so many fancies of his joyfully vibrating young mind, vanishes back into the mysterious depths of what-may-be. "Uh, sorry, Daddy."

Spence wipes sweat from the back of his neck. "How many did you find?"

"'Bout twenty."

Spence sifts through the nails in Russ's hands. "This one won't work. Or this one." Spence takes one that is saturated with rust and snaps it in half. "Or this one. But the rest of them are okay."

Veronica ambles over. She holds a worn hammer with a duct-taped handle, and her cheeks blossom pink from exertion. "Boarding up every door and window in the house is a falqing pain, Dad."

Russ's eyes bug out. He shakes his index finger at Veronica. "You cursed. You cursed."

Spence glances at Russ and then scrunches his eyes at Veronica. With a surreptitious wink, he says, "Language, Precious. Language.

"Besides, boarding things up is only smart," he continues. "We're just protecting our investment, so to speak—and Alma's, since the house is part hers. There's no one who will buy the old place right now, but who knows what could happen? Might as well try to keep things in as good a shape as we can. 'Course, I think we'll be so happy in Amazonis that we might just completely forget about the valley."

"Uh huh," says Veronica.

"Let's finish up so we can get going," says Spence as he hands Veronica some nails.

She nudges Russ and points. "Grab that board, short stack."

In another half an hour, the house is as boarded up as it's going to get. Spence, Veronica, and Russ walk over to their old clunker of a freedriver and stand there for several minutes staring at the gray house. A gust of wind whistles through narrow gaps between the boards and walls.

"It looks so weird all boarded up," Russ says in a hushed voice.

"Really weird," Veronica says. She sniffs.

"You grew up in this old house," says Spence. "So did I. And your mama and I spent many an evening on that porch swing looking at the stars." Spence pulls both his kids close for a moment, then they pile into the clunker. They'll stop at the graveyard one more time before they leave the valley.

9

The Late Bishop

"You are Peter. And you shall also be Paul." He hears her voice as clear as a dooper, as if she were lying right next to him.

After he crashes back into consciousness, the vivid dream memories persist long enough for him to hold onto some of them. He traveled to many places: big cities, countryside, a stark red desert. He broke bread before thousands. And, although he is no dancer, he danced. No, *they* danced, the two of them, together.

Though the images fade quickly, her words remain. Her voice sounded so distinct, so real. Peter rubs his eyes and draws a long, slow breath. Light streams into his window, and he glances at his time display. It reads: 09:52.

It reads: SUNDAY 09:52.

Sunday? Is it Sunday? How did that—?

Sunday, August 6, now 09:53. The Sunday service starts in *seven* minutes.

Oh Lord, and it's even a special day on the church calendar, isn't it? The "Feast of the Transfiguration," I think. Peter has never before overslept a service. After his humiliating meltdown last week, he certainly can't afford to be late today!

He leaps out of bed and begins pulling his pants on. *Why hasn't anyone come by to check on me? They know I'm always at the chapel by 09:15.*

By the time he dresses enough to leave his apartment, it's 09:57. He doesn't have time to shower or shave. He will have to get an update on Jasmine's condition before he starts the service, and that will cause a couple more minutes of delay.

A dagger of panic ices down his spine. *I haven't written a sermon.*

His panic immediately mutates into near-blinding anger . . . anger that his last foothold on faith collapsed when Jasmine did . . . anger at those who mistreated her . . . anger at the waste of his own life, in service to an elaborate Nothing . . . anger that he can't even do a stupid, useless job right.

I have no sermon. So what, really? Maybe I should just preach the truth to them: There is no God! Or if there is one, He surely doesn't give a damn about us! How about this for a sermon: Hey pals, let's just pull the plug on this failed religion nonsense right now. Tell 'em how I really feel! At that moment, he lacks even the wherewithal to punish himself with a mental image of a disapproving Priscilla.

Peter speed-walks down the street and hurries into the cathedral courtyard, still in a huff. He reaches the north entrance and tries to pull the door open. It's locked.

"What the—?"

There's no reason for it to be locked. Dorcas, Phoebe, and Martin all have credentials to unlock it. Then Peter notices a handwritten sign stuck to the door. It says only "MAIN ENTRANCE."

Scowling, Peter turns from the door and strides across the courtyard toward the front of the cathedral. As he turns the corner, his foot kicks something metallic and sends it flying. It tinkles against stone a few meters ahead of him.

The keys!

He reaches down and picks up the keys to the tabernacle, furrowing his brow. They clink together in the palm of his hand.

Peter looks up toward the cathedral's main entrance and finds another surprise. Someone has had the gall to remove Jasmine's tent while she's lying in the hospital. Peter's scowl deepens. Then his eyes grow wide as he moves forward and sees—No! Yes. For the first time in Peter's lifetime, the Ghiberti Doors are standing wide open.

"What the—! Who—?"

Disoriented and furious, Peter marches through the main entrance and into the nave. Then he freezes. Some part of his mind hears a set of metal keys fall to a stone floor.

Light streams in through every window in the cathedral.

Mosaics of color surround Peter, refracting every hue of the rainbow onto the nave's columns and floor. Before his mind can begin to recognize the people clustered around the high altar ahead of him, his eyes are drawn to the resplendent set of double stained glass windows immediately to his right. The windows' light falls upon the floor: red, gold, white, and several shades of blue. The patterns in the windows include small faces and names, but Peter's focus is drawn to the phrase written across the two windows in tall stained glass letters: "LIGHT AFTER DARKNESS." His breath catches inside him.

He swivels to look at the pair of windows on the opposite side. They hold a panorama of people, both men and women. Names such as "Jerome," "Luther," and "Gutenberg" stand inscribed on them. The tall stained glass letters spanning this pair of windows reads: "THE WORD OF OUR GOD WILL STAND FOREVER."

Peter slowly walks in the direction of the altar, gawking. The next set of windows to his left reads: "THE GLORY OF THE LORD CAME INTO THE HOUSE."

He turns back toward the main entrance and looks up at the Canticle of the Sun. The window is even more extraordinary than Thad described, and it spills every color of light into the cathedral. For a moment, Peter stands transfixed by its wild kaleidoscope of iridescence.

He pulls his eyes away from it and turns to survey the entire panorama—window after window, each a rainbow of colors, each lovelier than the next. Walking in the direction of the altar, he can now see the enormous, magnificent rose window on each side of the transept. Light streams through every window in the upper tier, too. And along with the rest of the cathedral, the Chapel of the Nativity is bathed in light. The golden doors to the tabernacle stand wide open.

Peter wipes away a tear and takes a deep, cleansing breath. *My God, this is who we were meant to be.*

And then he sees her. She's standing behind the altar table, which holds loaves of bread and vessels brimming with red. Grinning and gaping Christians surround her, silent in their own trances of wonderment. Felipe stands by her side, looking in all directions. Dorcas smiles broadly as she holds hands with a wide-eyed Nastya and a chuckling, wet-faced Martin. Thad weeps like a child.

Peter briefly glances back to where the keys lie, then he fixes his eyes ahead on Sophia. She beckons him forward and begins walking around the table toward him. "Peter, come join the feast," she says. Her face shines like the sun, and her garments are as white as light.

He falls to his knees and gasps, "My Lord and my God!"

PART TWO

If you think you have a right to certitude, then show me where the gospel ever promised or offered you that.

—Father Richard Rohr, O.F.M.

10

Light After Darkness

Sophia does something none of the Christians have ever seen before. She recruits someone to the Church. Then another person. And then another.

Peter searches his old codices and learns that some Christian groups called their initiates "catechumens."

Sophia brings in more catechumens. They come from the streets of Sanef, and they need more than a church service and lemonade. They need food; they need shelter. Their number includes recovering stim addicts, former sex workers, undocumented refugees, and homeless disabled people who reached their public assistance limits but haven't had the courtesy to die. Sophia inspires all of them to seek something more than what they have known.

The Church Council decides to revamp some of the old buildings on the cathedral grounds. Interior renovations on a Protected Multicultural Reservation do not require permits from Nation Hall, thank God. And it turns out they already have the necessary funds.

During the weeks of fasting in front of the cathedral, Sophia started listing many of the crypt's most valuable artifacts for sale on the net. She also personally visited wealthy collectors in Sanef at various times, such as the Sunday morning Peter saw Sophia dressed so fashionably. She somehow accessed the crypt and made good on the deals, taking on the role of agent for the cash-starved cultists.

Yes, Sophia did the unthinkable, Peter acknowledges. She did what he never could have done. She sold off pieces of the Church's heritage to people who would respect only the artifacts' historical and monetary value but never their religious significance. A part of Peter still mourns what has been lost. In those moments, he reminds himself: *People matter more than things. The present and future matter more than the past.* They're Sophia's words, of course. When Peter first heard them, he was shocked to realize he actually believed—for the first time since he was a child—that the Church *has* a future.

Dorcas seems to believe it, too. As activity at the cathedral increases, she begins to serve as a sort-of chief operating officer. "I was so wrong about Sophia at first, Bishop," Dorcas says. "I regret my doubt. I just never thought He would return as a, well, as a *feme*." She shakes her head. "The Lord *does* work in mysterious ways."

Peter puts an arm around Dorcas's shoulder. "You know, the Church never said that God, as such, is a male. Using male pronouns was conventional, but there was always a recognition that God is beyond gender." Peter even reads to Dorcas from a couple of venerable old church documents, including one which states: "We ought therefore to recall that God transcends the human distinction between the sexes. He is neither man nor woman: he is God." Dorcas nods in assent, but it's clear to Peter that she's still getting used to the idea of a God big enough to be encountered in a feminine face as well as a masculine one. It's just *different*, that's all.

Meanwhile, Phoebe of all people adopts another re-discovered word: "crusader." Peter explains the word's sordid history, but that doesn't deter her from calling on her friends to "crusade" against neurpro. She says the deepening community of the Church and its catechumens shows that "messing with people's minds" is not the way to solve personal or social problems. "People don't need their minds reprogrammed," the normally silent Phoebe declares loudly after one Sunday service, turning every one of the congregants' surprised faces toward her. "They need their *hearts* reprogrammed. And only God can do that."

All things considered, the last six months have brought a complicated but joyful renaissance to the Christians. As of this wet day in late February, sixty-one catechumens reside in newly renovated parts of the cathedral grounds. Many, though not all, have been baptized and therefore could actually be called "Christians." But for the time being, everyone still refers to the new people, baptized or not, as "catechumens."

Precipitation drizzles down outside the windows of the recently renovated Bishop's Office, but winter's last gasp can't dampen Peter's joy. Thanks to Sophia, upwards of seventy souls came to last week's service. After this morning's public netcast interview, he expects an even larger crowd to show up this Sunday. He's working on his draft sermon, occasionally returning to a word or phrase to erase it and replace it with another:

Draft for Sun., Feb. 25

My sisters and brothers, I am so happy to be here with you today (etc.)

Has it ever seemed like God is far away, hiding from us up in the heavens somewhere? Over the years, we Christians have sometimes asked ourselves why God doesn't just tell us what God wants. If God really exists and knows us and loves us and wants to be in relationship with us, why wouldn't God speak to us more clearly? Why the game of hide and seek?

Why, indeed? This question tormented Peter for so long. But now he has experienced its delicious and terrifying flip side.

Have you ever considered that God's distance may have been a mercy?

If God stood before you in the flesh and called you to follow and leave behind the things that give you a feeling of control and security, and you were certain the call was true, what would it mean to the way you live? What would it mean to your ego-driven plans and your social media presence and your career and your focus on your own clutch of family and friends?

How would you live? For those of us who have heard the call, it's like our houses have been burned to the ground. We have been stripped naked by the power of the call.

After Sophia's miracle on Transfiguration Sunday, Peter can't imagine ever doubting again.

For youths, taking marching orders from on high can sound appealing. But mature adults have invested years in developing attitudes, opinions, addictions, and programs for happiness. True faith has the power to unsettle all of these. Think about it, really do: When we lose our niggling doubt—the doubt that keeps us worried about death, that gives us permission to feel unworthy and lonely, that permits us to focus our energies on "success" and the practicalities of the "real" world—how radically must that change our lives?

You see, when God doesn't keep God's distance, we have no more excuses for valuing the passing things of this life more than what is eternal. Yet releasing one's grip on those passing things is hard, my friends. It is so hard that some might turn away even knowing they've found the truth! And having turned away, they would be

condemned to live in the painful knowledge of their own coward-
ice and lack of integrity.

O Blessed Distance!

Now he'll flip it around on the congregation. He'll remind them how special
they are and assure them they have the strength to meet the challenge.

Yet now, my sisters and brothers . . . just as God came close to
humanity in Jesus, God has once more come close—to us!—in So-
phia. She sustains us by Her pure and undefiled radiance, but She
also challenges us. Have courage! We would not have been given
the pure, glorious gift of Her presence if we were not ready for it.

For my part, I have faith that She will not ask more of us than we
can handle.

He pauses for a moment and sighs. Once he realized Her true nature,
Her biography began to make more sense to him. It had seemed so full of
ungodly suffering. But, now, he feels certain that Sophia never actually suffered like a human would have, because She is no mere human—She is no
less than the Almighty, Invulnerable God choosing to disguise Himself as
a fragile, mortal human woman. *Yes, that makes sense to me. That must be
right. Gloria in excelsis Deo!*

Peter smiles and turns back to his task. *I love writing sermons.*

While the bishop fiddles with his sermon notes, the woman with a scarred
jaw sits cross-legged on filthy, cracked pavement next to a teenage boy
with a blank expression. Graffiti artists have claimed the lower floors of
the neighborhood, except for a spot across the street where a video screen
alternates between ads for Stimmers Anonymous and "Exotic Amazonis."
An occasional gust of wind lofts stray pieces of garbage into the air. Few
pedestrians are out in the morning drizzle.

In contrast to the woman's simple clothes, the boy's apparel is stylish
in a cheap and flashy way which merely draws attention to his swollen black
eye. He appears to be staring absentmindedly at something across the street,
but he's listening to the woman.

". . . and after my mom died, I didn't even have that kind of protection.
He decided to make me one of his 'special ones.' That was his name for the
youngest girls. I later understood he could charge the most for us, because
of the risk. He only gave us to clients he knew really well.

"Luckily, I would often be left alone for days or even a week at a time.
I had plenty of time to read and re-read my great-grandma's books. There

wasn't any natural light in the basement, so I had to read by the light fixture. That oldtime light stopped working exactly three times over the years. Each time was a horror story for me." She shivers.

"The first time it happened, he acted like he was too busy to replace the illuminator. After nearly three days in the dark, I just lost it. I started screaming and throwing myself against the door. I broke everything in the room, except I didn't hurt my books. He finally came in to replace it, cursing and hitting me. The second time it went out, it didn't take him long to bring in a replacement illuminator, but that wasn't the problem. Part of the wiring had worn out. After he threw his hands up, I painstakingly took it apart, piece by piece. I eventually fixed it, feeling my way in the dark with just a few tools. I didn't have any choice. The third time was the illuminator again. They were supposed to last forever, but I had the light on all the time. That electric light—it kept the darkness from eating me."

The boy glances at her and then resumes staring into the distance. The drizzle has let up.

"When I got a little older," she says, "he would take me out and give me to clients at other places, like cheap roadhouses, off the grid. Sometimes, it would be more than one male. Sometimes, femes would be there, too. Sometimes, it would be two of us 'special ones' with just one male. We had to treat the clients he gave us to as our absolute masters, or we would be punished." She absentmindedly touches the scar on her jaw. "So I just hid as deeply inside myself as I could. I simply survived—it was all I could do.

"Then one day, when I was teenager, I was delivered to a male's house, maybe thirty kay from home, out in the woods. It was probably the farthest away from home I'd ever been until then. The male's partner was supposed to be away, but she walked in on him. The sudden screaming and fighting frightened me, and I ran out of the house and kept going, just to escape the scene.

"I was maybe half a kay into the woods, just running, putting distance between me and the ruckus, with no plan or idea in my head. And then I looked over, and there on a stump was a knife. Actually, it was a dagger—sharp on both sides of the blade, you know?"

The boy nods.

"It looked shiny, like it was brand new," she says. "I still have no idea why it was there or who left it. I stopped and picked it up. I realized I could cut out my tracker, the one he had put in my arm. I hadn't been planning to run. It had never really occurred to me before that maybe I could run and just keep going.

"But it would be hard. Even the worst situation has a certain stability, a routine, right? I was able to recognize that my situation was awful. I hated my so-called 'father', and I hated myself even more. But I knew where I fit in there . . ."

The boy's eyes meet Sophia's for the barest instant.

". . . and now I was suddenly thinking about going into the total unknown, by myself and literally with nothing. I mean, I was only wearing a bathrobe. So I froze, and I looked back in the direction I had come. And I asked myself, 'What would Jesus do right now?'"

The boy gives her a puzzled glance.

"Sorry. I'll tell you about him later." She takes a breath and says, "I took the dagger and, then and there, cut into my own arm. No anesthetic or antiseptic or anything. What did I know? It was a miracle I didn't faint or get an infection. But I did it. I pressed the bathrobe into the wound, and I ran."

She lifts her sleeve to show the boy the small scar on her arm. His eyes silently shift back and forth between her scarred arm and her scarred jaw.

"A lot happened after that, but the bottom line is I eventually made it to the big city, to Memphis. I had read books, but I had no personal experience of the System beyond my father's girls and clients. But there were people there—only God knows how I found them—who cared about lost children like me, who showed me there was more." Her voice cracks. "I learned that there are people who actually love other people *as people*, not just as objects to be used."

Resolve burns in her eyes. "And I swore to myself I'd never, *ever* let anyone use me like that again."

The boy's face holds no expression, but a single fat tear leisurely meanders its way down his cheek. She gently wipes it away with a finger. He doesn't move, but his eyes meet hers.

It's all she needs. She stands and reaches out a hand. Softly, she says, "You deserve better, too. You don't have to live this life. Come with me to our refuge. Come with me to Grace. There, you can find space and time. And maybe more."

She waits, hand extended, as he sits as still as a statue and stares at her in silence. A minute passes, then two.

Cautiously, he takes her hand.

11

Roots and Wings

The next day, Peter sits down on the cathedral steps with a catechumen named Lydia. While waiting for Sophia's daily lesson to start, they spend a few minutes enjoying the sunniest day Sanef has seen in a while. A smattering of clouds races across the sky high overhead, but Peter feels only a slight breeze on his cheek.

Lydia gets Peter talking about those first weeks with Sophia, and he regales her with one of his stories. ". . . and when I came out that day, I saw Her right over there." Peter points. "She was dressed up in very professional-looking clothes."

Lydia raises an eyebrow as if trying to picture it.

"At the time, I thought She must be going to a job interview." Peter laughs.

Lydia smiles at him. The twenty-six-year-old came to Grace as one of Sophia's third dozen catechumens. She's winsome, street smart, and almost as tall as Peter. She says, "And She was actually going out to sell your old things."

"Yeah. Well, not *my* old things or even *ours*. They were *God's* things, She said. They were God's things, and God wanted them to be sold."

"And do you doubt it?"

"I don't doubt anything now."

The ambient noise from the cathedral is getting louder as people congregate for the lesson. Phoebe walks past and waves before entering through the Ghiberti Doors. Peter shakes his head and smiles at the thought of introverted Phoebe inflamed to oratory by a political issue.

"What are you thinking about, Bishop?" asks Lydia.

"Oh, the 'crusade.' You know, even my uncle is joining in."

"Isn't he a normal non-metafiz person?"

"Non-metafiz, definitely. Not so sure about 'normal.'" Lydia smiles, and Peter continues, "Let's just say he's complicated. But he certainly does hate neurpro. He says he worries about the ways our culture and economy allow us to dehumanize one another—that the cleverer our technology becomes, the more it empowers us to treat one another as statistics or commercial opportunities or things to be 'programmed,' rather than as fellow human beings."

Lydia laughs humorlessly and stares down at the steps. "Boy, that's the truth."

Peter knows Lydia has hard-won knowledge in that area. He turns to her and lifts her chin so that their eyes meet. "I still don't really understand how divine love and divine justice are balanced, but I have faith in Sophia. And She says that each of us is a precious child of God, no matter what has happened to us or what we have done. That means you, Lydia, are eternally beloved."

She turns her head aside and sniffs. "I still can't really believe that. But . . . when I first met Her . . . well, no one had ever spoken to me like that before." She nods toward the cathedral. "And I see what's happening here, and I know it's something special."

"It is!" Peter says. "I've dreamt of this my entire life. I've never known such peace and joy. This old church has become a place of life and growth. Sophia has transformed us from a tomb into a womb."

Lydia smiles. They look on in silence as a middle-aged woman ascends the steps near where they sit. In the sunlight, the woman's hair shimmers somewhere between blond and gray.

They exchange greetings, and Peter asks, "How are you today, Alma?"

Alma gives Peter a quick, bashful smile. "Good. Really good. Just so thankful to have found this place."

"I'm thankful you're here, too—that all of you are here. You've been with us about a month now, haven't you?"

Alma nods. "Sanef seemed as dry and empty as the valley where I come from . . . until I met Sophia. Then I knew why I had come out here. I just wish my family could be here with me."

"Your family?"

"My brother and niece and nephew. They had to leave our valley, too, basically to keep from starving to death. They moved even farther away than I did." She glances toward the cathedral. "Oh, here I am running my mouth. It looks like She's gonna start soon. Guess we should go in." Alma moves to head inside.

"You go ahead," says Lydia. "We'll be there in a sec." She turns to Peter. "Before we go in, I wanted to tell you I really enjoyed your netcast interview yesterday."

He grins. "I still can't believe Sophia and I did a netcast. The host said the platform usually attracts an audience of around a hundred thousand in Sanef and ten thousand more in the neighboring nations."

"You were both extraordinary."

"Oh, no. *Sophia* was extraordinary . . . when She talked about faith, hope, and love. When She invited listeners to visit Grace Cathedral. When She told stories of people who had been marginalized by society but who are growing to understand that they are precious in the eyes of God. I just pitched in a few things about Church history. She didn't need me there at all."

"Say what you want, but I think you're brilliant." Lydia looks over her shoulder through the Ghiberti Doors. "She's about to start. Thank you for your words about being beloved." She turns to give Peter a hug, but he's already on his feet, gazing toward Sophia.

Stained glass windows splay rainbows of color across the nave's floor and colonnade. Peter and Lydia pick up the bible codices resting on two adjacent cushions and sit down. They join about fifty other Christians and catechumens arrayed in a semicircle around the periphery of the indoor labyrinth. Some of the elderly Christians are seated in chairs.

Sophia sits on a cushion in the center of the labyrinth, where the pastel hues of the "THE WORD OF OUR GOD WILL STAND FOREVER" window spill across Her lap. After concluding Her forty-day fast in August, She returned to Her normal healthy weight. Solid as stone and soft as a feather, She draws all eyes to Her without making a sound. When the nave is silent, She addresses the assembly: "Welcome, friends. What a blessing it is to be with you here today. Let us begin."

They start by saying a prayer together:

> *Holy, loving, lovely God:*
> *Let us glorify and adore you, great mystery.*
> *Sublime father, mother, teacher, lover, friend, deepest self,*
> > *you are ever present with us and in us.*
> *If it is your will:*
> > *grace us with another day,*
> > *give us passionate gratitude for your abundance,*
> > *heal our desperate brokenness,*
> > *send us the humiliations that will grow our souls,*

open us to serve as conduits of your grace, and
help us to see you in all;
So that we may incarnate your love.
Amen.

They raise their heads, and Sophia says, "Today, I'd like to talk with you about the Beatitudes, which we read in last Sunday's service. These are blessings Jesus gave at the start of his Sermon on the Mount, the first being 'Blessed are the poor in spirit, for theirs is the kingdom of heaven.' The Beatitudes can help us approach the heart of Jesus' teachings."

Peter can't help but notice once again that Sophia is speaking of Jesus in the third person. *I'm sure She's just waiting for the right time*, he thinks. *Then She'll say explicitly that She's the Second Coming of Christ.*

A young woman raises her hand. She's nineteen or twenty, and this week her frizzy hair has pink stripes.

"Please, Brooklyn," Sophia says. "Do you have a question?"

Brooklyn nods adamantly. "Sophia, it's been like so *wow* these last two months. I mean, I access a lot, you know. But the Christian 'good news' is so different and fascinating compared to anything I've ever encountered. I mean, this Jesus guy was like totally monkeynuts awesome. I mean, you know what I mean . . ."

Sophia nods patiently.

". . . so I guess what I don't get is why this religion had like millions and millions of people and then it basically folded up. I mean, how's that even possible?" She glances around. "Oh! I guess that's not really on-topic."

"We have time," Sophia says. She looks to Peter. "Would you like to answer Brooklyn's question, Bishop?"

"Uh, sure. Brooklyn, you're asking why Christianity went from being a huge religion to being a very small one?"

She nods.

"Well," says Peter, "it was part of a larger shift that affected all religions. Most modern historians think the problem was that metafiz conflicted with the scientific worldview. As things got more complex and technologically advanced in recent centuries, it was inevitable that people would lose their religious beliefs—again, that's according to today's historians. But if it's true, it means there wasn't really anything the Christians of past generations could have done to change what happened." Peter shrugs.

Following a few moments of silence, Sophia utters a single word: "Twaddle."

Peter stares at Her. "What?"

"Twaddle," Sophia repeats. "Hooey. Beware of myths that tell you certain things are 'inevitable.' Remember that God is free to make choices, and God created you to be free, as well."

"Um, okay." Peter swallows. "Perhaps you should answer Brooklyn's question, My Lady." After Transfiguration Sunday, Peter called Her "My Lord" several times before it occurred to him that the title's feminine form would be more proper. Many of the Christians now address Her as "My Lady," while most of the catechumens simply call Her "Sophia." Peter has never heard Her comment one way or another on how people choose to address Her.

"I am happy to tackle the question," She says. She winks at Peter, and he feels his lips spontaneously part in a smile. He can't help it—he loves it when Her attention is focused on him.

She turns to Brooklyn and says, "There is an old blessing: 'May your soul have deep roots and strong wings.'"

"How can you fly if you're rooted in the ground?" asks Brooklyn. "It sounds like a paradox."

"Truths of the soul can often sound paradoxical. The blessing means that people need both a strong foundation and room to grow. They need both a stable sense of identity and the ability to evolve. A healthy soul neither disintegrates nor petrifies. It is grounded but also free. Does that make sense?"

"Yes, I think so," Brooklyn says.

"So, to answer your question," Sophia says, "Christianity collapsed because it stopped offering people's souls both of these.

"With changes in technology and society, human culture became less and less rooted. It began to focus mostly on 'wings': individual freedom, technological innovation, mobility, and progress—all of which are blessings, to be sure. People became more critical of their historical and religious roots, which they came to realize too often had been bound up with the oppression of one group of people by another. And there was important truth in this recognition. But some went further, concluding that religion was just no good—that it should simply be cast off and forgotten. A few even argued that no overarching vision about reality should ever be trusted. They thought that any big-picture story about the meaning of existence could only lead to dogmatism and oppression.

"For religious folk, that perspective threatened to suck purpose and fulfillment out of life. The secular world appeared to be going off-track, moving people in a shallow, materialistic direction. And there was truth in this view, as well. But too many of the Christian churches reacted to the growing rootlessness by defending the roots at all cost. All across the different denominations, many Christians simply dug in. Their religion became all roots and no wings. Believers were not allowed to question traditions, propose alternate interpretations of scripture, or suggest that the group's understanding of God should continue to unfold. Such 'roots only' religion became almost entirely backward-looking, and the living, loving God of the Christian Gospel came to be seen as static and oppressive, ironically strengthening the arguments for God's obsolescence.

"What never evolves, dies. Eventually, these backward-looking forms of religion could no longer flourish."

Half a dozen cushions down from Peter, Alma raises her hand. At Sophia's nod, she asks, "Why didn't anyone put the roots and wings together, like in the blessing?"

"Excellent question," says Sophia. "There were those who tried. These Christians described themselves with words such as 'modern,' 'liberal,' or 'progressive.' They saw novelty and change as gifts of the Holy Spirit, and they knew that the Gospel was meant to be more than dead letter. They sought to proclaim the Christian message in ways that connected with science and humanity's ever-so-gradual spiritual evolution."

Peter wants so badly to understand. "Why," he interjects, "didn't they succeed?" How different his life might have been if they had!

"They were thoughtful and analytical but rarely visionary. Instead of preaching a new vision of God's unchanging love and presence in their changing world, they often just split the difference between the attitudes of the 'roots' people and the 'wings' people. Instead of *synthesizing* old and new, they often just cobbled together bits and pieces from both."

"I get it," says Brooklyn. "It's like the difference between baking a cake and just putting the ingredients in a heap. In the first case, you're synthesizing, you're putting something together that includes the ingredients but is more than just their sum. In the second case, it's just a mush."

"Nice analogy," says Sophia. "To bake their cake, those Christians needed a vision—a vision of reality that fit, on the one hand, with scripture and tradition and, on the other, with the changing times in which they lived. One might say that finding this vision was their missed destiny. If they had succeeded, it would have allowed them to proclaim a message to modern people that offers both roots and wings, just as the Gospel was always meant to do."

Brooklyn scans the faces of the Christians and catechumens sitting around the circle. She's almost shaking with excitement. She croaks out, "Maybe it's, like, *our* destiny to find this vision!"

Sophia smiles. "Let's not get ahead of ourselves, my dear." Addressing the group, She says, "Now, turn in your bibles to the fifth chapter of Matthew's gospel . . ."

After the lesson, Peter heads for his office to put some finishing touches on his Sunday sermon. He's crossing the courtyard when a strapping young man catches up with him. "Bishop!"

"Hi, Jason," Peter says. "How are you today, my friend?"

"Thirty-nine days clean and sober," Jason declares. His eyes, once bloodshot from stimming, now shine.

Stims are such a devastating modern form of addiction, Peter thinks. *As hard to shake as the narcotic substances of yesteryear.* "Bless you. You look so healthy. Do you want to pray together?"

"Actually, Bishop, I wanted to ask you a question about Sophia."

"Certainly."

The last of the Christians and catechumens are dispersing after the lesson. Jason raises his eyebrows and speaks in a secretive tone. "You and Sophia—I think I saw a few sparks back there."

"I'm not following you."

"I'm just wondering if you two've got something happening."

"Something—"

"You know, *something happening.*"

"Oh." Peter squeezes the other male's shoulder. "Jason, you need to understand that She's, She's special."

"I *know* she's special."

"I mean, She's not what you think."

Jason thinks for a moment and then nods. "Oh, I get it. She's a q-feme."

"That's not what I mean," Peter says. *He really hasn't put it all together yet, has he?* "I mean She's not a normal person, Jason. She's 'not of the world.'"

Jason strokes his goatee, confused.

"To put it simply," Peter says, "I don't think She's—I don't think She's available."

"You don't *think* she's available."

"Right."

"Because you've got something happening with her?"

"No! Of course not."

Jason smiles. "First-rate, Bishop! That's what I needed to know." He vigorously shakes Peter's hand and strides purposefully away. An image of Sophia locked in carnal embrace with Jason pops into Peter's head, and he hears a rush of jealous blood in his ears. To his horror, he also feels himself stiffen. Furtively, he hurries from the courtyard into what was once the diocesan headquarters building.

Entering The Bishop's Office, he stops and takes deep breaths to calm himself. After a few minutes, he walks over to his window. Two people are meditatively walking the outdoor labyrinth. Calmer now, Bishop Peter makes the sign of the cross toward the unseeing catechumens.

Bless you.

He turns from the window and sits down at his desk. Pushing the conversation with Jason out of his mind, he checks his messages. Three are waiting for him. He scans the list of callers, and his eyes bulge. *We suddenly seem to have everyone's attention.*

He fetches a cup of hot tea and then returns the first call on the list. A young woman's voice answers. "Mister Halabi, thank you for calling back."

"Certainly. It's not every day I receive a call from a program manager at the Western North American Social Foundation."

"Ah, so you're familiar with our work."

"Of course. You support social and health programs in a number of nations."

"That's right," the program manager says. "Our grants are highly competitive, and it's rare for us to proactively reach out to an organization. But our board has been hearing fascinating things about yours—that you're having success getting lowcontribs off the streets and, in particular, helping stim addicts."

"I suppose you could say so. Outreach to the poor and marginalized— 'lowcontribs,' as you call them—has once again become a central mission for us."

"Well, your success has attracted notice. The WNASF would like to invite you to apply for a support grant."

"A 'support grant'? What does that mean?"

"Potentially quite a bit of money. It would be a way to ensure financial security for your organization into the foreseeable future."

Wow, they want to give us money. We could stop selling holy artifacts. We could expand our missionary activities.

"That's very generous of you," he says.

"Bear in mind that I cannot guarantee you will receive a grant. You will need to go through the formality of the standard application process."

"Of course, understood."

"I'm so glad you're interested. We have an application package with five parts. First, an application form with questions about the organization's basic characteristics: mission, vision, governance structure, personnel, etcetera. Second, your most recent financial statements. Third, evidence of corporate registration with your national authorities, in your case the Independent Nation of Sanef Bay. Fourth, a standard Disavowal of Metafiz form. And fifth, a description of intended uses—"

"Sorry, can you back up? What is a 'disavowal of metafiz' form?"

"Oh, that's just a boilerplate legal form. Years ago, there were organizations that wanted to teach various forms of metafiz while obtaining funds from the foundation. Obviously, we don't allow that."

Huh? thinks Peter. "Do—do you understand who we are? We're the Christian Church."

"I understand. Your group emerged from a cult, and now you're moving into the social services space. It's happened before. Obviously, if you're going to successfully transition, you'll want to make it clear, especially for public relations purposes, that your program does not involve metafiz."

Peter sighs. "You don't understand. Our religious faith—what you would consider 'metafiz'—is what motivates us to care for the poor. We're not doing it to make money. We're doing it because our faith requires it of us."

The program manager goes silent for several seconds. "Are you saying," she asks, "that you're not allowed to help people unless you can indoctrinate them?"

"Not at all. We also help people who choose not to join the Christian faith. It has taken us centuries, unfortunately, but we've learned that God never uses coercion or fear to compel belief—and that the Church may never do so, either.

"That said, we cannot 'disavow' teaching the good news of our faith."

The program manager giggles nervously. "*God*—wow, I didn't expect to hear *that*. Uh, Mister Halabi, I may have been misinformed. I had thought your group was ready to become an efficiently contributing organization."

"I'm afraid that our outreach isn't about 'efficient contribution' or even only about meeting people's basic physical needs. Our, our . . . teacher, She says it's about reaching out to our sisters and brothers to help them know they are beloved children of *God*—that their souls have eternal value, regardless whether they are materially rich or poor."

"Oh—um. Okay. Well, I guess there would be no point in applying, then." She sighs. "You know, you're leaving a lot of money on the table."

"I understand. Thank you for your kind call. If you would ever like to talk about God, don't hesitate to call again."

"Sure."

She breaks the connection, and Peter leans forward with his head in his hands. *Was there some way I could have finessed that? How can we continue if we don't find some way to earn money apart from selling artifacts?* He rubs his temples and blows on his tea to cool it down. After some moments, he steels himself and returns the second call on his list.

A man greets him and introduces himself as the "deputy chief recruitment officer" for the Dempublican Independent Party of Sanef. After an exchange of pleasantries, the man says, "Your colleague, the woman on the netcast—Sophia, is it?"

"That's right."

"Wow, what charisma. I mean, she's got the gift of persuasion. Lots of politicians would like to have that kind of magnetism."

"I suppose you're right. It's because She is special. She's not just a normal person like you or me. She was sent by—"

"Yeah, so, has she ever thought about running for Parliament?"

"Has She—running for—sorry, running for Parliament?"

"You betcha. I think she could go far on the Dempublican ticket. We're the largest party in Parliament, as you know. She is a Dempublican, isn't she?"

"I, uh, I'm not sure."

"Hmm, she doesn't support the Meganational Identity Party, does she? Because their platform threatens Sanef's peace and prosperity in a huge way, let me tell you."

Peter must think for a moment. *Oh yeah, the Meganational Identity Party. They advocate a political reunification of the former US-American meganation.* That party doesn't have a majority anywhere in the former meganation, though, as far as Peter can recall. Most people still believe what everyone was taught in school—namely, that the earthwide wave of meganation disintegration was an "inevitable" consequence of a "freer" and "more robust" global economy. Now older and more jaded about politics, Peter suspects that the cartels orchestrated the old meganations' dissolution to avoid regulations and enhance their own power. But Uncle Jeff is the historian, not Peter.

"I don't think She is supporting any political party."

"Well, I'm sure if she read our platform . . ."

Sophia appears in Peter's doorway, and he asks the recruitment officer to hold.

"Phoebe and I are going out to preach," She says, "and I wanted to let you know. We should be back before dinner."

"My Lady, before you go, I have someone on the line who's trying to recruit you."

"Recruit me?"

"To run for a seat in the Sanef Parliament."

She puts a hand to Her mouth and then, with an earnest expression, says, "Hmm. What do you think? Should I run for Parliament?"

He laughs nervously. "I never really thought about it. I mean, I suppose it could be a way to bring attention to the Church and to make the System a better place."

"Politics matters," She says. "Transforming laws can help 'make the System a better place' . . . but only if those transformed laws are grounded in a transformed culture. Otherwise, humane laws will die because the soil in which they grow cannot continue to nourish them."

Peter nods.

"Remember that laws are ultimately about enforcing conduct," Sophia says, "and authentic transformation of peoples' hearts can never be forced. It can only be invited, again and again. So, Peter, if you and I dedicate ourselves to politics and laws, who will keep inviting the culture toward transformation?"

"I—yes, I think I understand. I'll tell him, 'No, thank you.'"

Sophia nods and leaves Peter to wrap up the call.

Unfortunately, the recruitment officer has a hard time taking no for an answer. "Look, just tell me what party she's going to support." Failing to elicit a definitive response from Peter, he ends the call on an ominous note. "I know you're doing some weird stuff on that old multicultural reservation. I hope you realize it's better to have friends than enemies in Nation Hall."

After the call, Peter sits in silence for several minutes. Even a political neophyte such as he can recognize a threat when he hears it. *This has been an unsettling afternoon.* It used to bother him that no one paid attention to the Church, but he's now realizing there were certain benefits to flying under the radar.

Okay, here's hoping the last call goes better than the first two.

After one ring, an automated voice answers. "Thank you for calling the International Christian Capitalist Club. All lines are currently busy. Please hold for the next available customer service representative or say the name of the party you wish to reach."

"Regional Chief Executive."

"Please hold. Connecting."

After some moments, a man's voice answers. "This is the RCE."

"Hello. Peter Halabi here. I'm returning your call from earlier today."

"Ah, Mister Halabi. Very efficient of you to call back so quickly. Are you related to Priscilla Halabi?"

"Yes, she was my mother."

"I take it she's no longer earning?"

"She passed away a few years ago."

"What a shame. Had no idea that your organization was under new management, or that you were a family business. Well, here we are. Now, Mister—excuse me—*Bishop* Halabi, when I learned of your recent netcast, I thought to myself, 'It's very enterprising of them to start trying to sell their message publicly again.' Really, my applause to you."

"Thanks for your support."

"Now, Bishop, the one, teeny thing that concerns the ICCC, and where I'd like to come to a negotiated settlement, is your associate, the woman, pushing some very bad, very harmful ideas and saying that they are 'Christian.'"

"I'm not sure what you mean."

The Regional Chief Executive chuckles. In a conspiratorial tone, he says, "The truth is I have a lot of sympathy for your cult. The ICCC started out as a cult, too, you know. In the old days, they believed in metafiz and worshipped your scriptures."

"You don't read the bible anymore, do you?"

"Sure, our members do, sometimes, in redacted form. First step was to replace the books of Luke and James—books of straw, for sure!—with the books of Ayn. Gave free market economics the status of religious dogma—very smart, that was. And the group's image continued to change to keep up with modern times. Largely thanks to the ICCC, the word 'Christian' has been liberated to encourage the unending pursuit of prosperity. That's one reason why we're one of the most influential private societies in the System."

"I'm not against 'prosperity,' Mister Chief Executive. But I would say that the Christian Gospel is about 'prospering' spiritually, not about accumulating material wealth."

"Ha! You turned that around on me quite poetically. Would hate to get in a debate with you, Bishop. But do you realize the ICCC has thousands of members across the System? What do you have? A few dozen lowcontribs? Your cult lost the marketing game a long time ago. Realistically, it's not even worth your while to go on netcasts."

"You don't want us to go on netcasts? I don't understand."

"I think you can understand that the ICCC needs to protect our brand. You see, unlike you, we give people what they want. And what they want is permission to focus on comfort and status, on playing the game and getting ahead." He chuckles amiably. "Also, let's face it, you can't do business in a civilization that takes seriously the sorts of ideas your associate was pushing on that netcast—'love thy neighbor' and that sort of naive sentimentality."

Peter can feel his heart pound. "Christianity is a spiritual path," he says, "not a social club. Its measure is not how much it just 'gives people what they want.' Its purpose is to help transform people into something greater than they can imagine."

"Bishop, let's be reasonable people and not dabble in metafiz."

"I'm afraid my *job* is to 'dabble in metafiz.'"

The Regional Chief Executive sighs. "I can see you're trapped inside your archaic worldview, and we're not going to get anywhere like this. Bishop, I thank you for the time you've spent speaking with me. Would you be so kind as to hold a moment for my associate?"

"Would I—well, if—"

The Regional Chief Executive places Peter on hold.

After a few moments, another man's voice begins speaking. In a flat monotone, barely pausing to take breaths, the man says, "Mister Halabi, I am Chief Legal Counsel for the North American Region of the International Christian Capitalist Club, hereafter referred to as 'the ICCC.' On behalf of the ICCC, I hereby formally demand that the entity doing business under the name 'One, Holy, Catholic, and Apostolic Church'—hereafter referred to as 'OHCAC'—including you its registered chief executive and each and every one of its directors, officers, employees, and agents, immediately cease and desist from publicly associating the term 'Christian' with the encouragement, aid, or abetment of lowcontrib status, given that such activities would more likely than not materially and substantially dilute the ICCC's legally protected brand. If OHCAC refuses to comply with our reasonable demand and we are forced to litigate the matter, we reserve the right to seek an injunction and damages from OHCAC, including but not limited to incidental, consequential, and punitive damages, as well as reasonable attorneys' fees to the greatest extent permitted by applicable law. You will shortly receive an electronic statement documenting the foregoing demand. Good day, sir." The lawyer breaks the connection.

Peter leans back in his chair, dumbfounded. He has no idea what the lawyer meant by accusing the Church of "diluting" the ICCC's "legally protected brand." But, clearly, they're trying to shut Sophia and him up.

He takes his first sip of tea, but it has gone cold. *The ICCC has lots of members in the cartels and could really cause us trouble, even apart from any lawsuit.* He resolves to discuss the matter with Sophia and the Church Council as soon as possible.

Three calls, three misunderstandings. One of them thinks the Church should simply be a secular charity. Another thinks we should be a wing of a political party. And the third thinks being "Christian" is about membership in an exclusive club. I'm still not certain exactly what the Church is supposed to be like, but I'm pretty sure it's not supposed to become any of those things.

During Peter's walk home that evening, he can't help but glance nervously over his shoulder.

12

Grace

Five dozen people climb the forty steps up to Grace Cathedral's main entrance. Their guide reaches the top first, and he practically shouts, "Good afternoon, Your Holiness!" Before Peter can do more than grimace, the tour guide whispers, "I think almost all of these people are on the tour just to see your attraction—amazing, huh?"

"Well—"

"You've got some locals today, not just tourists. You folks have really stirred up interest around town." He winks at Peter and, without waiting for a response, wheels around toward his tour group. As the main clump of them reaches the top of the steps, he announces: "Here we are at the historic Grace Cathedral you have all heard so much about. It is my honor and privilege to present to you His Holiness, Pope Halabi the Second of Sanef, Overseer and High Priest of the Ancient Church of G-Zeus!" He turns to Peter and bows deeply, splaying his arms out behind his back.

What a showman, thinks "Pope Halabi the Second." Putting on a smile, he faces the crowd. "Hello, friends. Welcome to Grace Cathedral. Please call me Peter. I've learned the hard way that all the fancy titles in the System can't tell a person who he really is." Peter surveys the group and sees various expressions, including interest, curiosity, and, in a few cases, open hostility. A serious-looking man and woman in the back of the group appear to be entering notes.

They're dressed a little too businesslike to be tourists.

Peter continues his address: "The building we're about to walk through is the current mother church, or headquarters, of the ancient Christian religion—what we call the 'one, holy, catholic, and apostolic Church.' Around here, we like the saying 'Everything old is new.' We are a very old religion, but we have been blessed to enter a new day. And it's a good thing, because our teachings are needed more than ever. Are there any burning questions before we go inside?"

The man in businesslike attire speaks up. "What are your teachings? Give us a summary." He sounds as if he is used to giving orders.

"That's tough in just a few minutes. But here's one teaching. Every one of us is a precious child of God, no matter what has happened to us or what we have done."

People in the crowd whisper to one another. The businesslike man and woman squint at each other and enter additional notes.

"Okay, then," Peter says. "There will be more time for questions at the end. Let's take a look around." He walks through the Ghiberti Doors, and they follow him to the indoor labyrinth. Dozens of cushions and chairs rest along the walls. "I'd like to start our tour right here so that you can get a panoramic view of this cathedral and its lovely stained glass windows, which date from—"

"Stained *glass*?" exclaims a thirtysomething man who is even taller than Peter.

"Uh, yes, indeed." The luminors are on, and Peter gestures toward the Canticle of the Sun above the cathedral entrance. "Each of these colorful windows is made up of tiny pieces of colored glass assembled by artists to create the images you see. Collectively, the cathedral's windows are made up of many thousands of them."

The tall man squints up at the window. "No way. That's got to be a holoprojection."

"It's not."

"Come on. No one would be that inefficient. No rational person would invest so much in mere ornamentation." A few of the other visitors nod their heads.

"There's a window at ground level over on the west side of the cathedral," Peter says. "Let's go over there first, and you can touch a stained glass window for yourself."

The man grunts. As the group follows Peter through the nave, he hears more whispers over the sound of their shuffling feet. Just as he's passing by the Chapel of the Nativity, a piercing scream startles him.

Ayeeyyyy!

He jerks around and realizes the sound came from beyond the open door to the courtyard. *What the . . . ?*

He asks his visitors to wait where they are and hurries over. As he exits the building into the sunny courtyard, the noise erupts again. This time, his ear identifies it.

It's cheering.

Sophia performs a pirouette as two clamorous young catechumens cheer Her on. Like Her, they're wearing dance shoes. They laugh and clap as She leaps and spins Her way through the courtyard, demonstrating dance movements. Her flowing white dress gives Her an angelic aspect, but Her face wears a broad, so-human grin. Oblivious to the bishop's presence, the two catechumens step forward to join Her dance.

After Sophia's fast, Peter learned that She loves to dance. And She's good. From what he can tell, She dances like one who has been professionally trained. Some days, She grabs Her dance shoes and says She's going out to "preach the kinetic gospel." Peter doesn't know an *assemblé* from an asparagus, but he guesses that most of Her dance movements could be described as "ballet." Although he's seen Her dance before, at that moment he finds he can't pull his eyes away from Her. Her every motion sounds a note in an ambulant symphony of grace.

"*Who's she?*" whispers a voice from behind Peter.

He turns and sees that the tall man from the tour group has followed him out the door. Like Peter, the man appears to be glued to the sight of Sophia.

"She's, She's—who is She? For now, let's just say She's like nobody you've ever met."

The tall man swallows and draws his gaze away from Her. His mouth curves into a lupine grin. "Don't think I've forgotten about that window supposedly made of little pieces of glass, Mister High Priest!"

Forty-five minutes later, Peter stands by the Ghiberti Doors and waves to the departing visitors. *Got through another one of those.* The tall man turned out to be not so bad. Upon touching the stained glass window, he converted. *Well, not to the Christian faith but to a more receptive demeanor.*

Sophia walks up to Peter. She's changed into day-to-day clothes and shoes. "Bishop Peter," She greets him.

"My Lady," he acknowledges, bowing his head.

She looks out on the departing tourists. "Are you enjoying the opportunity to show off your cathedral?"

"Yes, thanks to you." He pauses. "There's just one thing."

"What's that?"

"Well, when I talk to these groups, I always have the feeling that most of them think I'm insane."

She raises an eyebrow.

"They think that the stories I tell them are bizarre 'metafiz' and they have to humor me as if I'm from a primitive culture or have some sort of mental disorder—like maybe I need neurpro." He cringes.

"Not all of them, certainly. Our catechumen Elizabeth joined us after taking your tour."

"Yes, that's true, so I'm happy to play cathedral docent. But still, most of the people seem to think I'm—what did they used to call it? Ah, a 'religious nut.'"

She smiles and pats him on the arm. "Your path is one leading to a greater abundance of love and freedom. Those are the true criteria of sanity. If you're insane, then your 'insanity' is saner than the System's 'sanity.'"

"Thank you for your wisdom." He grins. "I have to say, when we first met, I never thought I'd be learning the true meaning of sanity from *you*."

She practically howls with laughter, infecting Peter. Soon, tears are running down their cheeks.

Their schedules permit them to spend another minute or two together in companionable silence broken only by an occasional chuckle. Given the demands of outreach, teaching, spiritual counseling, and overseeing the cathedral buildings' ongoing renovations, the Christians have suddenly found themselves with much to do. Sophia, Peter, and Dorcas, in particular, often find their calendars quite booked up. As lovely as it is to be needed, a part of Peter misses the days when he could sit on the steps and talk with Sophia at length with no one else around. *At least today She was able to steal some time to dance.*

As they're about to head their separate ways, Alma hurries around the corner of the cathedral toward them. She's breathing heavily when she reaches them, and her hands are shaking.

"What's wrong?" asks Peter.

Alma glances at him, but she plainly wants to speak to Sophia. "M—may I please talk with you?"

"Of course," She says. "Come sit down with me on the steps."

Peter nods at the women. "I'll let you two talk in private. I'll be in my office if either of you needs me."

"Thank you," Alma whispers. Sophia takes Alma's hand, and the women sit down and begin to speak in low voices.

Peter walks over to The Bishop's Office. When he arrives, he finds that new correspondence is awaiting him. He begins reading it and draws in a sharp breath. He wasn't expecting anything like this.

From: Tax Assessor, Government of the I. N. of Sanef Bay
To: Mr. Peter Halabi
Date: Tuesday, February 27 17:03
Subject: PMR STATUS/TAX ASSESSMENT
Attachments: 1

Dear Mr. Halabi:

The National Antiquities Administration has informed this Office that it is reviewing the continuing applicability of the parliamentary grant of Protected Multicultural Reservation (PMR) status to <u>Grace Cathedral, 1100 California Street</u>, I. N. Sanef (Attachment A). Under Antiquities Code Section 41.1156, PMR status is no longer legally applicable when one of the categories of "Changed Conditions" applies to a property. Please be informed that the National Antiquities Administration's review will be completed within <u>sixty (60)</u> days as mandated by statute. Should your property's PMR status be dissolved at that time, you will be assessed the following property taxes, payable within <u>fifteen (15) days</u> . . .

Oh my God, thinks Peter. The Church's PMR status might be taken away, and then they would have to pay property taxes . . . an on entire city block right in the middle of central Sanef. The potential tax liability is astronomical. *How many of the holy artifacts would we have to sell to pay that!?*

He doesn't know why this has happened. *Is it because people are living on the cathedral grounds now? Because of the renovations? Dear Lord! Could it be the ICCC? They're already threatening to sue us. Are the Dempublicans coming after us? They're the biggest party in Parliament.*

He goes home and spends that evening on the net researching regulations about PMR status and property taxes. It's around 23:30 when he finally drags himself to his bed and falls asleep. He plans to convene an emergency meeting with Sophia and the Church Council in the morning.

That night, at a time so late and so early that the city feels quiet and empty, a figure appears at the darkened door to The Bishop's Residence. No one sees the intruder somehow open the locked door and enter the apartment. The intruder noiselessly closes the door before moving through the apartment to Peter's bedside and standing over him, silently observing the bishop as he sleeps. His chest rises and falls with the rhythm of his breathing.

Trinity wakes up. As soon as the rabbit sees the intruder, she begins to jump around with frantic energy. Peter continues to sleep, unaware that anything out of the ordinary might be happening.

A hand reaches toward Peter. Just as the intruder is about to make contact, one of Peter's eyes cracks open blearily.

"Ahhhh! Sweet Jesus! What the—!?"

Peter manages to scramble up against his headboard, stretching his hands in front of him in a defensive panic. Then he recognizes Sophia.

"Peter, it's all right! I'm sorry I startled you." She's wearing a lightweight jacket and a backpack, and She's holding a small light in Her hand. "I'm sorry. But you need to wake up."

"My, My Lady?" He looks at his time display. It reads: WEDNESDAY 03:06. "It's the middle of the night," he whines. "Wha—what are you doing here, in my apartment?"

Sophia lifts the rabbit from her cage and strokes her. She immediately calms down and nuzzles against Sophia. "It's technically morning," Sophia says. "And it's time for you and me to take a trip. I thought we might take it a little later, but it seems that now is the right time. Dorcas will manage things here in Sanef while we're away."

He shakes his head, trying to banish the sleep from his brain. "Go away? Now? But, where?"

She points straight up.

Peter's eyes widen. For a second, he thinks She wants him to ascend with Her to heaven.

13

Everythingness

A light moves upon the face of the deep. It shines in the darkness, and the darkness does not overcome it.

The Earth-Meres Commercial Shuttle *Rick Husband* is approaching the halfway point of its five-day run to Meres. The spacecraft carries ninety passengers, each of whom has a berth in one of six identically-sized modules: one first class, one business class, and four economy. Six well-heeled passengers divide the space in the first-class module, while twelve passengers divide the one for business class. In each of the economy modules, eighteen passengers share a sleeping tube bank and a common area.

The bright orange of Peter's bedding contrasts with his tube's gleaming white walls. The soundproofing is good, and he's accessing data about Meres and taking care not to bump his head. *My God, I still can't believe we're doing what we're doing.*

Only Sophia could have convinced Peter to leave Sanef now, when the Church seems to be under attack. He suspects that the letter from the tax assessor's office is some sort of retribution, and it makes his blood boil. But he has exchanged messages with Dorcas, and she's tracking down a lawyer to advise the Church on that and on the letter from the ICCC. Peter tells himself that they have some time and that Dorcas is certain to be handling the situation as well as he could. For Her part, Sophia left no room for doubt that his duty lay in following Her aboard this shuttle to Meres.

In the meantime, Peter was embarrassed to realize that all of his "knowledge" about Meres comes from entertainment vids, so he's trying suck up as much data about the place as he can before they arrive. Sophia, on the other hand, spends almost all of Her time in their module's common area interacting with their fellow passengers.

The *Rick Husband* has used constant acceleration to provide a Merian gravity level during most of the trip. Once the Earthers onboard got used to maneuvering in the weaker Merian g—Peter rammed himself into ceilings twice the first day—they were eager to congregate in the common area and talk. Most of the passengers in their module are immigrating to work in one of the various Merian nations. Few, if any, of these immigrants have ever traveled offearth.

It's late afternoon according to the ship's time, which reflects the slightly longer Merian day: 24 hours and 37 minutes. As Peter accesses data about their destination, he occasionally comes across references to the planet's old English name. Yet it seems that marketing has mostly murdered "Mars."

The early offearth development companies concluded they could charge slightly more to resettle customers if the destination were *not* named after a bloodthirsty god of war. An enterprising marketeer came up with the idea to soften the Latin "Mars" by interweaving a hint of "Ares," the equivalent Greek god. He thereby created "Meres," which is pronounced like "marries" or "Mary's." English speakers widely adopted the name, and the planet now sounds to them more like grandma's house than a kennel for the dogs of war. In Peter's view, this is one case in which two wrongs do seem to make a right.

Meres, he has also learned, has a population of several hundred thousand, with more arriving almost daily. The planet has a disproportionate economic importance, as do the Stations in Earth orbit and the settlements in the Stroids between Meres and Jupiter. As for the far inner and outer System, a few cartel alliances maintain crewed facilities and outposts there. In any event, the teeming populations who will live out their lives on Earth still dwarf the wispy tendrils of humanity that stretch out into the System.

Speaking of which, it's time to stretch my legs. Peter pulls on his shirt. His next scheduled turn in the star lounge will begin in a few minutes.

As he passes through the module's common area, he tells Sophia where he's going. He climbs up through the spacecraft's central passageway, passing a crew member who nods at him, and enters the star lounge at the appointed minute. He takes a seat in one of the less comfortable of six chairs arrayed in a circle—the one marked "Passenger: Economy Module 4"—and leans it back for a better view. An inconceivably vast panorama of bright stars and nebulae spreads out before him.

Located at the bow of the vessel, the star lounge provides a 180-degree view of outer space. Peter has been assured that nothing the spacecraft might encounter between Earth and Meres could possibly penetrate its transparent dome. He's still a little skeptical given the zeal with which the crew insists that the hatch connecting the star lounge to the rest of the vessel remain closed when not in use. Regardless, Peter's awe of the magnificent view eclipses his lingering trepidation, and he wouldn't dream of skipping his two half-hour daily allotments of star-lounge time.

The pink little sphere that Peter recognizes as Meres has grown modestly since his early-morning time allotment. He's learned the names of some stars and their locations relative to the disk of the Milky Way, and he could easily access all the facts and figures he wants. But most of the time, he just stares at the naked stars without any technological contrivance in the way, apart from the transparent material protecting him from hard vacuum and deadly cosmic rays.

Peter's eyes scan vast swaths of interstellar space. He holds a hand half an arm's length from his face and makes a circle with his thumb and forefinger. With keen enough eyes, one could see more stars and planets than one could ever count, just within that little circle. He murmurs, "O Lord, how manifold are your works."

A voice to his left asks, "First time?"

Jogged out of his reverie, Peter leans over to respond to the man seated to his left. "It is my first interplanetary trip. You?"

"Ah goodness, I've lost count. My bosses make me come back to Earth twice every Merian year."

So about once per Earth year. If he's a regular interplanetary traveler, he must be some kind of manager for a cartel.

The man holds out his hand. "Thomas Delaney—call me Tommy. Pleasure to be making your acquaintance." Tommy Delaney is handsome with a strong jaw, probably taller than Peter, and more muscular. Being a man of stature is a disadvantage in the cramped spaces of the shuttle, but Tommy's cartel must have paid for one of the roomier modules—his chair looks more comfortable, and he was already in the star lounge when Peter's time allotment started. Like Peter, he's fair and has dark hair. Peter guesses he's in his early forties.

"Peter Halabi. The pleasure is mine."

"And where are you from, young Peter?"

"Sanef, actually."

"A lovely nation, truly!" says Tommy, loudly. "Every time I'm there, I enjoy it. Almost makes the old Earth gravity worth it."

One of the other passengers, a white-haired woman, clears her throat and turns to give Tommy and Peter a pointed look. Peter returns his attention to the view, and Tommy follows suit. They sit in silence for several minutes, gazing out into the void of space. Peter sighs. *I can't get enough of this.*

Tommy glances over at Peter and chuckles. Only slightly quieter than before, Tommy says, "You seem rather taken with the cosmos."

Peter tries to keep his words to a whisper. "I've spent my entire life in a city, surrounded by tall buildings and light pollution. I had no idea the stars could be so beautiful." Peter's first time in the star lounge dredged up a long-forgotten memory of going to a planetarium show with Priscilla and Jeff. Peter must have been nine or ten years old. Like any city-dwelling child that age, he was awed by the bright stars projected onto the planetarium dome. But that experience was nothing compared to the view of the stars from space.

"Hmm. It's good you feel that way," Tommy says. "I once saw a lad lose his mind sitting right there where you're sitting. Well, same seat, different shuttle."

"Lose his mind?"

"Not permanently, most likely. But he sure did flip out."

"Flip out? Why would he flip out?" Peter forgets he's trying to whisper.

"He was like you, spent his life earthside in a big city, but he had a different frame of mind. An especially honest one, if I may." Tommy arches his eyebrows and waves a hand toward the void. "He looked out there into that vast, vast emptiness, and I'm supposing he realized he, all of us in fact, are just teeny, random specks in an infinite nothingness. It really flipped the lad's switch."

"Is that what you believe, that we're just random specks in nothingness?"

"Believe? Friend, it's pretty well proven. We know the cosmos is tens of billions of light years across, at least, and it sure seems there aren't anyone else out there. We've been listening for signals for generations now, and we haven't heard a peep from anyone. I figure you pretty much got to accept that we're a little glitch in what turns out to be a big, dead nada."

"You sound like—" Peter stops himself.

"Like one o' them Isnotist loonies? No, no. You don't have to be a fruit-cake to realize everything is just one big, random splatter of emptiness. Just take a good look out there. I'm not the first one to say this. There used to be an entire religion back on Earth based on 'emptiness.' That was their whole starting point."

Peter notices that Tommy said "religion" rather than "cult." Peter says, "Actually, there are still some Buddhists on Earth and in the Stroids."

"That's it. 'Boodists.'"

Tommy's reference to a "starting point" makes Peter think. *Sophia keeps talking about "abundance." Is that Her spiritual "starting point"? Not Emptiness, like the Buddha's, but rather Fullness? Not Nothingness, like the nihilists', but rather "Everythingness"?* Peter rubs his chin. *The Buddhists say all forms are impermanent, and they're certainly right that all things change and die in the passage of time. But what if all things are also, in some way, eternally present to God beyond time? What if nothing is ever truly lost?*

Tommy interrupts Peter's thoughts again. "Sounds like you know something about philosophy."

"Hardly. But it is my job to think about . . ."

Peter almost says "metafiz."

". . . bigger issues."

"Sounds like a fun job," Tommy says. "Are you a professor?"

Peter quickly glances around. At least two of the four other passengers in the star lounge are likely listening in on their conversation, including the white-haired woman. Regardless, Peter starts to give Tommy his well-rehearsed opening statement. "I'm the leader of a group. You have probably been taught to call groups like ours 'cults,' but we call ourselves 'Christians.' We are a very ancient—"

"Christians! Mercy me," Tommy says. "What a small System. *I'm* a Christian too!"

"You—"

"I was the last baby in the I. N. of Cennsalach who was, who was—what do you call it when you pour water on someone to make them a Christian?"

"Baptism."

"Right! I was the last baby baptismed, maybe the last one in all the Irish nations. My great-grandmother insisted. Then she and the old priest both died, and that was it for the baptisms."

Peter stares at Tommy in wonderment at this turn of events.

"Naturally," Tommy continues, "I don't believe in God or G-Zeus or any of that tofu sausage."

Peter frowns.

"Sorry about that, my friend. I know there's no 'meaning' to life, but I can get on with things anyway. I'm certainly not needing to blow myself up or to drink blood to deal with it—no offense. Where I live, we have a different way . . ." He raises a middle finger. ". . . of saying 'falq you' to the cosmos."

Before Peter can come up with a response to *that*, the crew member on duty announces it's time for the economy and business-class guests to rotate out of the star lounge. In the passageway, Tommy asks, "Where are you going once you get to Meres?"

Peter stares blankly, realizing he has no idea where exactly on Meres they're going. It's a big planet with many settlements, of course. *Score one for blind faith.*

"I'm not sure, actually," he says. "My companion is the leader."

"I thought you said you're the leader?"

"Well, sort of. It's complicated. At any rate, when it comes to where we're going, She's the leader."

"Right, taking directions from a feme—poor lad. Been there many a time, I'm afraid, 'fore my girl left me. Now she's half a world away in Argyre." Tommy pauses and then says, as brightly as ever, "I work in a little place named *Eden*. You've heard of it?"

"A place on Meres named 'Eden'? No, I'm sorry, I haven't."

"Gracious, lad, you really don't know much about Meres, do you?"

Peter shrugs apologetically.

"Well, I'll transmit my contact data to you. Eden's not too far from Kistrob, where we'll disembark." Tommy leans in toward Peter. "Come visit if you have a chance, and take a look at the future."

14

Bloody Anselm

The Independent Nation of Amazonis has flesh-and-blood customs officials, but they do their best to imitate automatons. One of them numbly recites scripted words: "As you are in possession of a non-trivial data volume of content flagged on the INA Restricted Metafiz List, entry permission requires that you attest to, and I file, an RML slash 3 slash C Declaration of Intent. Kindly repeat after me: 'I—state your legal name . . .'"

"I, Jasmine S. Chandevi."

Peter made it through customs first and stands waiting for Her. He notices that Her hair and jumpsuit look slightly askew. The ride down from orbit was bumpy.

"Solemnly declare," the official drones, "that my materials on the Restricted Metafiz List . . ."

"Solemnly declare that my materials on the Restricted Metafiz List."

"Shall not be used to proselytize any religion or other antisocial ideology . . ."

"Shall be used to proselytize any religion or other antisocial ideology."

"Shall *not* be used to proselytize any religion or other antisocial ideology . . ."

She pauses and furrows Her brow.

"Let's start again," he says. "I—state your legal name . . ."

"I, state your—I, Jasmine S. Chandevi."

She sounds woozy, Peter thinks. *She should have taken some of the motion sickness meds they offered us.* Peter opted for the extra strength version.

"Solemnly declare that my materials on the Restricted Metafiz List . . ."

"Solemnly declare that my materials on the restricted metabolism."

The official clears his throat and presses on. "Shall *not be used* to proselytize any religion or other antisocial ideology . . ."

"Shall be used to proselytize any religion but no other antisocial immunology."

The customs official looks up at Sophia for the first time. "Turbulent entry from orbit?"

She slowly nods, looking as if She might throw up on his shoes.

Crisply, he says, "I'll indicate that your RML slash 3 slash C declaration is attested. Welcome to the Independent Nation of Amazonis and to the planet Meres. *Next!*"

"Thank you," She whispers.

Sophia gives Peter a discreet wink as they exit the customs hall into a large concourse. Then Her eyes widen, and She bolts for the nearest restroom, covering Her mouth.

Peter grimaces. While he waits, he walks out into the concourse and stares like a tourist. Considering his personal circumstances, he always assumed he would never be able to travel anywhere interesting on Earth, much less beyond it. He can hardly believe he's standing in Kistrob, Amazonis, Meres! *Who knows how many entertainment vids set on Meres I've seen in my life? But those were fiction. This is real.*

Peter accessed that this equatorial Merian city—a conglomeration of several interconnected concourses—takes its official name from an oldtime author who wrote classic novels set on this planet. To Peter, Kistrob's Concourse Three looks like a large indoor shopping mall, but each concourse also contains housing, services, schools, medical facilities, and other things one might expect to find in any city. Kistrob also boasts the busiest spaceport in the Independent Nation of Amazonis, which is one of the planet's dozen or so nations and colonial mandates.

Sophia rejoins Peter where he stands gaping.

"Are you all right?" he asks.

"Much better," She says, clearing Her throat. "How are you?"

"Enthralled." He points. "Look at the ceiling. There's natural sunlight coming in through those transparent panels so we don't have to feel like we're just in a big, artificial cave. But it's not enough light since we're so much farther from the sun, so they installed artificial lights between them. And the combination is tweaked to produce daylight as it would look on Earth."

"And look over there at the garden zone running along the center of the concourse," Sophia says. "The plants seem to be thriving."

"Yes. I think these gardens must be for recreation. I accessed that the Amazonians produce their food in regolith farms and hydroponic greenhouses in the countryside." Peter pulls his eyes away from the greenery and faces Sophia. "Anyway, what now, My Lady?"

"It's Monday afternoon local time. Let's check into our hotel. I'll confirm the time we'll get our rental vehicle tomorrow and a few other things. It would be good if you could pick up dinner and some provisions while I'm doing that."

We somehow skipped Sunday, Peter realizes. *I'm missing a Sunday service—weird.* No doubt his flock would, or did, come together despite the absence of their only cleric. He considers calculating the date and time in Sanef, but he feels too tired.

The hotel is only a short stroll down the concourse. Although Sophia reserved the cheapest accommodations She could find, Peter's tiny room is extravagant compared to his sleeping tube. He stows his things in his room, confers with Sophia about food and supplies, and sets out for the nearest grocery store, located two hundred additional meters down the concourse. Thanks to spending several days at a Merian gravity equivalent aboard the *Rick Husband*, he's found a reasonably efficient gait for the new g.

During Peter's short but invigorating walk, he notices a great variety of people. It seems that Kistrob is home to emigrants from many earthside nations. Some people wear simple jumpsuits while others are dressed in expensive business attire with collars and frills. The latest Kazakh and Neapolitan designs dominate the more stylish apparel here, much as they do in Kistrob this season.

The grocery store and several other establishments ring a cobblestone courtyard. A small, bone-dry fountain stands at its center. In the sunlight that filters down from the concourse ceiling, the courtyard looks like a village square from an entertainment vid set in Europe, with one major difference: the fountain and cobblestones are made of polished crimson Merian rocks. Peter doesn't much care for that. *It's as if someone created a picturesque European courtyard and then painted it in blood.*

About fifty people mill about the courtyard. A woman who resembles Alma the catechumen walks by, and Peter silently rebukes himself. *Another pastoral failure. I was going to ask Sophia what Alma was so upset about the other day. In the excitement of the trip, I completely forgot to follow up.*

He falls in behind a large family that's shuffling into the grocery store. A brief shoving match between two brothers slows their progress. As Peter takes a step back, he hears a young man's voice ring out a few meters behind him.

"MAN SEES EVERYWHERE THE ABSURDITY OF EXISTENCE—"

Peter's head jerks around.

"—AND LOATHING SEIZES HIM!"

Peter doesn't consciously realize what's happening. It's as if his body just moves without waiting for his brain to catch up.

"I DENOUNCE ALL VALUES!"

Several people turn toward the man with puzzled expressions.

"THAT WHICH YOU THINK IS—is—that which—THAT WHICH YOU THINK IS, IS NOT!"

Peter hears the final words right in his ear as he tackles the man from behind, grabbing frantically at the man's arms. In the weaker gravity, Peter has leapt farther—and hit harder—than his reflexes anticipated.

"Wha—" the man huffs out.

Peter's brain finally catches up. He's lying on his side, on the cold red cobblestones. With all their strength, his arms clutch the thrashing, cursing young man. Terror lances through Peter when he feels a hard apparatus strapped beneath the man's shirt.

The bomb!

"Don't let go, don't let go, don't let go," Peter mutters to himself as the two flail back and forth across the cobblestones for an eternity. He never hears the voices that call out: "A nun! A nun! He's over there!"

Every part of Peter's body suddenly burns, and darkness engulfs him.

Blind, thrashing numbness. Nowhere to run. *Run?* Someone wants to kill. *Who?* It's too dark to find out. Too dark . . .

After an unknowable stretch of time, a glimmer of light enters the darkness: self-awareness. *I'm breathing. I'm here. Somewhere.*

Something touches his forehead, and he smells perfumed soap. He languidly opens his eyes, and the face of an attractive feme comes into focus. She has ebony skin and exceptionally white teeth, and she's wearing a medical uniform. "Shh, take it slowly," she orders as she examines his readings.

A biotech?

Peter realizes he's lying in bed in what appears to be a hospital room. He flops his head over and sees Sophia at his bedside. A middle-aged man wearing an officer's uniform and a woman dressed in crisp business attire stand in view over Sophia's shoulder. Peter can see that Sophia's hand rests on his, but he can't feel it.

"Everything is okay," Sophia says. "How do you feel?"

"Bad."

"You just woke up. Do you know where you are?"

"Not The Bishop's Residence."

"No. Remember, Peter, we're on Meres."

Ah. It all floods back: The shuttle. The Milky Way. The customs hall. The hotel. The cobblestones . . .

Peter jerks upward. "The nun!"

The biotech puts a hand on his shoulder. "It's not time to sit up yet."

"You stopped him," Sophia says, with a quick glance toward the middle-aged man in the officer's uniform. "You stopped the nun. No one was hurt."

"Sir." The officer steps forward. "You prevented an atrocity. I'm sorry, we had to shockcock you both so the terrorist couldn't set off his charge. What you're feeling is just your body waking up again. There won't be any permanent damage, I can assure you."

The woman in business attire adds, "Mister Halabi, you're a hero."

"A hero? I just was, I just found myself on top of that guy."

"Fine, but it's a damn good thing for us that's where you found yourself," says the woman. "Good work."

It doesn't take long for the pins-and-needles of returning sensation to spread across Peter's body. The officials and the biotech leave the room, but Sophia remains by Peter's bedside. When the biotech returns sometime later, Peter says, "I'm feeling better now. Can I get out of here? I'd rather spend the night in my hotel room than here. No offense."

"Yes, you'll be as good as new after a night of sleep," the biotech says. "But the commissar and the officer want to speak to you again before I discharge you."

The woman in business attire and the middle-aged officer return to Peter's room fifteen minutes later. A younger officer follows them, accompanying a mobility chair that holds a man immobilized with a series of tight restraints around his legs, torso, and forearms. The detainee stares resolutely at the floor. His hands tremble.

The commissar turns to the younger officer and says, "Begin recording. . . . In the matter of criminal suspect number kay one eight four four eight, Amazonian resident number zero zero zero four five zero three one, name: Bouville, Jean-Pierre." She takes a breath and turns to face Peter. "Mister Halabi, for the record, do you disagree with my identification of this man as the person whom you were forced to tackle in Anselm Square at approximately seventeen-twenty this afternoon?"

"Uh, 'Anselm Square' is the name of where I was? The small courtyard with the blood-red cobblestones?"

"Yes."

Peter examines the detainee. "I got a better look at the back of his head."

"Turn your head," orders the younger officer.

The man jerks his head to one side, still refusing to meet anyone's eyes.

Peter recognizes the stringy mullet that repeatedly convulsed backward toward his face as the man thrashed in Peter's arms. "I can't be a hundred percent sure," he says, "but I think this is him."

The Denunciator never looks up at Peter. He works his jaw silently.

"Thank you, Mister Halabi," the commissar says. "That's more than sufficient evidence to convict. I want to thank you again, on the record, for your heroism. You, a foreigner, have done a great service to the Independent Nation of Amazonis . . ." She glances sideways at the middle-aged officer. ". . . and, of course, the municipality of Kistrob. End recording." The commissar nods at Peter and starts for the door.

"The young man here," Sophia asks. "What will become of him?"

The commissar stops and looks at Sophia for the first time. Her eyes seem to focus on Sophia's scar. She sneers. "It'll take a few weeks to process and finalize the conviction. After that, I'm afraid he'll get a lot better than he deserves, thanks to the gentleness of our laws."

"Prison?" asks Sophia.

"I'd put this garbage out an airlock if it were my personal choice. But federal policy is to redeem these people's minds."

"Neurpro," Peter murmurs, glancing at Sophia.

The commissar gives a curt nod.

"No," Peter says flatly, surprising himself.

The detainee finally looks up, wide-eyed. His red face is wet. He's, at most, sixteen years old.

"No," Peter repeats. "There must be a better way."

The commissar's sneer reappears. "You already know *my* 'better way.'"

"Madame Commissar, respectfully," Sophia says. "He's just a boy. We're leaving Kistrob tomorrow to go out into the desert. Release him into our custody. Peter and I will be responsible for him."

The commissar's eyes bug out.

So do Peter's.

"You simply can't be serious," the commissar says. "You want me to turn over a dangerous nun terrorist to a couple of civilian aliens? I'm afraid not. Good day." She turns toward the younger officer and gestures at the prisoner. "Take Mister Bouville away."

Sophia gives Peter a look that says, *It was worth a try.*

Peter nods and struggles to hide his relief. *I hate to think of such a young person being subjected to neurpro, but how could we possibly deal with someone so disturbed ourselves? How could She even consider it?*

As the others leave, the middle-aged officer tarries a moment. "Sir, for what it's worth," he says quietly to Peter, "there's a lot of opposition to neurpro in Kistrob. We're the most progressive part of Amazonis." He bobs his head toward the door. "But when the feds get involved, it's in their hands."

"You really did save the day, sir. I'm sure you'll get a call from the mayor's office tomorrow. She'll want to do something to honor you."

"Any chance she would be willing to help find a more humane way to deal with that young man?" asks Peter.

"I'm afraid there's no chance the mayor would intervene with the feds right now, however much she might want to." The officer hesitates. "This kid almost killed you and dozens of other people. If I may be frank, why would you give one hydroponic fig about what happens to him?"

Peter glances at Sophia.

"Peter is a friend of his Father," She says.

The officer knits his eyebrows and slowly nods.

"I'm sure Peter would love to tell you more about it," She continues. "I expect that he will be back in Kistrob next week. Perhaps you two could chat over teas then."

"Sure," the officer mumbles. He gives them a quick bow and leaves.

Sophia and Peter walk out of the hospital a few minutes later. Peter asks, "Do you think the mayor of Kistrob will really want to honor me?" He wonders what kind of recognition it will be. *Do they give medals on Meres? Maybe she'll host a reception in my honor . . .*

"It doesn't matter, because we won't be here."

"Oh." He stops. "Do we have to leave so soon?"

She rounds on him. "Peter, is it honors you seek? Is that why you're here?"

"No! Of course not." *I have no idea why I'm here, except you told me to come with you.*

Holding his eyes with Her own, She asks more gently, "Do you want to stay in Kistrob another day in case the mayor calls?"

"I just want to—to do your will."

"In that case, I will for you to get a good night's sleep and to meet me at nine tomorrow morning in the hotel's breakfast room—ready to go."

As Peter lies in his bed half an hour later, he can't stop picturing the tear-soaked face of the desperately troubled teenager who almost murdered him. It occurs to Peter that Sophia still hasn't offered him a theodicy. He still cannot begin to understand why a loving God would permit so much evil and suffering in the System.

Later that night, a nightmare briefly unsettles Peter's otherwise sound slumber.

Praying that the bomb won't detonate, he feels his hips press into hard cobblestones as his sweaty arms tightly grasp a thrashing body.

Don't let go! Don't let go!

He turns his head. The stones beneath him change from crimson to light gray. A rainbow of colors—red, gold, white, and several shades of blue—illuminate a portion of the gray floor beside him. He manages to look upward, and he recognizes the vaulted ceiling. He's struggling with the suicide bomber on the floor of Grace Cathedral.

No! Not my Church!

In his sudden panic, Peter loses his grip on the thrashing body. He wakes from the nightmare only after his adversary jumps up from the floor and turns toward him, staring through him coldly as She triggers Her bomb.

PART THREE

Who is this woman striking as dawn, pure as the moon, fiery as the sun, and as terrifying as an army marching with banners unfurled?

—SONG OF SONGS 6:10

15

Morning, Afternoon, and Evening

Today he will follow Her into the desert.

He wakes up hungry and realizes he has no idea what passes for breakfast on Meres. Fortunately, the food in the hotel's breakfast room doesn't look terribly alien. Soy-based sausages, yogurt, and rye bread are among the items on offer. Half a dozen hotel guests eat at small tables. Peter grabs a plate and begins to load up.

Sophia flows into the breakfast room with Her customary combination of grace and confidence. Although She makes no sound, several heads turn toward Her. Peter feels his lips turn up in a smile. One glance at Her face quiets the residue of the nightmare he now realizes was throbbing in his mind's recesses. *Her demands are sometimes so unexpected or persistent that I feel like I'm being invaded.* He remembers Her standing over him in The Bishop's Residence, patiently insisting that they catch a shuttle to another planet. *Yet She never forces anything. Very rarely, She will express frustration, but She never takes offense, never holds a grudge, never acts out of anger. Talk about Godlike powers.*

"Good morning," Sophia says. "How are you feeling?"

"Much better—good as new, actually." He looks down at his overfull plate. "Just hungry!"

"Clearly."

After breakfast, they check out of the hotel and walk over to Concourse Three's public garage. Sophia has reserved a "landhog": a rugged camper vehicle outfitted for both roads and moderate off-road environments on Meres. The public garage has room for twenty landhogs, and about half of the stalls stand empty.

As with all vehicles on Meres, the landhog has freedrive capability as well as the standard autodrive mode. Neither Sophia nor Peter has any experience freedriving, but Sophia says they might need it when they venture beyond the main trunk roads. In other circumstances, the prospect would seem unthinkably dangerous to Peter, but he puts his trust in Sophia. They both take the rental agency's ninety-minute "crash course"—*ha, ha*, thinks Peter. Then the agency gives them a temporary rating and enables their vehicle's freedrive setting.

The landhog is a boxy thing—aerodynamic efficiency matters less in Meres's thin atmosphere. The front of the vehicle is a driving compartment with large front windows, and it can comfortably seat two adults. Behind the driving compartment, there is a larger, windowless living compartment. The front of the living compartment contains a galley for preparing food, which includes, bolted to the floor, a small metal table with two stools. The galley's left front wall has a screen which can display audiovisual feeds from the landhog's external security cameras. Farther back, there are two sleeping nooks, one on each side of a center aisle. Storage lockers fill the areas above and behind the nooks. A washroom with a toilet, a small sink, and a tiny shower area can be found at the very back of the vehicle. Handrails run along the top of the living compartment.

The landhog has three exits: one on the driver's side of the driving compartment, one on the passenger's side, and one on one side of the living compartment. Sophia issues a command, and scintillating, transparent curtains stretch themselves across the exits. "Comes with nanomesh," She says.

Peter nods and stares wordlessly at one of the curtains. This is his first experience with nanomesh, which allows people to transition between pressurized and unpressurized areas without donning cumbersome suits. When a person walks through a nanomesh curtain, a layer of the intelligent nanorobots making up the curtain either clings to her or peels off, depending on whether she is going out to the planet's surface or coming back inside. The thin, nearly transparent layer of flexibly interconnected nanos can provide a human body with pressure, heat, and protection from standard levels of radiation as effectively as a pressure suit. The nanos cannot manufacture breathable air, but they can channel and circulate it, working with any air supply on a person. They also provide radio connections between mesh wearers: the nanos automatically connect wearers within one another's line of sight, roughly mimicking an experience of speaking in the open air.

Peter pulls his gaze away from the mesh curtain and begins helping Sophia compare the landhog's manifest to the items in the storage lockers. They confirm that the rental agency stocked the landhog with a week's worth of consumables, including topped-off air and water supplies. While

Sophia makes final arrangements at the rental desk, Peter takes one more detailed inventory of the food.

"It's all there," Peter says when Sophia returns.

"Excellent. Thank you."

"Your will be done, My Lady."

She sighs. "All right, let's journey forth."

They climb into the driving compartment, and Sophia enters the coordinates of their first destination into the MGPS navigation system. The autodrive maneuvers the landhog through the garage's airlock and toward the trunk road running along the southern edge of Kistrob. Taking the on-ramp marked "Gordii," they head eastward, accelerating to about ninety kilometers per hour. Just beyond the environs of Kistrob, rust-colored desert engulfs them on all sides.

Peter stares at the exotic landscape, feeling like one of the wide-eyed tourists he has so often seen in his own beautiful nation. He feels a twinge of guilt, knowing that this strange pilgrimage is being funded by Michelangelo and Velázquez. Still, he wants to take it all in. Vast dunes roll across the landscape, occasionally broken by red stone rills and outcroppings. The sky is nearly white near the too-small sun and pastel pink near the horizon, which he thinks appears slightly nearer than an Earth horizon would. There is no green or blue in sight—just rust, umber, red, pink, gray, and more rust. Despite all the images of Meres Peter must have seen over the years, this wilderness doesn't feel familiar at all. It's disconcertingly barren, stark, and alien.

"What kind of weather are we supposed to have?" he asks. "Assuming they call it 'weather' here."

"I understand that the weather in eastern Amazonis is usually calm this time of year," Sophia says.

"No deadly windstorms?"

"You've watched too many entertainment vids. Remember that the atmosphere is still much thinner than on Earth."

"Right."

Peter accesses data on Merian meteorology. It remains a bitterly cold planet, but it's slowly warming with each passing year. Humans have made modest but real strides in heating and thickening the atmosphere using various terraforming methods, but Meres is by no means Sanef, or even Siberia, yet. Any human standing on the Merian surface without nanomesh or a pressure suit would quickly die of asphyxiation and hypothermia.

"Peter."

"Hmm?"

"There are netstories about the nun incident."

Intrigued, he accesses them. One header reads: "Courageous Earther Stops Denunciation Attempt." Peter straightens and smiles. Another one reads: "North American Saves Thousands in Kistrob." He grunts. *Thousands!? They'd better check their sources.* Before he can access the full article, he hears Sophia snicker.

"I can't help it," She says. "The header is 'Earth Son Turfs Nun.'"

Peter smiles and accesses the article. Then he groans.

"Problem?"

"It says my name is 'Peter *Halibut*'!"

"That's fishy."

After a while, the landhog turns off the trunk road and heads north via a narrower one. They begin to gain altitude. The MGPS reports that the road runs roughly north-south along the spine of a formation called "Gordii Dorsum," and Peter accesses that "dorsum" is the term used on Meres for a ridge or range of hills. Gentle slopes fall away in the distance to the left and right of the landhog.

"This part of Meres is not a tourist destination," Sophia says as they sip tea. "The dramatic landscapes most popular with tourists are found in places like Marineris, a canyon the length of North America. Here in eastern Amazonis, one mostly finds flat plains scattered with detritus from eons of meteor impacts. But Gordii Dorsum stands out as a prominent formation rising over the plain. Erosion caused by terraforming has created some steep cliffs. I think you'll find that Gordii has some good views and interesting features."

"Didn't you talk to a fellow on the shuttle who said he was going to take a job at 'Gordii Dorsum'?"

Sophia looks down at Her hands. "He changed his mind. He's going to the Independent Nation of Argyre instead."

"Argyre" is yet one more place on Meres Peter knows nothing about, apart from the fact that Tommy Delaney's ex-partner moved there. He smiles and shakes his head. "I never thought I would be vacationing offearth."

"I would avoid getting too attached to the idea that this is a vacation. We have work to do here."

"Of course. But what sort of work, My Lady?"

"Among other things, the work of learning. I am planning to share some important lessons with you."

Peter stares out at the darkening landscape. The stars are beginning to come out, and there is no sign of human life anywhere in Peter's field of vision. The sensation of absolute isolation turns out to be surprisingly novel and unnerving. "And these lessons—*this* is the place where they need to be learned?"

"Are you questioning me, Bishop Peter?"

"No, of course not!"

She nudges him. "Then that's another thing you'll have to learn."

They stop for the night after a final stretch during which Sophia freedrove the vehicle for the first time, in the dark. Following this "exhilarating experience" (according to Sophia) or "harrowing ordeal" (according to Peter), both travelers are tired.

They eat a no-frills dinner, then Peter claims the passenger-side sleeping nook while Sophia takes the driver-side nook. After they settle in, Sophia quickly falls into a deep slumber, but Peter has a hard time nodding off. For one thing, he's used to sleeping in the dark, and the light in Sophia's nook is illuminating the living compartment. But the real problem is that his mind is racing. It swirls with thoughts of Sophia, the Christians, Lydia, Uncle Jeff . . .

Uncharacteristically, Jeff avoided Peter for a week or two after Peter showed up at Jeff's door proclaiming that God actually had become incarnate in the person of Sophia. Once Jeff was able to regroup, he began cautiously doing what he could to show support, notwithstanding his concern that Peter was being grifted. Jeff even showed up after a recent Sunday service to get intelligence on what was happening at Grace and to confer with Phoebe about her "crusade" against neurpro. Given Peter's sudden departure for the spaceport with Sophia, they were on their way to Meres before Peter had a chance to send Jeff a message letting him know. Jeff hasn't responded yet.

Still, Peter knows what Jeff would say right now. *What are you doing on Meres? Why did she take you away from Sanef just when things were getting interesting? There are people who want to threaten everything you've been building, and she just takes off? Why do her "lessons" have to be taught in a desert on another planet?*

For a moment, Peter permits himself to entertain doubt. *What if this journey is the product of an unbalanced mind's erratic behavior?* He considers Sophia's suggestion that they take a disturbed terrorist with them into the desert. While Peter shares Her sympathy for the boy, Her suggestion was impractical verging on irrational. *What if Sophia isn't fully rational and I'm nuts to believe this woman is Who she thinks she is?*

He draws a deep breath. *Enough.*

Peter chooses to shut down this line of thought and starts silently repeating the Lord's Prayer until he feels himself dozing off. His last waking thought is of Trinity. He hopes Felipe will follow his instructions and resist the temptation to indulge her insatiable desire for carrots.

~

Just then, not many kilometers away, Russ's supervisor finally tells the boy his shift is done. As usual, Russ's hands are covered in grease. He'll wash them in the dormitory—he never stays in the environmental maintenance room longer than he has to.

"Thank you, sir," he says. "Goodnight, sir."

The supervisor grunts. Apart from orders, threats, and terse calls of "you're dismissed," the only thing he's ever said to Russ, on Russ's first day, was: "Expendable, small hands—good tool."

Casting cautious glances around the hallway, Russ quickly walks toward Veronica's janitorial closet. Her shift is also ending, and they'll walk back to the dormitory together. The halls are relatively empty at that time of night. The only thing scarier to Russ than the emptiness is when the halls are filled with staff.

As he approaches the closet, a male's gravelly voice issues from inside. "Country biscuit, I wanna sop up your gravy."

Russ freezes. He knows his dad can't help: Spence won't be finished with his double shift until later in the night. Russ looks around frantically for something he can use as a weapon. *'Course, the staff doesn't just leave things like that laying around.*

Russ hears a sharp *pop.*

"Ow!" the male yells. "Gooddamn it, ya little whore!"

Russ rushes over to the closet and sees the male standing just inside, rubbing a shoulder. He has Veronica trapped. Crouching slightly, she holds a mop in both hands and brandishes the handle like a club. She's staring at the male with wild eyes.

"Falq. That hurt," he says.

"It's gonna be your balls next time, asshole. You got no privileges to me."

"Maybe not, ya little tease, but—" The male notices Russ out of the corner of his eye and gives him a quick, hard look.

Russ glares back. The male is a pale, big guy. He has fat cheeks—*like a big baby,* Russ thinks—and a receding hairline. His eyes are bloodshot.

The male turns back to Veronica and shrugs. "Let's catch up later, bitchy little biscuit. I might just give ya another chance to climb aboard the Frank train."

"Falq you." Veronica mimes a thrust at him with the mop handle.

Frank breaks into a broad grin. As he steps out of the closet, he reaches out and ruffles Russ's hair, not gently. "You keep an eye on that sister of yours, kid. She's a feme who likes it rough. Just how I like 'em."

Russ ducks aside and snarls at him.

As Frank strolls away, Veronica emerges from the closet, still clutching her mop. Her hands shake. "We never shoulda left the valley," she mutters.

Russ hangs his head. "You already said that a thousand times."

Veronica steps back into the closet and carefully puts the mop back in its place. She places a hand against a wall to steady herself.

"Veronica—"

"It's okay, bubbie. Let's just get back to the dormitory."

As she closes up the closet, a floor supervisor appears. Russ has seen this one before, but he's never had to talk to him. The floor supervisor glances at the numbers on their uniforms and addresses Veronica.

"Refugee 439, it is time for you to report to your dormitory, is it not? You are not authorized to remain in this location after your work shift."

She and Russ both stare at the floor supervisor's shoes. Her face is red, and she holds her trembling fists close to her side. "I'm sorry, sir," she says in as meek a voice as she can achieve. "We were just leaving, sir."

"You're not interested in a different assignment, are you?" He sneers. "A couple have just opened up."

"No, sir," Veronica says.

"Then move it."

As they scurry away, the floor supervisor calls out, "And you, boy, wash those filthy hands."

Peter wakes up to the aroma of sizzling soy bacon. Morning light streams in through the driving compartment's front windows. To his relief, he can't recall any nightmares involving cobblestones or thrashing bodies. Sophia stands in the landhog's galley, heating up the bacon and a couple of the other breakfast foods from their inventory.

"Good morning, My Lady. That smells good."

"We need to fuel up. We won't be sitting in the landhog today."

"No surprise there. Following you does not seem to involve much sedentariness, regardless of the planet." He stretches his arms and yawns.

"Thank you. Now get those lazy bones out of bed and get ready. Breakfast will be done in a few minutes."

Peter freshens up in the washroom, then the two of them enjoy a pleasant meal. "I have a hike mapped out for us," She says as they chew the last of the bacon.

"That sounds great. It'll be nice to get out of the landhog and explore. How long is the hike?"

"About thirty kay."

His eyes widen. "Thirty kay? I've never hiked that far!" He swallows. "My Lady."

They arrive at an overlook around the twenty-fourth kilometer of the hike. There, on the southeast side of Gordii, an expansive view of the Eastern Amazonis Plain spreads out before them. Peter estimates that they have another hour of sunlight, but then it occurs to him he might be judging the Merian sky by earthside standards. It's early evening, in any event.

He feels pretty good despite the long trek. Sophia pointedly reminded Peter that they're in less than four-tenths of Earth's gravity. She was right, as always. *The weaker gravity certainly helps once one finds a good stride.* The sky is clear of dust, and various shades of rust, red, pink, and white swirl in their view, along with an occasional metallic glint from a human-made object. Peter looks hard at the horizon through high-resolution magnification spectacles, panning back and forth. He notices a speck of green, perhaps a greenhouse, in the far distance.

"Are you looking for something in particular?" asks Sophia. "Out here, we'll see lots of red but no redwoods, I dare say."

Like Peter, She is protected by nanomesh, which is nearly invisible on Her skin and clothing except for an occasional metallic scintillation. Peter has *almost* gotten used to the idea that a thin layer of cleverly programmed motes is all that stands between them and frozen, bloody decompression.

"I'm searching for Olympus Mons." He continues scanning the horizon with his magspecs. "I accessed a lot about it during the passage from Earth. At twenty-five kay, it's the tallest mountain in the whole System. Its summit is so high that it's above the atmosphere. A mountain reaching into space!"

"You're looking in the right direction, but Olympus is hundreds of kay away. At this distance, the summit is below the horizon."

"Ah, right. Well, could we go there?" He feels like a child asking his mother to go on a ride at a recreation park.

"I know the lure of a high summit is thrilling, but your time on Meres must first focus on conquering the foothills."

He isn't listening to Her statement for any message deeper than its literal meaning. "I don't understand. If we have to be here, we should at least be doing something. I mean, we're just aimlessly walking around a desert, for God's sake!" He feels the heat of embarrassment rise in his face before he's even done speaking. *Who am I to talk to Her like that?*

Of course, Sophia is not offended. "It's been a long trip, I know. And you probably feel that the people back at Grace need us, and our place is there."

He nods mutely.

"I feel it, too. But I can *tell* you only so much. There are some things I must *show* you. We're doing more than just 'walking around a desert.' We're beginning to walk around a *mystery.*

"Peter, the spiritual path ultimately is not about storing up merit or getting God's 'attention.' It is more about shedding things than acquiring them. It requires us to spend time in a desert."

"Okay. But I lived in a desert for a long time. Before you came to us."

"So you did." She touches his arm. "And I also know what it's like to live in a metaphorical desert. Because we both know what it's like, we're now ready for our explorations in this desert.

"Here on Meres, there is true wilderness. And here we can have something we cannot have in Sanef—a place where we can take a short break from pastoring the others around us. We can take a breath and allow the chains of fear, desire, and obligation to loosen their hold on our hearts."

"You're saying those things have a hold on *your* heart?"

"I hope not. But I struggle with them, too. I, too, need silence, simplicity, and contemplation." She sighs. "Yet our overactive, unfocused minds invariably resist. The mind hates to simply abide in presence. It prefers to compete and contend, rush and accumulate, and serve what I call 'the grasping ego'—the self-centered, insecure, covetous part of the soul—rather than rest in faith."

"Faith," Peter says. "Faith is hard."

"Ah, yes. You're right about that, Bishop. But faith is not only about 'believing' things, especially believing absurd things. Your Church collapsed in large part because you bought into this idea."

He opens his mouth and then closes it. He would like to protest, but he can't.

"Faith is much bigger than that, much deeper," Sophia says. "It grows and changes. Faith has a morning, an afternoon, and an evening."

Faith has a morning, an afternoon, and an evening? He asks, "How do you mean?"

"This morning, when you first woke up, what did you know about the wilderness of Gordii Dorsum?"

"Um, I knew a 'dorsum' is a ridge or a set of hills." He cocks his head. "And I knew this particular dorsum starts just north of the equator and runs basically north-south. And that it's part of the I. N. of Amazonis. That's about it."

"Right. Most of what you knew, you had accessed. Your mind knew abstract facts and information you had been told, but you didn't have any personal experience of what it's like here. Now, after hiking around the Gordii Dorsum wilderness all afternoon, what do you know about it?"

"Well, now I know it has gorgeous sand drifts in some places. I enjoyed how they were sculpted by the wind. One of them looked like a dolphin." He touches a rock. "And I know that these craggy rocks are all over the place, and I wonder how they got here and how much the terraforming has started to affect this landscape. I also know that the sand here is not exactly a single 'red' color—there are slight variations of lighter and darker shades. And I know that this incredible overlook is here and that we're quite a ways above the plains, although unfortunately not high enough to see Olympus."

"So the facts you already knew this *morning*, before the hike, gave you a basic framework for understanding this place. But by this *afternoon*, you had actually experienced something of it. And now it means more to you, viscerally."

"Yes, I suppose so."

Sophia leans in toward Peter. Their respective nanomesh layers automatically negotiate contact, and, for a second, their two biospheres unite into one. His eyes bulge as Her lips briefly touch his.

She steps back. "After this *evening*, what will Gordii Dorsum mean to you?"

His heart jackhammers. "It will be the place where you, you kissed me." He swallows. "My Lady."

"In the *morning* of faith, our faith is primarily about beliefs," She says. "I call it the 'morning' because this is where most religion starts. It begins with rites of group identity, rituals, stories, rules, creeds, and doctrines. These can provide an excellent starting point—you could think of them as the maps of where you want to go. But merely having a map, even a very well-drawn one, does not mean you have experienced the journey. A purely 'morning' faith will still be dominated by what one might call 'chronic compulsions.'"

Why did She kiss me? Was it just part of Her lesson? Was it something more? Aloud, he asks, "What is a 'chronic compulsion'?"

"Anything opposing growth in love which nevertheless obsesses and captures us. Many chronic compulsions spring from the main instinctive drives each of us is born with: consuming, conquering, and copulating."

"Consuming, conquering, and cop—copulating. What do you mean?"

"By *consuming*, I mean not only the need to eat and drink but, more broadly, the drive to acquire and devour *more*: more material things, more entertainments, more self-focused experiences—including those provided by stims, alcohol, drugs, and other vehicles of addiction. Jesus called the drive to acquire and consume 'serving Mammon.' *Conquering* is about insecurity, envy, ambition, the need to feel special and better than other people, and the need to be in control. It expresses itself in the desire to have prestige and to wield power over others. *Copulating* is, of course, the physical drive to reproduce, which some mistake or try to substitute for deeper forms of love, intimacy, and eroticism."

"And these drives are bad?" asks Peter.

"They are not 'bad' in any absolute sense. The drives to consume, conquer, and copulate stem from basic human biology, and they form part of the foundation of human existence. But a building is not merely a foundation. As one looks upward, the question becomes how long such drives will dominate one's heart and mind and life. As long as one consents to being dominated by any chronic compulsion, it can be exceedingly difficult to grow beyond the morning of faith. Religion may be in one's culture or in one's head, but there may be little room for the love of God in one's heart."

"Okay," Peter says. His nerves are still abuzz from the kiss, but he perseveres. "The 'morning' of faith is when faith is mostly about 'beliefs,' which are ultimately just thoughts. I think you're saying that just having beliefs, even true and good beliefs, isn't the end of the faith journey."

Sophia nods. "The *afternoon* of faith corresponds to a greater opening of the heart. By God's grace, one begins to recognize the grip of chronic compulsions on oneself and seeks to turn the energies one has invested in them toward higher purposes. This creates the space to connect more deeply to beauty, joy, and suffering beyond one's own fears, needs, and desires. Proving that one is 'correct' or 'justified' starts to become less important than living in love and charity, both with those like oneself and with those who are different. Afternoon faith is less about beliefs and thoughts and more about wisdom and lived experience."

"And there's an 'evening' of faith?" asks Peter. He glances eastward where some type of aircraft or spacecraft twinkles near the darkening horizon.

"By grace, some souls taste, already in this mortal life, the *evening* of faith—the culmination of religion, beyond 'religion' itself. In the evening, God—not rules or ideas about God, but God's living presence—becomes the soul's most fervent desire. The soul seeks to remain open continuously to the touch of a beauty beyond words. Such souls allow themselves to be seduced by God, and they adore God in return. Their relationship with the Eternal becomes a passionate, committed love affair."

"A love affair? That's very—well, that's not the way our tradition usually thought about how God behaves."

She purses Her lips. "Hmm. Do you think it would be 'unorthodox' to teach such a thing?"

"In principle, no. Christians have always believed in a God who is so loving that God in some sense actually *is* love, but . . ."

"But?"

"But in practice, we have not talked much about a 'love affair' or used this image in our worship. So, even though it's orthodox, as a practical matter it was treated as if it were *un*orthodox."

Sophia smiles. "Mature faith is more about how you love than what you think. Strive for 'orthophily'—correct *love*—and then 'orthodoxy'—correct belief—will usually take care of itself."

Later that evening, Peter lifts his head and gazes across the narrow aisle separating his sleeping nook from Sophia's. She's already drifted off to sleep with Her light burning. Her mouth is open slightly.

Peter ponders the teenage nun in Kistrob and wonders what motivated the boy. *What was his name? Something French . . . Bouville? What sort of personal demons would make a young person like Bouville decide that life is meaningless, that it has no value, no sacredness?* Peter lets his head fall back onto his pillow.

Are religious leaders partly responsible for the nihilism of this age? Did we spend too much time trying to limit sacredness? We would tell people that sacredness could be found only in a certain institution, or in a certain book, or in a certain way of thinking—and that everything else was profane. But our criteria for separating the sacred from the profane were always imperfect and sometimes arbitrary. People could see that. So they began to believe nothing was sacred. They converted to the myth of Nothingness.

Maybe the deeper truth is that everything is sacred, that everything has the potential to hide and reveal God. Is that what we should have taught?

Or is that just fluff-brained nonsense?

A soft beeping interrupts his brooding. It's a voice message from Earth. He cues it up and listens:

> *Hello, Bishop Peter. This is Dorcas. Across the light-minutes of distance, I'm sending you blessings from your flock in Sanef.*

I had a chance to talk to a lawyer. You know that tour guide who comes to Grace? It turns out he's a retired one. I showed him the letters from the tax assessor and the International Christian Capitalist Club. I also conferred with Socrates since he seems knowledgeable about such matters.

As for the first one, it looks like we can ask for a hearing to defend our PMR status. The tour guide is going to refer me to a former colleague with experience handling this kind of case, but it's going to cost money. I'll let you know how things develop.

As for the ICCC, these people have somehow managed to register the word "Christian" as part of their protected trademark. None of us are sure how their threat is going to play out. We really need you and Our Lady to come back, to help handle this.

Meanwhile, even though She is not here, we still have more people coming to the cathedral for help almost every day. Jason and Felipe brought in two in the last two days. I'm worried that we're running out of room to take more people in, at least until the renovations are complete. And even if we keep our PMR status and the ICCC doesn't take us for all we're worth, our budget is getting strained, unless we're going to—

Dorcas sighs.

—sell even more of the holy artifacts.

So, I'm not sure where our current path is headed from an operational point of view. What's next? We're in a holding pattern until you and Our Lady come back. We need you, so please don't delay. If you can let me know when you expect to return, please do.

Peter thinks the message has finished. *We've got to return to Sanef. Everything we've been building is so fragile.* Then Dorcas starts to speak again.

I, I also want to ask for your judgment, as bishop, on something I've been thinking about a lot.

Our Lady is always pointing to Jesus, teaching what He taught, but I don't think She is Jesus. It just doesn't feel right to me to say She is the Second Coming of Christ. Setting aside the whole gender thing, it doesn't feel like She's saying we're at the "end of days." It seems more like She's saying the opposite—that history and the Church are still at their beginnings! That God has much more in store for us.

So, Bishop Peter, if God's Word can become incarnate, why not also His Breath? Didn't Jesus say He would send another Advocate to remind us of the things He taught? Is there something that says the Holy Spirit can't take on flesh like Christ? Isn't God free to do something like that?

Maybe the Holy Spirit has been speaking to the Church all these generations but we stopped listening. Maybe the only way She could get our attention back was to become flesh and dwell among us?

I'm no theologian, and I know I'm out of my depth. But, Petey, when I pray, I feel like the Father is telling me to listen to His Spirit.

Well, that's it. We all miss you. Give Her my love, and please respond without delay. End message.

Peter rolls over and looks across the aisle at Sophia again. Her chest rises and falls beneath Her blanket with Her rhythmic breathing.

If God's Word can become incarnate, why not also His Breath?

It's a compelling theory, but Peter knows he can't give Dorcas the confirmation she craves. He has no infallible answer. Like her, he's struggling to interpret everything that's happening as best he can.

I know Sophia won't just give me a straight answer, that's clear enough. But I've got to figure it out. I've got to understand!

16

Vast Abundance

When Peter wakes up the next morning, Sophia's nook is empty, Her bunk neatly made. He climbs into the driving compartment to look out the windows, and he sees Her sitting perhaps thirty meters away with Her back to the landhog. Turning back toward the living compartment, he notices something on the table that wasn't there the night before. It's a piece of heavy paper folded in half. Sophia scrawled the words "BISHOP PETER" across the paper.

He unfolds it and scans what She wrote. Then he slowly re-reads the text. He absentmindedly wolfs down half a snack bar while changing clothes, clips an air cartridge onto his belt, and exits the landhog.

As Peter approaches Sophia, he realizes She pressurized the self-standing nanomesh dome that came in one of the landhog's storage lockers. Occasional metallic shimmers and the boxy air supply and temperature regulator sitting in the dust give away the dome's presence. The dome extends to about four meters in diameter and stands over two meters high. Sophia sits in the center on a mat.

As Peter enters the dome, the nanos that cover him merge with the dome's mesh, leaving him exposed to the air within. It makes Peter feel as if he's simply standing on the open surface of Meres, red gravel crunching beneath his boots. Although it's warm enough in the dome, the thought gives him a shiver.

Gingerly, Peter sits down on the mat next to Sophia. Mat or no mat, they'll get dusty if they spend the morning in the dome, but he knows the nanos will clean them off. A person wearing mesh could walk through a dust storm then walk back inside through a mesh curtain and expect to find no more than a few stray dust particles on his skin, if that. Or so Peter accessed.

Sophia sits with Her eyes closed and looks as if She's praying. He's anxious to discuss the news from Sanef, but he doesn't want to interrupt. After a few minutes of silence, Sophia opens Her eyes and briefly places a hand on Peter's arm.

"Good morning, Peter."

"Good morning. I—"

"When you look out there, what do you see?" She gestures toward the desert.

"Um. Not much. Dust, mostly. Some rocks."

"Look deeper."

"I see—I see a, a desert, a dusty, sandy, gritty, freezing, lifeless desert."

She smirks. "Emptiness?"

"Yes, for sure."

"Look deeper, and you will see a blank canvas. You will see possibilities waiting to be lifted into actuality. Mark my words. Someday, this will be a garden world filled with more history than Earth can boast today."

Peter stares out at the Merian desert and struggles to imagine such an age. After a respectful amount of time passes, he says, "My Lady, I wanted to let you know I have news from Dorcas."

She holds up a hand. "Later. There's nothing Dorcas cannot handle there that we can help with from here."

"It's just that she's really worried . . ."

"Do you think," Sophia says, "that because Dorcas is elderly, she has nothing more to learn, no more to grow?"

"Uh. I hadn't thought about it. I suppose not."

"Then let her grow."

Peter frowns, but he decides not to press the issue.

Sophia slides around so that they face one another while sitting cross-legged. "For the next few days, I am asking you to focus on foundational matters rather than the latest events in Sanef."

"Foundational matters? Okay. Does that mean we'll discuss the Holy Trinity? That seems pretty foundational to our faith, and I have some theological questions about you—about that."

"We must start at the beginning."

"The beginning?"

"The most basic *what*, *how*, and *why* of God's action and presence. This will allow you to clear away some of the deadwood that has accumulated in your thinking—before you delve into the *who* of God seen by Christians in the Trinity."

Hmm. "Okay."

Sophia points at the piece of paper Peter still holds in his hand. "Do you know what you have there?"

"A prayer."

"Yes. It's one of three prayers I would like to share with you over the next three mornings, beginning this morning. I've never shared these with another human being."

"I'm, I'm honored."

"These prayers attempt to celebrate divine truths using mere words. But understand: words about God can give you only a map of metaphors of the mystery."

"A map of metaphors of . . . the mystery?"

"Yes, and I'm afraid that you'll find this remains true when you pass these teachings on to others."

"When *I* pass these teachings on . . . ? You make it sound as if I'll be teaching by myself. But when I teach, you'll be there, too, right?"

"Peter, I will always be with you."

He raises his eyebrows. "Um, okay. But—but I don't just mean—"

"Please say the prayer aloud."

"I—uh. Okay." He holds up the paper, takes a breath, and recites the prayer:

> *Almighty God of vast abundance:*
> *Tireless one, in freedom and joy*
>   *you cultivate orchards of unimaginable variety.*
> *Behold, you have said* yes *to every imperfect existing thing.*
> *I give thanks that you chose even me, a soul-broken orphan.*
> *Majesty beyond all glory! Artist of novelty!*
> *We suckle at your breasts,*
>   *your worlds without end.*

Sophia joins Peter in a concluding "Amen."

The prayer's imagery surprises Peter. Not the reference to suckling at God's breasts—he knows the bible includes images of God as a mother and as a woman in labor. No, what startles Peter is the prayer's reference to being "soul-broken." *Could Sophia really have been referring to Herself?*

They sit quietly for several minutes until Sophia breaks the silence. "Let me tell you a story," She says. "Or perhaps we could describe it as a 'thought experiment.' I call it 'The Parable of the Apple Orchard' . . ."

"Apple trees have a lot of genetic variability. Lots of different kinds of apples are possible. With a big enough orchard and plenty of time, a farmer could grow trees with thousands of combinations of colors, shapes, sizes, and flavors of apples, including very sweet ones, very sour ones, and everything in between.

"Consider a farmer who operates a small apple orchard and does not have much money. She must use her skills and energy to grow enough apples to sell so that she can afford the things she needs to survive. How does she decide which variety of apple trees to plant in her orchard? Since she has limited land, time, and money, she must maximize her orchard's productivity and efficiency.

"Let's say that big, red, sweet apples from the variety known as 'Angelic Magnificence' earn the most money per kilo. These apples are uniformly flavorful and juicy. They grow without blemish and are never sour. Some might say the Angelic Magnificence apple is the perfect apple. It doesn't cost any more to grow Angelic Magnificence apple trees than other kinds of apple trees, and our apple farmer can earn the most money from their apples. So, naturally, she plants only Angelic Magnificence apple trees. The apple farmer lives in a situation of scarcity, and she acts accordingly.

"*Scarcity* is when you have a limited amount of something you need, like the farmer's limited land and money. The apple farmer must deal with scarcity, and so must we. It's part of the universe where we currently find ourselves. Indeed, scarcity is a foundational condition that people simply take for granted. The processes of nature and society are fundamentally structured by the fact that all things—food, space, material goods, time—are limited . . . that there *is not enough* to go around, at least not forever. The deep urges to hunt, to acquire, to expand; jealousy; wounded pride; fear of loss: these and many other realities of human life are closely bound to the condition of scarcity. It's like air or gravity for one who has spent his entire life on Earth: scarcity is so thoroughly woven into human experience that we normally do not even recognize any alternative. Scarcity affects what jobs people do, whom they spend their lives with, what they accumulate, and what they strive for.

"Now, let me tell you about a different apple farmer. This one is not subject to scarcity at all. She is not limited in any way. Her reality, rather, is one of *total abundance*. This apple farmer has unlimited land, money, time, and resources. She has no mortgage to pay. She will never die. She can farm for the pure enjoyment of bringing forth living things from the soil and for the delight of experiencing the varied tastes, hues, and textures of the apples.

"This apple farmer loves Angelic Magnificence apples, so she plants thousands—millions!—of trees that grow them. Why shouldn't she? But with her limitless time and energy and her love of apples, she decides to plant other varieties, as well: green apples, yellow apples, apples of every shape and size, all of them very sweet. And does that exhaust her desire to grow varied and interesting apples? No! This is an apple farmer with *unlimited* time, energy, and resources—nothing can exhaust her. She knows that apples can offer sweetness and unique beauty even if they also have some sour or ugly parts. The apple farmer wants to experience that unique beauty, even if it means planting some 'imperfect' apples.

"Let's think about one of those varieties. Perhaps we could call it 'Variety H. Sapiens.' These apples are not as lustrous as Angelic Magnificence apples, but they have a fascinating texture that gives the farmer goose bumps when she touches them. They are not as sweet as Angelic Magnificence apples, but they have a tang that creates a unique taste. They have blemishes, but they are unlike anything else in the farmer's astronomically huge orchard. All in all, the farmer is quite pleased that she planted trees with Variety H. Sapiens apples to enhance the diverse beauty of her orchard.

"Now imagine the apples can speak to the farmer. One of the Variety H. Sapiens apples asks the farmer, 'Why did you breed me to be so sour? Why don't I have a bright red hue, instead of a dull green one? And the other apples on my branch—they're far too sour and ugly, too.' From his limited point of view, the farmer is negligent or even cruel in allowing the sourness and ugliness on his branch, the only world he can see. He may even start to believe he grew in the wild—that no farmer could exist who is so stupid or evil as to cultivate a branch with so many flaws.

"But the farmer delights in the Variety H. Sapiens apple, and the apple's branch, and his tree. The farmer knows that there are much uglier and sourer varieties she could have chosen to grow. Some varieties would be so sour that the farmer does not even want them in the orchard, but Variety H. Sapiens is not one of them. The farmer also knows that if she gave the H. Sapiens apple his heart's desire and transformed his tree in the way he wants, the tree would simply become another Angelic Magnificence tree. But the farmer already has plenty of those. Although the tree would be more 'perfect' according to the way that apple sees things, it would be of less value to the orchard and the farmer.

"You see, from that apple's limited perspective, his branch is flawed and perhaps should even be used for kindling. From the farmer's much larger perspective, the H. Sapiens apple is precious and unique, and she loves him for what he is and what he will become in his own right.

"She loves him more than he loves himself."

After a time, Peter says, "Let me see if I understand the parable. The apple farmer who lives in total abundance is obviously God, and you're saying God's creation is inexpressibly large and diverse—it extends beyond the System and beyond even the whole universe as humans know it. So far, so good?"

She nods.

"And if we could see our particular existence—our tree or branch, in your parable—as God sees it, then we would have a different perspective on its value."

"Yes."

"It sounds as if you're finally proposing an answer to the question I asked in our first serious conversation. I mean, the Parable of the Apple Orchard is a theodicy, or at least part of one, right? I asked why God allows evil and suffering, and you now answer that the difficulty of seeing things from God's broader point of view is part of the problem."

"You're on the right track," She says. "Jesus tried to give you a glimpse of this broader point of view. Why do you think he used so many images of banquets? Why did he multiply loaves and fishes and say his Father's house has many mansions? In these and many other ways, he told you and showed you that reality contains extraordinary vitality, fecundity, and abundance."

"Abundance," Peter repeats.

"God's vast abundance is one of the great truths of everything that exists or ever will exist: Almighty God's ongoing creation of copious, diverse potentialities for life, raising mere possibilities into actualities within universes and civilizations and souls."

Peter sighs. "I'm trying hard to imagine that this is true, that for God there is no scarcity—there is complete abundance and endless creation. But, forgive me, I'm finding it really hard to believe. This vision is just so *big*. It seems too good to be true."

She smiles. "All good religion sounds 'too good to be true.' But what I've told you is also hard to accept because it demands something from you."

"It does?"

"The grasping ego loves scarcity, not abundance. Scarcity formed it, after all. The grasping ego prefers a small world where it can more easily feel like it is an important part or even an indispensable one."

"Well, if I'm being honest, I have to admit that something within me does like my world to be small. Then I can feel important and central. It's scary to think that the world is unbelievably huge and complex. It challenges my understanding of my life's significance."

Sophia nods. "By design, the unfolding of human history has continued to reveal a bigger and bigger world, a world of previously unimaginable abundance. In recent centuries, your horizons were rapidly expanded by the scientific method, technology, and the cross-cultural exchanges they made possible. You found out that the universe is very much larger, older, and more complex than your forebears dreamed. These revelations scared and threatened many people."

"I think you're going to say that these 'scared and threatened' people included Christians."

"Many Christians were among those threatened by the expansion of horizons. They denied the vision of vast abundance the Holy Spirit was opening up."

"The—the Holy Spirit?" Peter stares at Sophia, wondering if She will reveal something about Herself.

"You continued to hold tightly to a small world," She says. "You fought science. You fought anything that threatened long-held identities. You focused on defending clear but arbitrary moral boundaries. Your God became a small god intended to prop up a view of the world as being small. But, over time, the harder it became to deny the bigger world, the less relevant the small god became. People came to see this small god as merely a lie."

She's talking to me again like I'm responsible for everything the leaders of the Church have ever done. It still makes him cringe.

"So," he says, "the Church was called to embrace and proclaim God's abundance. But the Church . . ." He sighs. ". . . often denied it."

She nods. "You see, Peter, it was *part of the plan* for humanity to encounter a large, diverse, and constantly evolving universe: a realm of immense space, deep time, and mind-boggling multiplicity; a vibrant, interconnected web of life; a complex dance of human histories and cultures. These truths do not oppose or undermine God. They reveal God's nature as wellspring and lover of vast abundance."

"Okay. You're saying God's abundance has no limits. And God doesn't want to cultivate only unblemished 'Angelic Magnificence' trees. Even with all its imperfections and bitterness, God chose to make this *possible* existence *actual*."

"God passionately desires this existence—what it has been and what it will grow to be in the coming ages."

Peter reaches down to scoop up a handful of cold, rusty Merian dirt. He watches it trickle through his benumbed fingers as he tries to wrap his mind around the enormity of the vision She has proclaimed to him. *Our existence is complex, diverse, abundant—when we deny this truth, we deny the power and vitality of the living God.*

After a time, Sophia glances at the sun's position in the sky. She stands up and casually brushes red dust from Her pants legs. "Come," She says. "We have an appointment."

They encounter no other vehicles on the road that winds down Gordii's spine. Sophia freedrives them southward for several kilometers, once steering around a small rock that had rolled into the roadway. She then turns right and descends the dorsum's western flank, taking a twisting road down to the plain west of Gordii. Initiating autodrive, the landhog follows the curve of Gordii north again toward the coordinates Sophia provided.

By early afternoon, they reach the corner of a huge fenced-off zone abutting the western side of the dorsum. To the west, only a few outcroppings dare to disturb the plain's monotonous flatness. The fences march toward the horizon until the eye loses sight of them.

The landhog turns westward and drives along the fence line until a dull gray structure comes into view. The modest utilitarian building comprises a meshed garage with attached office or storage space. The landhog enters the garage and rolls to a stop.

"Here we are," Sophia says.

The garage holds a few vehicles of various shapes and sizes. A young man sits at a desk in front of the faded flags of Amazonis and the Gamma cartel alliance. Sophia and Peter exit the landhog and walk over to the young man.

"You must be the Lead Engineer's guests," he says. "He's on his way."

To Peter's surprise, Tommy Delaney soon emerges from a doorway. He waves as he strides over to them. Outside the narrow confines of a shuttle, Tommy seems even taller. Well-groomed and dressed in practical but stylish business attire, he looks rather dashing.

"What a pleasure to be seeing you again so soon, my friends," he says. He gives Sophia a long hug. *A little too long*, Peter thinks to himself. Then Tommy turns to Peter and grasps his hand. "Welcome to Eden, the both of you!"

Peter glances around the gray garage. "Oh, this is Eden. Looks quite, quite nice."

"Huh?" Tommy looks over his shoulder. "Oh no, this isn't *it*." He turns to Sophia. "Haven't you told him anything about it?"

She smiles and shakes Her head.

"A woman who makes a plan and takes charge. Now, I like that. I like that *very mooch*, I do." His eyebrows dance up and down.

The sexist comment furrows Peter's brow, but Sophia continues to smile broadly at Tommy. *A little too broadly*, Peter thinks.

"Alright then, kiddos. Follow me down the stairs here, and I'll give you the 'Edenic' tour." To Peter, Tommy says, "Like I was telling you, working at Eden's my way of saying 'falq you' to the cold, empty cosmos." He bows his head apologetically to Sophia. "Excuse me, ma'am."

"I've heard worse in my time," She says dryly.

Tommy leads them through a doorway and a special mesh curtain designed to clean contaminants from visitors. Bypassing an elevator, he takes them down six long flights of sturdy metal stairs and through yet another mesh curtain, into an underground room. A wall-sized metal airlock stands sentry before them. Picture windows on the left and right sides of the room open onto extraordinary vistas of a massive underground chamber.

The chamber is large enough that Peter cannot quite gauge where it ends. His efforts to do so are complicated by tall stands of foliage, much of it growing almost to the ceiling and obscuring the walls. The ceiling emits light that looks like sunlight as seen from Earth. A flock of birds flies across his field of vision. Beneath the cold Merian desert, a tropical jungle thrives.

"It really is like Eden," Peter whispers.

"It is," Tommy says. "And it's the serpent we're interested in."

Peter cocks a questioning eyebrow.

Tommy turns from the window and says, "Right, before we go in— the basics. This astounding chamber is a 'holistically monitored ecological environment.' Unlike a 'closed ecological environment,' visitors may enter. But we do keep track of every biological activity that occurs here. And I do mean 'every.' Respiration. Anything you would happen to eat or drink. Trips to the loo. Just like your man Adam and—what was her name?"

"Eve?" Peter says.

"That's it. Nice name. Not as nice as 'Sophia.'" Tommy gazes at Her. "Just like your Adam and Eve had, there's an all-seeing being in our garden here, which in our case is our omnisensate surveillance system. So once we step into this intelligent airlock here, there's no privacy. We would need to go to my quarters for that." He pauses. "Did I mention I'm the Lead Engineer here at Eden?"

Wordlessly, Sophia steps into the airlock. It scans Her, weighs Her, and pricks Her skin with a tiny needle. Then it cycles the air and discharges Her out the other side onto a platform overlooking the chamber's floor.

Peter follows, submits himself to the same process, and steps into Eden's fecund humidity. After more than a week in hermetically sealed environments, the mingled aromas of tropical fruits and flowers overwhelm his senses, making his eyes water with delight. He can hear the calls of tropical birds and the croaking of frogs. His eyes pan across the dewy jungle, and he catches sight of something totally unexpected. "Penguins!" he cries.

Below, a dozen comically skinny penguins lie on their bellies around a small pond. Several of them raise their heads to spot the source of the commotion interrupting their naps. They relax again after a few seconds. Apparently, lurking humans are old news for these creatures.

"Junguins, version four-point-oh," comes Tommy's voice. He's already standing behind them on the platform. "Classic penguins genengineered for the jungle heat. That is not the weirdest thing you'll see today, my friend." Tommy pats Peter on the shoulder.

As they descend a set of metal stairs to the jungle floor, Sophia asks, "Tommy, why would you engineer Antarctic animals to live in a jungle?"

"It's the serpent, you see. We're always looking for the serpent." He grins at their puzzled expressions. "I know what you're thinking. 'What's the bloody serpent you keep going on about, Tommy?' You ever seen that ancient symbol of a snake eating its own tail, going around in a circle forever? That's the *ouroboros*, the serpent we're trying to find in this garden."

They reach the chamber floor, and Tommy begins leading them along a dirt path. He says, "See, living on exoplanets—worlds circling other stars—won't be like living on the Stations or Meres or the Stroids. If we have a crop failure on Meres and start to run low on food, we can get supplies from Earth within a week. But faraway colonies on exoplanets will have to be self-sufficient. They'll be flying without a parachute, agriculturally speaking. This means an exocolony will need to be able to maintain an ecosystem that is simple enough to establish on a new world yet robust enough that it will not collapse."

Peter gazes at Sophia while Sophia gazes at Tommy.

"In the most extreme theoretical case," Tommy continues, "you would try to transplant a whole ecosystem as you found it on Earth, including creating exact earthlike conditions—light, heat, water, etcetera—to support it. Assuming you didn't overload it with too many humans, you would have an *ouroboros*, a balanced system that can eat itself indefinitely and not die. But taking a naturally occurring ecosystem with you to the stars would require a lot of species. Absent some huge technological breakthrough, it would be too complicated to establish properly."

Peter tries to follow Tommy's scientific explanations, but he keeps getting distracted by creatures he spots in the chamber. An insect that looks like a cross between a beetle and a cicada is crawling across his jumpsuit. He guesses that Tommy's people haven't seeded their ecosystem with bugs poisonous to humans, but he still gently flicks the thing away.

"What we're trying to do here at Eden," Tommy is saying, "is to find simpler recipes for *ouroboros* ecosystems, recipes requiring fewer ingredients, fewer species. It's easy to genengineer individual species, but finding the recipe for an entire stable, economical *ouroboros* ecosystem requires time and experimentation. Engineering such an ecosystem is an exercise in managing chaos. It's incredibly complicated."

"How many recipes have you found so far?" asks Sophia.

"In one sense, five. In another sense, zero. That is to say, we've found five solid ones so far. But they're all five still pretty complex. We believe there are more economical recipes to be discovered." Tommy waves his hand. "This is one of six chambers here at Eden, each with a different climate and each testing and tweaking different recipes."

Peter looks around the massive chamber again. *There are five more like this one!*

"Meres is the perfect place for this kind of science," Tommy says. "For a while yet, at least—until terraforming reaches the point that it screws it all up. On Earth, you just can't get away from the risk of unmonitored contamination. You can never be sure you're keeping out all the microbes, fungi, etcetera, that are always trying to worm their way into your ecosystem. For now, those issues are still manageable here. And it's also been good here because the subsurface of Meres has the basic building blocks you need to start up an ecosystem: nitrogen, carbon, calcium, water, and the like."

Tommy falls silent, and they keep walking. About halfway across the chamber, they briefly greet two passing researchers who appear to be about Sophia and Peter's age. The researchers bow deeply to Tommy, who gives them a shallower bow in return. As Sophia and Peter follow along, Tommy describes the energy output of the "tovramium-powered radiative emitters" that provide the chamber's sunlight. He also points out several interesting species. Sophia asks what Eden does to respect and protect the life forms it stewards, launching Tommy on an extended description of their ethical protocols governing the treatment of the animals.

"I'm not following all the technical details," Peter whispers to Sophia, "but the implications are fascinating. These people are at the cutting edge of the Ecological Revolution's latest wave. This kind of creating is really holistic, really complex."

"We're fortunate to have the chance to experience this," Sophia says. "It was providential that you met Tommy on the shuttle and introduced him to me, no?"

"I suppose so," Peter says. He cocks his head. "Wait a minute."

He stops.

"There's a pattern to what we're doing," he mutters. "We've now moved from the 'morning' to the 'afternoon,' haven't we? This is a place where people are exploring the abundant possibilities offered by time and space. You told me about the Apple Orchard and God's vast abundance this morning, and this afternoon you want me to actually *experience* something like it. Am I right?"

Instead of answering Peter's question, Sophia turns and addresses Tommy, who has stopped to wait for them to catch up. She asks, as one might inquire about the weather, "How exactly is something this beautiful a 'falq you' to the cosmos?"

Peter stares at Sophia with wide eyes, shocked that She would repeat the vulgarity.

Tommy grins. "Life is short and we're all going to die, no?"

"Yes, this life is exceptionally short," Sophia says softly.

"Well, if the cosmos is going to hit us with cold emptiness in all directions," Tommy says, "then I say, let's hit it back. Even though emptiness is all we can look up and see during our lives, we're going to seed this cosmos with so much life that someday humans—or someone descended from humans—will be able to look up at the stars and know they're teeming with other lives.

"That's why this is 'Eden.' We who work here believe life is at the beginning of its spread outward to the stars. And we're doing things here that will mold the fate of the cosmos and outlive us all—the cosmos's indifference be damned! If we're a flame surrounded by darkness, then the work we do here at Eden will someday set the darkness ablaze with life."

Sophia seems utterly absorbed in Tommy's spiel, and Peter thinks, *I bet he's gotten more than one pretty young thing into bed with little speeches like that.* As they approach an intersection of several paths, Peter starts whispering to Sophia again. "My Lady, I think there may be important moral and theological implications to the ecological experimentation happening here. I mean, aren't these scientists—what did they used to call it?—'playing God'?"

Tommy stops and turns toward Peter. "I wonder if you would be so kind as to do me a favor?"

"Um, of course," Peter replies.

"I need to walk around here and check on a few things. What I want you to do is to keep going down this path until you come to the wall." Tommy points toward the far wall opposite where they entered the chamber. "You'll see a formation that looks like a cliff with some metal stairs embedded in it. Go up the stairs, and you'll see a plastic tray with important insect samples on it. Grab it. One of the junior researchers accidently left it there last shift, and I said I'd make sure it gets back to the airlock side."

"All right. Okay."

"Miz Sophia, I'll need you to help me monitor a few things."

She nods.

"Thanks, Peter. We'll head this way." Tommy points down one of the branching paths.

Peter nods and begins walking down the trail to the cliff, frowning. *Tommy has neatly cut me out of the picture for a while.* He decides to complete the assigned task but to be quick about it.

The trail does not cut a straight line to the far wall. Rather, it weaves back and forth and merges with other trails. Peter perseveres, but he can't help but make brief stops to gaze at feathered flying squirrels, a mob of scintillating green kangaroos, and a tiny, screeching creature resembling a pterodactyl with a five-centimeter wingspan. This last specimen rests on something that resembles a blue sunflower.

Sophia's lesson about God's vast abundance, Tommy's ecological expositions, and the exotic sights of Eden conspire to put an idea into Peter's head. *If God's creation is unimaginably vast and diverse, then could there be an "ecological" way to view religion?*

If so, it would not be like a monolithic, hierarchical model of religion— where God reveals a message to an authority such as a prophet or apostle, then the authority proclaims the message to the people, and then everyone believes the same message or else is considered a heathen or heretic. Is that model a "small world" understanding of revelation? In a vast and diverse creation, won't different messages be needed for the vastly different contexts, at least to some extent?

He's accessed enough to know that every great religion in its heyday was a sort of ecosystem of ideas and practices. Whether a person was a universalist or a nationalist, a conservative or a liberal, a rule-follower or a freedom-seeker, a fundamentalist or a mystic, every great tradition had branches, sects, orders, or denominations to fit. *To think of it in a positive sense, sacred stories like the story of Christ were so powerful that they could invade a large array of "ecological niches" in the sense of different orientations. People with all sorts of different bents read the bible, attended church services, and identified as "Christians." And as a person progressed through life, they might evolve—for example, from a purely ego-serving view of religion to a loyal fundamentalist view to a mystical view seeking unity with all creation.*

Fine, but . . . there's a clear problem with this line of thought: it strikes Peter as the sort of relativistic thinking that that can easily slide into Is-notism or other forms of nihilism. *If different teachings are appropriate to different contexts, how can one judge what the "right" teaching is for a given place and time? Even if the details may differ in different contexts, surely there are broad universal standards for true, healthy religion? If there really is an overarching truth about God, then there must be.*

A tiny furry creature darts across the trail, startling Peter. He realizes he's been standing in one spot, making no progress toward returning to Sophia and Tommy. *I meant to hurry.* Peter continues down the trail as quickly as he can without breaking into a run. Only a few minutes later, he reaches a small cliff with a set of metal stairs bolted to its side.

Tommy told the truth. Up on the cliff, Peter finds a tray with several compartments holding various dead insects. He surveys the jungle chamber to get his bearings. Through a gap in the foliage, he can just make out Sophia and Tommy in the distance, sitting together on a log. Judging by their gestures, they seem to be engaged in energetic conversation. He sees Sophia appear to throw Her head back in laughter. *No doubt at some colorful homespun witticism.* Peter stomps down the stairs. It takes him fifteen minutes to navigate the twisting trails and emerge into the clearing where they're sitting.

Despite Tommy's purported need to "walk around," he and Sophia are only meters from the spot where Peter parted from them. As Peter approaches, he sees that they're facing one another, talking intently.

Peter's spine stiffens. *Her hand is on his.*

Sophia sees Peter and waves.

Tommy quickly wipes something from his cheek.

Peter approaches Tommy and mumbles, "Here's your tray."

"Thank you. . . . Truth is . . . *truth* is I didn't need the tray that badly. I was just trying to get rid of you for a while." Tommy doesn't appear to be dismissing or mocking Peter—his voice is filled with sincerity. "I'm sorry, my friend. Will you forgive me?"

"I—" Peter looks at Sophia and then back at Tommy, wondering what transpired between them. "Of course."

To Sophia, Tommy says, "I'll think about what we discussed." They lock eyes for a moment, then he says, "I suppose we should start heading back toward the entrance." His flamboyance has transformed itself into a surprising earnestness.

She nods, and they both stand. The three of them begin walking in the direction of the airlock, Peter following Sophia and Tommy in silence. As they walk, Tommy's natural exuberance begins to reassert itself. He shares some stories of dramatic failures at Eden, such as the time when introducing a few geese resulted in the death spiral of an entire chamber's ecosystem. "That was a rough one," Tommy says.

When they reach the airlock, Sophia takes a long last look at Eden and steps in. As She cycles through, Tommy says, "Peter."

"Yes?"

"That feme. She's special."

"*I know* She is."

"She was telling me you two are close and you protect her."

"She—She said that?"

"She did. And I'm telling you I want you to do a good job. The System needs her and what she has to say."

Peter deflates. *I really am the worst pastor ever.* He spent the visit stewing in jealousy while Sophia apparently took pains to evangelize the man. "Yes, it most certainly does. I will protect Her, always."

Tommy claps him on the shoulder, then the men pass through the airlock.

Sophia and Peter part with Tommy in the garage, with hugs all around.

"Keep your eyes on those stars, young Peter," Tommy says.

Sophia selects coordinates that will take the landhog around to Gordii's eastern side via the trunk road to the south. They pull out while Tommy waves and the garage attendant salutes listlessly.

After Eden's surface-level building recedes from view, Peter finds he can't resist a probing comment. "You and Tommy seem to have a connection."

She must have noticed an edge to his voice. "You feel that a profane atheist is beneath consideration? *You* spent too much time trying to keep God's grace out of the hands of the supposedly unworthy. Do you not know that the wind blows where it wishes?"

Peter clears his throat. "I guess I wasn't thinking in precisely *religious* terms."

Her brow furrows, then Her eyes widen. "Oh."

If ever asked, Russ could now name two beliefs he holds to be certain: One, hell is a real place. Two, the demons aren't nice to you just because you're a kid.

He holds himself rigidly in place and tries not to cry. The cluttered room smells of an oily residue. Wrenches, crowbars, and electronic odds and ends lie strewn across a row of tables, each of which sports a big metal clamp. The overhead lights make a low buzzing noise. This room is as scary as the environmental maintenance room where he works.

"I'm sorry," he whimpers.

"You're sorry *what*?"

"I'm sorry, *ma'am*. I got lost, ma'am." Russ is careful not to look in the direction of the suit locker. His hands shake, and his legs feel as if they might, at any second, break out into a run on their own. But he knows if he runs away it will be much worse.

The woman slaps him again with a beefy hand, on the other cheek. She grabs his collar and pulls him close. Her worn gray uniform coveralls smell like the insides of Spence's shoes.

"Who's your culpable adult?"

"My daddy, num—number 438, works in the tooling mill, ma'am. He hasn't been back for three shifts, ma'am. I was—I was looking around for food, ma'am."

"You think I leave food lying around for rodents like you to steal?"

"I guess not, ma'am."

"You know, a little falqer who goes poking around places he's not au-thorized to be in could get his whole family *reassigned*. You know that?"

Russ's eyes widen. He shakes his head, and a tear rolls down his cheek. Veronica did her best to prepare him for getting reamed out if someone caught him here, but he's still terrified.

"I'll have to think for a while about whether to report you sneaking around here. Now get the hell out of here, and stay out of my sight."

"Yes, ma'am, I promise, I promise!"

The woman lets go of his collar, and he flees down the hall toward the dormitory, his courage now pushed past its breaking point.

Aunt Alma's gonna help us, Veronica said, *but first we need to help our-selves.* Russ got reamed out, but he was able to swipe an access fob just how Veronica told him to. The fob pokes him in an uncomfortable spot, but he doesn't let the discomfort slow him down.

~

Peter can't help but notice that the man in the mirror looks rather scrawny and poorly dressed compared to Eden's dashing Lead Engineer. *Definitely in his forties, and not a single gray hair. I wonder if he dyes it?* Peter sighs. He straightens and emerges from the washroom, saying "I hope you enjoyed the dinner I made—My Lady?"

She's not in the landhog. Mildly concerned, he strides over to the se-curity screen mounted in the wall that separates the living compartment and the driving compartment. They stopped the landhog on the plain east of Gordii just before sunset. Unobscured by Meres's thin, unpolluted atmosphere, bright stars now illuminate the landscape. He looks at the screen and is reassured to see Sophia standing near the landhog.

Suddenly, She leaps into the air.

She's dancing! After a moment's hesitation, Peter clips an air cartridge to his belt and joins Her outside.

He gapes as She performs a stunningly fluid high leap with one leg stretched forward and the other backward—a *grand jeté*, if he knew what to call it. In the low gravity, She has leapt high enough that he can see Her frame silhouetted against the bright starscape as if She were flowing along with the Milky Way itself.

Like some goddess of the starry expanse.

With a smile, She bounds over and holds out Her hand. "Come join me."

"No, no," he mutters, shaking his head. Peter is no dancer.

"Come dance with me," She insists. "It's what you're meant to do."

He sighs and takes Her hand. *Thy will be done.*

At first, he fears he'll make a misstep and go sprawling across the regolith. Eventually, though, he feels his inhibitions flow away, and he begins to enjoy the dance. For a long time, they dance and laugh together, bounding joyfully across starlit alien sands.

Two messages are waiting for Peter when he returns to the landhog. After getting ready for bed, he sits down in the driving compartment to listen to them. The first—no surprise—is Dorcas asking once again when they'll return to Sanef. Hearing an uncharacteristic note of panic in her voice, he shoots off a short reply telling her that they'll be on Meres for at least two more days. *Sophia said there are two more prayers, one for each of the next two mornings.* He also assures Dorcas that the Christians and catechumens remain continually in his thoughts. The second message is from Lydia—a short greeting also asking when they'll return.

He steps out of the driving compartment and walks over to Sophia's bunk, where She's already sleeping soundly. A "paper" magazine, which was actually made using fungus that grows in greenhouse waste, lies open on the blanket in front of Her. Peter picks up the magazine—the latest issue of *Scientific Merian*—and lays it aside, resisting the temptation to turn off Sophia's light. He doesn't know how She would react if She woke up in the middle of the night to complete darkness.

He lingers for a moment and then sits down on his own bunk. *It's hard to believe I didn't see how beautiful She is the first time I looked at Her.* His feelings are a complex braid of worship, the love of a disciple for his teacher, and romantic longing.

Is this how it was for Mary Magdalene?

Slumbering there, Sophia looks not only lovely but also as fragile as any mere human being. Earlier that day, it felt to Peter as if She were teaching him so that he could go out and teach others on his own. *But She has no need for a middleman.* She can teach the Gospel much better than Peter ever could, and surely She'll stay with him—with the Christians, that is—for a long time. Yes, surely.

Wasn't Jesus of Nazareth the once-and-for-all sacrifice for us? Sophia has already experienced enough suffering during Her time in this world. Surely, She won't have to follow in His footsteps. Surely!

17

Deep Presence

By the time Peter wakes up, the early bird has already gone outside and set up the nanomesh dome. Peter scans the table for a piece of paper, but She didn't leave one there this morning. He quickly freshens up, changes clothes, and exits the landhog.

Camped east of Gordii, they're too far from the dorsum to see it in the distance, particularly as the wind is kicking up fine dust. The plain itself looks as flat and barren as the landscape above Eden. Here, though, Peter sees some small boulders and rocky detritus in the morning light. He enters the dome and sits down next to Her.

"Good morning, Your Holiness," She says with a smile.

"My Lady, please don't call me that. I'm nothing compared to you."

She places a hand on his for a moment. "Nothing is nothing."

They sit in contemplative silence for several minutes. Then Sophia turns toward Peter. "How do you feel after our discussion yesterday morning?"

"Truthfully?"

"Always. Truth is my middle name."

"At first, I was excited. But the more I think about it, the more the idea of 'vast abundance' really does make me feel *insignificant*. If reality is unimaginably vast and diverse, then what difference does one person make? I'm just one among a million googolplex souls in a billion trillion universes, or whatever?" He shakes his head. "The vision of great abundance is beautiful, I'll grant you. I can see it running like a thread through Jesus' life and teachings, and it explains something about why God would create an existence like ours.

"But it makes me feel totally unimportant. At best, an individual soul is a little bauble, a trifling plaything for God . . . just one little apple on a gnarled tree lost somewhere in the vastness of an inconceivably huge orchard." He sighs. "Maybe I'm one of those people who wants a 'small' world because such abundance is terrifying."

"Wow, Peter. That's heavy stuff."

His eyes grow large. "*You're* accusing *me* of focusing on 'heavy stuff'?"

She laughs. "Fair point."

He can't stop himself from smiling at Her. Even under pink sunlight filtered through an alien atmosphere, She is . . . lovely.

"When you talk about being an apple on a tree lost in the vastness of the Apple Orchard," She says, "you're thinking of a small 'god' who can only be walking in one part of the orchard at a time."

"Yes, I suppose I am. I think you're going to say that God is everywhere in the orchard, so I can't be lost from God's sight."

"Indeed, God is everywhere. Even, Peter, within each of the apples."

"Huh?"

She produces another piece of heavy paper like the one Peter found yesterday morning. "This is the second prayer. Read it aloud for me."

Peter takes the paper and begins to recite the prayer:

All-vulnerable God—

He stops and peers at the paper. With a confused glance in Her direction, he starts again:

All-vulnerable God of deep presence:
In your merciful desire to redeem us from nothingness,
*   you choose to sojourn within the limits of mortal existence.*
Glory to you, consciousness within all beings, deepest me!
When I hate, I hate you; when I eat, I eat your flesh.
You have allowed yourself to be bound and beaten,
*   cut and raped and broken—with me and in me.*

Peter's voice shakes. "Sophia—"

"Finish the prayer, Peter."

With trembling lips, he says:

Before Abraham was, I Am.

"Amen," says Sophia.

They sit in silence while Peter considers Sophia's prayer. Finally, he asks, "What does it mean, 'deepest me'?"

"Excellent question. It means our boundless God experiences every-thing from the inside, too—as *Emmanuel*, 'God with us'—not only as an outside observer. Saint Catherine of Genoa is said to have exclaimed it: 'My deepest me is God!'"

"Oh, come on. For you, okay. And maybe even for an ancient saint. But surely *my* 'deepest me' isn't God?"

"Who else would it be?"

"I don't know. I guess just *me*."

"And who are *you*? Are you just your physical body?"

"Of course not. I'm also my mind. 'I think, therefore I am,' right?"

"Certainly, you have thoughts. But *are* you your thoughts?"

"Mm, it doesn't feel right to say I *am* my thoughts. There's an underly-ing *me* who has thoughts that come and go."

"And your feelings? Are you your feelings?"

"No, same for feelings. I get wrapped up in them, and I identify myself with them: I say, '*I'm* angry' or '*I'm* happy.' But *I* am not just my feelings. I am a person who has feelings that come and go."

"Are you your experiences and memories?"

"That's a little harder. In one sense, I am my experiences and memories."

"Without them, your own incomparable, utterly unique soul would not be what it is. But is that the entirety of who you are, a database of experi-ences and memories?"

It takes Peter a minute to frame a reply. "There is something else there. It's my, my—I don't know—'consciousness.' If I had amnesia and didn't re-member anything about myself, I would still have the sense of knowing I exist—I would still be a conscious being. I think I would still know that *I am*."

"I am," whispers Sophia. She gazes at him.

Peter's eyes widen, and he mutters, "*I Am*. That's a divine name first revealed in, uh, in the Book of Exodus, when God spoke to Moses out of the burning bush. Moses asked for God's name, and God said, 'I Am Who I Am.' And then God ordered Moses to tell his people, 'I Am has sent me to you.'" Peter stares into the distance. "And you're saying that the divine name 'I Am' hints that God may be identified with, among other things, *consciousness itself*?"

She smiles.

"Huh. So you're trying to tell me," he says, "that there really is a 'divine spark' in each of us—that a soul's deepest, most foundational consciousness is, is also God's?" Peter remembers now: some Christian theologians and authorities—Blessed Pope Francis I, among others—insisted that a spark of divine light is within each of us. But this had always sounded like poetry to

Peter. *Sophia seems to be suggesting that the "divine spark" is a metaphysical reality—that the presence of God inhabits the core of every creature as its very sense of being a subject: that which can say "I am."*

"That's powerful," he says, "but it's, um, very abstract and, well, deep. It's hard to wrap my mind around it."

"I warned you that we would be trying to sketch a map of metaphors of the mystery using nothing but clumsy words. Yet we have no choice but to use words as long as we abide in this mortal existence." She looks out toward the desert and then returns Her gaze to Peter. "*You* erred . . ."

He winces.

". . . when you insisted that only one person, Jesus of Nazareth, possessed the spark of God's divine presence in his soul, and that only his suffering was the suffering of God. But Christ is not so small: he is 'the way, the truth, and the life' of *all* that is. What is true for him is true also for you, including the deep truth that God dwells within you and participates in your joy and suffering."

"Oh," Peter says. "I think I read something about this. There was a monk back in the twentieth century . . . his name was Martin—no, Merton—and he wrote something like, 'The truth I must love in my brother is God Himself, living in him.'"

"Indeed."

"So . . . God lives in every creature as its deepest sense of 'I am'? God dwells in, I don't know, dogs and lizards and redwoods?"

Looking at his face, She smiles. "You don't like the thought of that, do you? You'd rather your God just remain seated on a heavenly throne, scepter in hand, surrounded by power and glory."

"I don't know about that, necessarily. But it does seem disrespectful to suggest that God is in me or in a dung beetle. It seems sacrilegious to say God could be in things that are imperfect and small and weak."

"That's because you early Christians are just beginning to—"

"*Early* Christians!?" His jaw drops. "You mean 'late Christians,' don't you?"

"You *early* Christians are just beginning to fathom the central revelation of your tradition. For so long, you understandably wanted to focus only on God being *Almighty* . . . to know that someone was in control of this broken world, this 'gnarled' branch of reality. That made it hard to fully see *Jesus*, the heart and icon of your religion. Peter, in a world where gods were thought to throw lightning bolts and rule as kings, Jesus allowed himself to be tortured and killed in a humiliating public execution. What kind of extraordinary, unexpected God is that? It is the God who participates in all suffering, who allows Godself to become the very image of *vulnerability*.

"You may have noticed that those who are strong are the ones who can trust themselves to become vulnerable."

Peter thinks of his mother. Priscilla never feared to cry. She didn't hide her vulnerability from others. She never needed to, because even in moments of suffering she seemed to tap into a mysterious wellspring of strength. "I suppose that's right," Peter says. "When we're strong, we can allow ourselves to be vulnerable."

"God *is* Almighty—inconceivably strong," Sophia says. "And that very strength empowers God to choose to become *All-vulnerable* as well. When we suffer, God suffers with us. Always. God both cultivates the 'Variety H. Sapiens' apple and *lives within* the apple. This is one of the great truths of everything that exists or ever will exist: All-vulnerable God's extravagant presence in the deepest depths of existence, choosing to exult and suffer with and within us, never abandoning us."

They sit in silence for a few moments while Peter reflects. Then he says, "This is another part of the theodicy. In God's vast abundance, God chooses to create realities that allow suffering, like the apple farmer who wants fascinatingly tart apples. That might be cruel or callous if God were standing above it all like a voyeur or a mad scientist conducting an experiment. But you're saying God objectively, truly dwells within us, not only 'above' us. As the H. Sapiens apple's deepest self, God 'exults and suffers' with him throughout his life. And even though the H. Sapiens apple might sometimes feel as though his existence is not worthwhile, the apple farmer—who has an inconceivably broader perspective—felt that it is. Is that basically what you're saying?"

"Yes. He's so much more than just a bauble."

Peter stares out into the desert and tries to calm his breathing while he seeks to adjust to the explosive change in perspective Sophia is offering. He begins to mentally catalogue the many ways he has treated other creatures as if they somehow stood separate and apart from God's deep presence.

After some minutes, Sophia interrupts Peter's reverie. "We've covered enough ground for this morning. We need to get started on other tasks early today."

"Right. Okay," Peter says. "Where are we driving this afternoon?"

"Who said anything about driving?"

Midafternoon finds Peter lifting himself to peer over a fat, crimson boulder. He focuses his magspecs on the crest of a distant ridge, guided by Sophia's instructions.

"I still don't see anything," he says.

His target is a few kilometers away—an easy enough distance for the magspecs. But he must find the right spot to zoom in on. The breeze is picking up again, and it will soon loft more fine dust into the air, further eroding visibility.

She perches Herself next to Peter and peers over the boulder with him. She points. "See where there's an incline over to the right? It's about a third of the way down that part of the ridge."

Peter steals a quick glance at Her. She's not using magspecs. Like him, She's dressed from head to toe in a burnt red jumpsuit with extra air cartridges hanging at the waist. It seems She picked up the jumpsuits—Merian camouflage—while they were in Kistrob. Dressed that way, Sophia and Peter look vaguely like some kind of Merian special-forces soldiers: stealthy outer-space ninjas.

Of all the preposterous images.

They hiked—bounded, almost, in the g—nearly nineteen featureless kilometers from the landhog to their current position. The ridge they now spy appears to be one of the sheerest parts of the Gordii formation, rising steeply above the plain. Peter can see, about a hundred meters ahead of them, a long stretch of fence topped with razor wire. Signs bolted to the fence at regular intervals warn: "PRIVATE PROPERTY. TRESPASSERS WILL BE PUNISHED TO THE FULLEST EXTENT OF THE LAW."

Peter still has no idea why they've come to that spot, but he trusts that Sophia will show him what She wants him to see. *I'm guessing this will be an "afternoon" experience of God's deep presence, just as yesterday's time at Eden seemed to be an "afternoon" experience of vast abundance. I wonder if our "evenings" will also fit into this pattern She's creating for us.* He remembers the kiss She gave him—he can't forget it—to symbolize the "love affair" She says takes place in the "evening" of faith.

Using a hand to block the rays of the distant sun, he eventually identifies a point along the top of the ridge whose redness stands out slightly from the surrounding landscape, exactly where Sophia described it. He zooms in on it.

The red pixel resolves into a massive, rectangular building, perhaps four stories high. He zooms in further.

No windows. A control tower on top of the building. *No, some sort of watchtower.* At high resolution, Peter can make out two people in gray uniforms. It looks as if they're monitoring the area below.

"I see it," he says. "Is it a prison?"

"No."

"I think I see nanomesh sheets shimmering around the perimeter. Hmm, is it a military installation?"

"No."

"It certainly looks like some kind of high-security compound or something. It's—wait, there's a group of—what? There's a group of children outside. They look as if they're school age. And I see some adults too. Is this some sort of military school?"

Sophia's breathing sounds ragged. She sits with Her back against the boulder. Peter looks at Her and absentmindedly notices a thin vein of crystal that runs through the rock—it looks like chalcedony. "No," She says. "It's a processing facility and housing for the refugees who work there."

"Processing facility? It looks more like a prison. Why would there be a 'processing facility' so far out in the middle of nowhere?"

Sophia does not answer.

Peter looks through the magspecs again. After a few more minutes, all of the refugees, both adults and children, start walking back toward the building complex at a brisk pace.

"They're all going back into the building," Peter says. "A lot of them look hunched over like they're exhausted, but they're all moving quickly."

"Break's over," Sophia says. "They'll get another one in six hours."

Peter puts the magspecs aside and kneels next to Her behind the boulder. "My Lady, based on what you've said—and the secretive way we've approached this place—I take it this is an illegal operation. Are these people being exploited?"

"Exploited, yes, very much so. Illegal? Technically, it is illegal, because Amazonis signed the same human rights treaties as everyone else. But processors like this one are effectively a law unto themselves: the Merian governments don't interfere. The substance being processed is important to certain research the governments value."

Peter stands, lifts the magspecs to his eyes, and looks at the compound again, but all of the people are now back inside. "Is the work dangerous?"

"Yes, the substance is hazardous until it's fully processed. Working near it causes permanent damage to human tissues after only a few weeks. The staff quarters are a safe distance from the processing center, of course."

"Perm—permanent damage? So, the refugees are being poisoned? Here, in a civilized nation, in our century?"

Sophia nods.

"If a refugee comes here, how long do they have to stay?"

"As long as they survive," She says. "There's no procedure for transferring refugees elsewhere, if that's what you mean. They work until they die."

"Until—until they die? And there are other places like this?"

"About a dozen across Meres."

"A dozen! How can this be true?"

Sophia stares out into the distance. "There's a race among the cartel alliances, and they are each working with client nations like Amazonis to win that race. The substance that is processed here plays a crucial role."

"You said these are refugees. I take it they come from Earth?"

"From especially impoverished nations—the Riyadhs and Oslos of the Earth—and from among the destitute in more prosperous ones . . . from anyplace where there are desperate people who can be lured here by promises of a better life on a new frontier."

"There's no way the refugees can escape? I see mesh up on the ridge, but I don't see any fences."

"They don't need fences to keep people *in*. The refugees can't control the mesh, and they're not permitted access to pressure suits. As you know, anyone who pushes through the mesh barrier without protection would suffocate just before she had a chance to freeze. And some refugees choose to do just that. That's their escape."

Peter sits down heavily on the ground. "Tell me what can we do to fight this."

She reaches out and places Her hand on the back of Peter's head, then She momentarily touches Her forehead to his.

"You're a caring person," She says as She sits back. "One of the worst parts is that they use proximity to the unprocessed substance to control behavior. To punish disobedient prisoners—refugees, I mean—the operators reassign them to work requiring them to be near it. In effect, the operators have the absolute power of life and death over these people. Disobedience, not working 'hard enough,' refusing sexual advances: any of these can lead to being assigned work that will kill you."

Peter's eyes bulge. "How do you know so much about this?"

"I have private sources of information, but the conditions at these places are an open secret among those who manage the affairs of certain nations on this planet. Knowledge hardly matters when a spirit of duplicity rules those with the power to change things."

"Again, what can we do to put this place out of business? Is there someone we can go to? Is there some way we can expose this more?" Peter is ready to drive back to Kistrob and march into the mayor's office to demand she help them. *Then we would need go to the capital of Amazonis, wherever that is—*

"Not today," Sophia says. "Be patient."

"We have to do something! Or is this place one of those so-called 'sour apples' you say God loves so much?"

She sighs. "You do not realize now what I am doing, but later you will understand."

The words are familiar to Peter, but he can't quite place them.

Sophia looks toward the ridge. "Come. We've seen what we needed to see. We should leave before we attract the attention of a security drone."

Peter repeatedly glances over his shoulder as they start back toward their camp. The dorsum looks darker and somehow jagged in a way it hadn't looked before. After a couple of silent, brooding kilometers, he says, "Were you *really* going to take that Isnotist boy with us into the desert?"

"I never said I was going to take him with us into the desert. That wouldn't have worked out. There's somewhere else I would have taken him."

"Oh. Okay. Where?"

"I'd rather show you than merely tell you, Peter. I expect that you will see soon enough, if you can trust me that far."

A sore and fatigued bishop lies on his back and stares at the paste-colored ceiling of his sleeping nook. It was late by the time they returned to their campsite on the plain east of the dorsum. The long hike would have been harder on Peter if Sophia hadn't prepared him by dragooning him into the first hike on Wednesday. *In retrospect, that must have been part of Sophia's master plan for the week,* he muses. He gazes across the aisle at Her sleeping form. She's breathing gently and rhythmically.

Peter thinks about the suffering of the people he saw through the mag-specs, especially the children, and it angers him. *I can't believe that advanced nations tolerate such evil. And the "Apple Farmer"? Does God really love rotten apples like the guards who exploit those poor refugees? If anyone deserves to burn in hell, they do.*

Despite what Peter saw that day, or perhaps because of it, this quiet moment also endows him with a feeling of his own blessedness. *What a miracle it is to be who and where I am, not only free and safe but here—with Her. What a blessing just to lie near to Her, to listen to Her breathe.* He has to believe She is a special manifestation of God—of the *living* God! So unpredictable, so intense, so alive! Out of all the billions who have lived, out of all the times and places in God's creation, he was chosen to meet Her face-to-face. He's the one right here, at this moment, breathing the same air as She. She chose *him*. And he did nothing to become worthy of it. It was pure grace.

Pure grace. Pure grace. Pure grace . . .

Just as Peter starts to nod off, Sophia begins to make fitful noises. He returns to wakefulness and looks over at Her. She whimpers.

She's having a nightmare!

Her noises become louder and more plaintive, and She makes little jerking movements. He thinks he hears Her say, "No, please, no."

He debates with himself for a few moments, then he gets up and sits down on the edge of Her bunk. He gingerly touches Her arm. Eyes still closed, She stiffens. "My Lady," he whispers. "It's okay. It's okay, you're safe." He tries to hide his embarrassment at seeing Her like this.

She abruptly bolts upright and jerks away from him. Then Her eyes focus on him, and She leans back against the side of the sleeping nook and draws in a deep breath.

"You were having a nightmare."

"Yes. Thank you."

He sits back on the edge of his own bunk. "Do *you* have nightmares often?"

She smiles at him humorlessly. Her breathing is becoming more regular. "These nightmares are recurring visitors. They often stay away a long time, but they never completely stop dropping by. I think this is just the price I'm paying for showing you the compound today." She touches Her heart. "So much innocent suffering."

"But isn't there something *you* can do to make the nightmares go away?"

"You think strength means being untouched by the suffering we are approaching. You still don't know me, Peter Halabi."

"I still don't understand you, and I probably never will. But I want to, very much." Then it occurs to him. *Of course, She's vulnerable, too. That was sort of the point, Peter.*

She takes his hand and kisses it, saying "Thank you for comforting me." He feels his face grow warm.

"We should try to get some sleep," She says. "Tomorrow is another big day."

18

Incarnate Love

Peter reads the third prayer aloud:

All-embracing God of incarnate love:
You patiently purify our longing,
  toppling our idols of success and false certitude
  and gracing us lovingly with glimpses of your wholeness.
Help me to put away my infantile fears and appetites.
Strangle my blinding, grinding over-and-against-ness and
  my thirst to be separate and special and admired.
Entangle my most passionate desire with your own.
Amen.

He raises his head and gazes over Sophia's shoulder toward Gordii. By Merian standards, the wind is especially strong this morning, and it pelts their nanomesh dome with dust.

"God's incarnate love," Sophia says, "is the last of the three truths we must discuss. When I say 'incarnate,' I mean love that is not merely abstract or otherworldly, but rather that interweaves itself into the very fabric of life's unfolding."

Peter nods and fixes his eyes on Her beautiful face.

"Mere words cannot do justice to God's motivations," She says, "but we can at least make a start by speaking of 'incarnate love.' One might describe it as inconceivably patient, boundless, selfless benevolence at the heart and center of the divine life. It is an unequivocal desire for life's embodied flourishing."

"'Love' is at the center of God's motivations?"

"Love is at the center of everything."

Peter looks down at the dirt. "Love," he repeats. He rubs his jaw. Last night, he ground his teeth for the first time in months. "'Love is at the center,' you say. Well, it is written in the bible that 'God is love.' And even lots of non-religious people are always going on and on and on about *love*. But . . ."

"But?"

"But how can that really be true if we're talking about the Christian God? If God really is so benevolent—if God is free to love unconditionally—why did Jesus have to die? Why was his crucifixion necessary for God to forgive our sins? I guess I've always thought there must be a *balance* in God between wrath or justice, on the one hand, and loving mercy, on the other. And Jesus had to suffer and die to appease the Father's justice, because of human sin."

"Mm, a balance," She says. "You're suggesting that God's need for justice—or, as you put it, God's 'wrath'—is as powerful and central as God's love. You believe that the 'Fall of Man' angered the Father, and he was going to allow everyone to be tortured in hell for all eternity. But then Jesus stepped forward and 'took the hammer blow' for humankind—or at least for the part of it who became Christians—by substituting himself as a perfect sacrifice. This transaction provided the satisfaction demanded by the Father's offended honor and justice. Isn't that how that story goes?"

"Yes, and it's true that it has never quite made sense to me," Peter says. "I don't understand why a God who is good and loving would *torture* anyone forever, no matter what they had done—even, I suppose, the guards at that compound, although the thought of getting revenge on them is appealing. And I don't really think it makes sense that any one person can or should suffer vicariously for another person's wrongs. But I don't know of any other explanation for why Jesus had to suffer and die."

"Bishop, the idea that Jesus served as a scapegoat to appease his Father and save fallen humanity from an eternity of torture was but one understanding of Jesus' death, albeit an all-too-popular one. Other understandings flourished at various times in Christian history."

"Really? I always assumed that understanding was the only orthodox interpretation of why Jesus came. It seemed so broadly accepted in the Christian writings I've accessed."

"Yes," She says. "That theory became particularly entrenched during the centuries of global colonialism by predominantly Christian meganations."

"Colonialism? But that's politics. What could that possibly have to do with the theology of Christ's suffering and death?"

"It's easier to justify invading foreign lands and dominating their peoples if you can convince yourself you're saving their souls from eternal torture by converting them to your religion."

"Oh." Peter hopes She's not about to start speaking to him as if *he* did those things.

"You can see the usefulness," She says, "of declaring that God brutally punishes those who don't fall into line—at least for those doing the declaring. But the widespread acceptance of this teaching slowly twisted the Gospel until it became barely recognizable. The idea of atonement through torture placed an abstract ideal of law or obedience above God's love and freedom. After you began insisting . . ."

Peter winces.

". . . that God was an eternal torturer who demanded blood sacrifice, was it any wonder people were unable to give their hearts to that diabolical 'God'? How could anyone trust or fall in love with such a one? No, Jesus' Father was not sitting up in heaven waiting for a debt to be paid in blood. God has always been free to forgive and to love.

"Remember the 'God' your friend Dan called an 'asshole'? The 'God' who would demand the death of his own Son? The 'God' who has all of eternity to help his children grow into fullness but for some reason is stingy with salvation?"

Peter nods.

"That so-called 'God' is not, was not, and never will be."

Silence fills the space between them as Peter reflects on all the times he prayed with trepidation to the "God" which Sophia just declared to be a nullity.

"Okay, so there is no 'balance' between justice and love," he says. "Love is squarely in the center."

"Love alone stands in the center of God's relationship with each creature. This does not mean God condones injustice. Truly, the Divine loathes injustice, and the fruits of this loathing are sometimes encountered as wrath. But this is not wrath in the sense of spite. It is rightful, suffering anger fueled entirely by God's love for each creature. God's steadfast mercy and passionate justice are both manifestations of an unqualified, central, and reliable benevolence, which has never required atonement through torture."

"So Jesus didn't have to die to appease God's wrath," Peter says. "But then why did he have to suffer and die at all? Why couldn't he have just come and preached about love and lived to a ripe old age? Maybe he could even have fallen in love and had a family—" Peter's face flushes, and he looks away from Her. The strong wind picks up even more. Airborne particles collide with the dome's nanomesh walls, giving rise to a low roaring sound.

"Jesus came to reveal the great pattern of all that is," Sophia says. "His incarnation, ministry, crucifixion, and resurrection reveal the flow of life between eternity and time, heaven and creation, what-is and what-may-be. Among other things, he came to show the intimate relationship between the Divine and all creatures. He came to show that those who are poor, who are different, who don't fit preconceived ideas—that they are to be embraced, not discarded or destroyed. Among other things, he came to model the death of the grasping ego's dominion over the soul, a death which offers resurrection into greater freedom and life. Jesus came to make these, and so many more things, visible and known to you."

Peter can look up at Her once again without hiding his face in embarrassment, and he nods as She continues to speak. The wind gusts harder, giving rise to a richer roar.

"His mission was transformational, not transactional. He did not come and do all the things he did to change God's mind about humanity. He did them to change humanity's mind about God."

Peter spends a moment absorbing those words. Then he says, "So, Jesus was a living message to us . . . in everything He did, including His crucifixion?"

"Jesus' path reveals the deepest truths of our own selves and the path of spiritual growth. He is not simply some idol to worship. He's more than that. . . . Peter, how many times does the bible record Jesus saying 'worship me' to his disciples?"

"I can't think of a time."

"What he said repeatedly was 'follow me.' But that was much harder. So you acted as if Christ were merely a miraculous, one-time event thousands of years ago without also seeing that he is the deep pattern you are called to follow, here and now. You often worshiped Jesus without also following him. Why?"

"Because it's easier," Peter whispers.

"Yes. Because if you also follow Jesus—if you take him seriously as 'the Way'—you will *change*. And the grasping ego hates change. It wants to believe it can become everything it is meant to be while remaining in thrall to chronic compulsions. The grasping ego resists the crucifixions that lead to resurrection."

"And God beckons us into the pattern of crucifixion and resurrection out of God's incarnate love, not out of wrath?"

Sophia nods. "God's incarnate love is one of the great truths of everything that exists or ever will exist: All-embracing God's progressive shepherding of all things, through birth, life, death, and resurrection, from apparent separateness to holy connection and flourishing."

Peter reflects on Her words. He says, "*Really* believing God is so loving . . . that God's mercy doesn't depend on anything I do . . . that it's not about worthiness or some heavenly transaction . . . that there's no need to 'buy' God's love or have someone else buy it for me . . . that blows my mind."

"If your mind has never been blown, then you've never encountered the Divine."

The wind has calmed. Despite how overwhelmed Peter feels, he's also experiencing a new lightness.

"Let's conclude our discussion of God's incarnate love by recalling the Parable of the Apple Orchard," Sophia says. "The apple farmer delights in that stubborn 'Variety H. Sapiens' apple. She cultivates him because she loves him as a unique creation and knows his life is worth living. It's good he exists, even with the suffering and limitations he must endure, even with his flaws, even if he doesn't know it yet. She looks with love upon his trials and failings."

"God loves him even though he's—he's scarred."

Sophia smiles ruefully and nods. "And, Peter . . . God loves *you* more than you love yourself."

Peter burns with a desire to lean forward and kiss Sophia. But he is afraid.

They're driving southward by late morning. While they're in transit, Peter enters some notes into his personal journal.

By early afternoon, Peter finds himself admiring the expansive main exhibit hall at the "Amazonis Museum of FTL Research and Development." The hall's soaring ceiling reminds him of Grace Cathedral, although its thin columns look too frail to support the structure, at least through the eyes of one used to buildings engineered for Earth's stronger gravity. Every surface gleams bright white as if the edifice was built just yesterday. Various displays, holographic videos, and hands-on activities populate the hall, which reverberates with noise. Fifty or sixty schoolchildren and half as many adults move about the hall.

"Well, what do we do here?" asks Peter.

"We just look around," Sophia answers.

"Uh huh." Peter now knows well enough that Sophia never "just" does anything.

The major exhibits are arranged to tell the story of Amazonian research into hypothetical Faster-Than-Light travel. The first major exhibit presents a video setting out the context for the settlement of Meres and the advent of

FTL research there. Sophia and Peter stop to listen as historical holograms and dramatic music accompany the narration:

> . . . as the Great Stim Crisis posed another challenge. At that time, much of Earth's population became addicted to Sensory-Targeted Immersive Mindtech, also called "stims." These, of course, are powerful digital technologies that allow one to withdraw from reality into a highly realistic virtual environment.
>
> As great swaths of humanity plunged into solipsistic digital addictions, resulting in the so-called "Lost Generations," interest in participating in the outer world diminished. But when governments finally began to undertake massive legal and technological interventions, space once again became a priority. Governments found that the saga of space exploration gave citizens an especially engaging way to relate to the real world as a place to be encountered and explored.
>
> While stim addiction still afflicts the international community, experts believe that the promise and drama of space exploration helped civilization to survive the Great Stim Crisis . . .

Peter is familiar with this history. He follows Sophia toward the next major exhibit, which dominates the middle of the hall. A holographic banner displays: "THE PHOBOS EXPRESS: TO A MOON IN A HEARTBEAT!" It centers on a transparent tube rising from a meter-tall platform all the way up to the ceiling. As they approach, Peter sees that the tube spans perhaps three-tenths of a meter in diameter. It bears bright yellow warning stickers identifying the space within as an unpressurized zone. A smooth sphere a little smaller than the tube's width rests at the bottom. The sphere is also transparent except for a thick webbing of metallic filaments at its core. Peter wonders if the sphere and tube are made from the same impenetrable material as the star lounge's dome on the shuttle from Earth.

"Good timing," says Sophia as dramatic, mood-setting background music begins to play. About twenty-five other visitors close in around the exhibit, including a teacher and his class of schoolchildren. A holographic persona of an attractive middle-aged feme appears next to the tube. She floats in midair, sitting with her legs crossed.

"Welcome, citizens and guests, to the star attraction of the Amazonis Museum of FTL Research and Development." The persona favors them with a dazzling smile. "The hardworking scientists at Amazonis's main FTL research facility, adjacent to this museum, are making dramatic progress toward realizing Faster-Than-Light travel within our lifetimes. As of this year, the fastest velocity attained in uncrewed interplanetary test flights has exceeded nine percent of the speed of light—a tremendous achievement for humanity. But we are still only at the cusp of the FTL revolution.

"We affectionately call this exhibit the *Phobos Express*. The cylinder extends past the roof of the museum, pointing toward space itself. We will have an authorized launch window in exactly ninety seconds. At that moment, the sphere in front of you will launch from this spot, travel in a straight line past the orbit of our moon Phobos, and return to the same spot. This round trip of over twelve thousand kay will take . . ." The persona pauses for dramatic effect. ". . . less than two seconds."

A few *oohs* erupt from the schoolchildren as a hologram of an oldtime-style digital clock appears before the visitors and begins counting down the seconds until launch. Some of the children hold their breath while others count down the ticking seconds in ever higher decibels. When the clock hits zero, the sphere disappears and a hush falls.

What happens next occurs almost too quickly for Peter to process. A brightly throbbing red sphere appears in the spot from which the transparent sphere disappeared. Immediately, the tube goes completely white. Peter keeps his eyes trained on the spot where the sphere was. After many seconds, the white within the tube begins to break apart, and he realizes it's steam. The sphere now glows a pale pink, and Peter can see it pale further with each passing second. He can also see that the sphere sits in a few centimeters of clear liquid which still produces wisps of steam.

The persona resumes her monologue. "Believe it or not, the *Phobos Express* just made a round trip of over twelve thousand kay—to the orbit of Phobos and back!—in approximately one point seven seconds."

Several of the children make delighted noises, but one of them exclaims, "It didn't go nowhere! It's a trick!" The teacher shushes the children so that the persona can be heard.

In the meantime, the persona smiles and nods, blissfully unaware of the budding conspiracy theorist standing before her. "And the *Phobos Express* traveled at only two percent of the speed of light," she says. "Our most recent experimental flights would leave it in the dust!"

The sphere has finally transitioned back to a transparent state, and the tube is now almost free of steam.

"How did the *Phobos Express* move so quickly?" the persona asks. "Why didn't it burn up in our planet's atmosphere? How did it turn on a dime and return right back to where it came from? To learn the answers to these questions and more, see the next major exhibit: 'Tovramium: The Miracle Material.'" A line of arrows appears on the floor, pointing the assembled visitors to the exhibit.

"Until next time, adieu!" The persona flashes her gleaming white teeth and winks out of existence as a dramatic melody reaches its crescendo.

Sophia and Peter move on to the next major exhibit. This one comprises a wall of images, vids, and holograms narrating and describing the special properties of "tovramium," a substance first discovered on Meres. *I don't think I've heard of it before*, Peter thinks. *Or have I?* When properly processed, tovramium exhibits extraordinary properties in terms of material strength, heat dissipation, and energy production. The exhibit warns that interacting with unprocessed tovramium can harm humans, but it assures its audience that the substance can be handled safely with the right precautions.

Departing the tovramium exhibit, Sophia and Peter find themselves directed onward to the far end of the exhibit hall. Above their heads, a domed ceiling features glittering white stars on a jet-black background. Motion-actuated displays allow visitors to learn about the first exoplanets likely to make good targets for settlement. The starry ceiling makes Peter think of the starscape painted behind Mary and Jesus in the Chapel of the Nativity, now impossibly distant.

Along the far wall of the domed area, natural daylight enters through a panoramic window that offers a stunning view of the lab complex downslope from the museum. Peter can pick out perhaps twenty interconnected buildings of different shapes and sizes. In contrast to the virtually monochromatic landscape, the buildings boast a rainbow of wild, playful colors. Sophia joins Peter at the window and looks out with him in silence.

"The tovramium," he says. "This 'miracle material.' That's what the people at that compound are processing. It's what's killing those people. That's what you wanted me to see."

"That's part of it. I also wanted you to see how close we are."

"How close we are . . . ?"

"To exploding."

Peter shoots a quick glance toward the *Phobos Express*. "You're saying tovramium explodes?"

Sophia shakes Her head and walks alongside the panoramic window. "Whatever else may happen, the research is not going to stop. Today, vessels to journey between the stars are still too slow, too impractical, too expensive. They will be for perhaps a couple more decades. But then, when higher velocities are achieved, starships will depart the System and begin spreading humanity throughout the galaxy. *Humanity* is going to explode, outward into this universe, farther than you can now imagine."

"Where I come from," Peter says, "most people take it for granted that we're nearing the end of history. With Earth's ecosystem so fragile, and most of the System so hostile to life, and the stars so distant, and the ongoing wars, it seems like most people expect a secular version of the apocalypse. But you're telling me we're standing at the beginning!" Peter looks out at the colorful, friendly-looking buildings of the research center.

"Wait," he says. "Tommy said Eden uses tovramium to create its artificial sunlight, didn't he? Does he *know*? Do those people down there know? Do they know where the tovramium is coming from?"

"Tommy had no idea until I told him," Sophia says. "He's an ethical person, and it was painful and confusing for him to learn the truth. But out of that pain may come good—Tommy is in a position to enlist help from some who might exert influence. As for the scientists here, tovramium features more prominently into their work. Do they know? Most of them know what they want to know.

"Most evil does not come from villains maliciously conspiring, twisting their moustaches while they laugh wickedly. Most evil isn't that sexy. No, it comes from duplicity, from willful ignorance. Places like the compound are not exactly a secret, but they're not talked about either." She nods toward the window. "These people are simply focused on making money while creating what they believe will be a better future for humanity."

"But how can our future be better if it's built on the exploitation of vulnerable people?" asks Peter.

"They think it will be. Who are you to say otherwise?"

"Who am—who am I? I'm a Christian. Isn't that enough?"

She nods Her approval. "It is." She continues, "While better technology can help create a better future, it cannot replace the human soul. So the question is this: When humans head out there, what will they take with them? Selfishness, violence, and a belief that the universe is theirs to rape? Or knowledge that all creation 'belongs to God,' which is to say that it reflects a higher transcendent reality? Will they go out there with seeds of wisdom and love—a wisdom and love that cannot thrive in a culture that reviles all so-called 'metafiz'?"

"You're saying metafiz—spirituality—is necessary for morality?"

"Not exactly. Individuals and groups can be very moral without faith in transcendent reality, there is no question about that. But, in the long term, a moral *culture* requires spirituality. Morality without spirituality ultimately becomes untethered. It cannot sustain itself generation after generation. That's a major reason why we've seen a resurgence of organized human rights abuses across the System. Human civilization has been spending down its moral capital. Without dynamic, meaningful, true spiritual stories, everything eventually comes down to competition and economics, eroding the moral underpinnings of a society. There is no check on the materialistic culture of status, accumulation, and exploitation."

Peter takes a deep breath. His feels his head throb. "So it's our responsibility to convert the System before this soon-to-be explosion happens? Sophia, if I spent the rest of my life, I couldn't convert most of the people in this exhibit hall, much less most of the System."

"Fear not, Bishop. It's not all on your shoulders. It never was. God is at work all around the System, not only at Grace Cathedral. The Christian church will have an important role, but not the only one."

"It feels like we'll be lucky if some group like the International Christian Capitalist Club doesn't manage to shut us down."

"You'll find that neither the ICCC nor the Sanef tax assessor will have the power to 'shut down' the Christian church. Cease to worry about that. You will overcome greater challenges than these."

"Okay. If you say so, then I—I trust you. I'll stop worrying about it." Peter stares out the window. "So, you're showing me two sides of the same coin. Humanity is making dramatic technological progress, and soon it will enable us to set out for the stars. But we obliviously use infrastructures of cruelty to achieve our goals. People need to be shown the truth: that love is the heart beating at the center of reality . . . and that when we fail to reflect that love to others, we hurt our very selves. If people's hearts open to this truth, then perhaps we won't carry our sinful ways out into the universe."

"It is unlikely," Sophia says, "that *homo sapiens* will ever free itself entirely from chronic compulsions. Even impossibly well-programmed neurpro zombies probably couldn't achieve that ideal in this complicated branch of the Apple Orchard. But I am saying that human civilization needs the spiritual resources to grapple with brokenness, fear, and grasping desire. One should not send a child into the wilderness naked. Your descendants will need nourishment for their souls as well as their bodies."

Peter stares at Sophia and then lifts his eyes to the domed ceiling. Countless stars twinkle at him. "This is why you came now," he whispers. "This is a pivotal era in cosmic history."

"Your lives in history are so significant," She whispers in response. "Each person's every action will ripple out into a future of countless worlds. You will seed the very stars with what's in your hearts."

Peter holds his breath until Sophia takes him by the arm and pats it to calm him down. Leading him forward, She says, "In the meantime, let's grab a tofufurter."

He nods wordlessly as his eyes roam across the starry dome.

∾

"Burgundy."

"Carmine."

"Cardinal."

Frank often plays this game to pass the time. He thinks about how the Inuit people supposedly have dozens of different words for snow. On Meres, it's dozens of different shades of rust and red. A keen observer—or one with a lot of time on his hands—might pick out a fair number of different shades, depending on geology, the angle of the sun, and the amount of dust in the air.

"Falqin' oxblood," he says, peering at a particular spot on an outcropping. He drinks the last gulp of water from a disposable bottle and throws it over his shoulder into his vancruiser's empty storage compartment. It bounces off the floor and rebounds against the back wall. A spot of dried mustard adorns Frank's pink chin.

He belches. "Just as good coming up as it was going down."

He hasn't always talked to himself out loud, but long days alone in the wilderness have a way of inviting it.

Frank chuckles. "I guess if ya think ya might be crazy, then you're not."

He checks the time. Days like this one are boring, but he doesn't have much to complain about. He just drives around the Gordii wilderness and gets paid better than he ever did back in North America when he held down jobs there. He's decent at bookkeeping, not bad at writing, and one hell of a bouncer, but he'd get lost in his stims and forget to show up to work. He can't afford to no-show at Gordii, though. *As boring as it is, this is the best gig I've ever had. Good pay, plenty to eat, and people mostly leave you alone.* He doesn't get privileges to the refugees like his boss does, but he has what he needs to get by, which is an unaccustomed feeling for Frank.

He's not allowed to stim on duty, of course. But he mentally replays this morning's victory as he drives his vancruiser through the wilderness. Inhabiting his favorite strategy stim, *Denunciation IV*, he took out eighty-three spectators in a football stadium—a personal record.

"Got some skills, hell yeah!"

But now, after so many hours unplugged, he's itching to get to the new stim in his queue. The Tharsis studio that made *Olympia's Mount* usually produces sexy damn stuff, so Frank has high expectations.

"Some hot digital personas will ride the Frank train tooonight."

He sighs and stares off into the distance. Frank's job is both easy and boring, for the same reason.

"No one ever falqin' comes out here."

Well, there was the time a couple of months before. A sandstorm buried a fallen length of fence, and a family got lost and accidentally freedrove onto company property. *A dad, a mom with a nice ass, two precious kiddies. I called the company assault team in on 'em just for the fun of seeing them scared out of their falqing minds, facedown in the dirt.*

"Electric crimson," he mumbles to himself, grinning at the memory. He glances in another direction. "Fire brick."

He checks the time. He plans to arrive back at headquarters at the earliest time he can credibly claim he completed his full patrol route. The prior week, he managed to get himself assigned to the vancruiser with the broken MGPS. That means headquarters currently has no clue where Frank actually goes while he's on patrol. *They just have to trust I'm doing my job by the book! Don't know how long I'll have until the damn thing gets repaired, but for now I'll milk it for all it's worth.*

Frank isn't worried about getting into trouble for failing to complete his assigned route—he likes his odds that nothing he can get blamed for is going to happen. His job is to monitor for external security threats, after all. In this goodforsaken desert, he's as likely to see a little green man as a real threat to the company. He certainly isn't one of the paranoids who thinks I. N. Daedalia is going to send agents to blow up headquarters. Frank has common sense, and he knows better than anyone that there's no one banging about out there.

So he speeds toward headquarters, swapping a shortcut for the northern loop of his assigned route. Forgetting about his color-naming game, he's already erect at the thought of plugging into his stim.

～

Sophia and Peter stopped for the night just south of Gordii. He's lying in his bunk, gazing across the aisle at Her slumbering form, lost in his thoughts.

Incarnate love. That's what She is to me.

After some minutes, he rolls over to face the other direction and tries to calm his breathing. As he finally begins to drift off, he hears a whimper.

She's having nightmares again.

He hears a rustling noise. As he looks over, Sophia sits down on the edge of Peter's bunk. She's shaking.

Peter quickly shifts himself around to sit next to Her. He wraps his arms around Her shoulders, and She holds onto him tightly.

"Are you okay?"

"Much better, thank you." She takes deep breaths in and out.

After a time, he says, "I'm surprised you're comfortable being close to a male like this, after all you've been through in your life." He grimaces. *Maybe I shouldn't have brought that up.*

She touches his hand. "I know the good and gentle when I see it."

"You know that's not really true. I'm so far from being who I'm supposed to be. I'm filled with pettiness and selfishness. And judgment. And fear."

"We're all broken," Sophia whispers. "We're all broken parts of the Whole. But when some of our broken edges fit together—well, then it's a foretaste of heaven, right here."

"*You're* broken?"

"I'm human, too, remember?" She sighs. "Thank you for your love." She kisses him lightly on the cheek and moves back to Her own bunk. She clicks off Her light, plunging the landhog into darkness for the first time. "Goodnight, Peter."

"Sophia? The dark—isn't it hard for you—?"

"Yes. But love redeems every divine descent into the dark depths."

After some moments, Peter mumbles, "Goodnight, Sophia." He still doesn't understand Her. But when he holds Her, he feels connected to everything.

Love!

19

Ecstasy

Sophia often appears in Peter's dreams, usually as a wise guide, occasionally as an intimidating presence, always through the eyes of a disciple. But that night's dreams cannot be called *pious*, nor even merely *romantic*. His dreams are *carnal*. Tangled bodies touch one another in the manner of lovers.

Peter wakes up facing the far wall of his sleeping nook. Daylight streams into the landhog through the front windows. He doesn't hear any movement—perhaps She's still asleep, or, more likely, already outside. He turns over quietly, hopeful he can get to the washroom without Her noticing the embarrassing physical manifestation of his arousal.

But She's still in Her bunk, awake. She's lying on Her side, facing him and propping Her head up on one arm. The sunlight refracts through Her mussed-up hair. Her radiant face and bright eyes cause him to stiffen further.

"Uh, morning," he says. His blankets cover him, but he can't stay under them forever.

"Good morning. Did you sleep well?"

"Pretty well."

"Me, too."

Peter glances at the time. "It's almost nine."

"We needed the extra rest." Sophia sits up, brings Her feet down to the floor, and stretches Her arms. Her modest nightshirt slides up to Her knees, and Peter finds himself staring at Her calves. He wants so badly to touch Her.

She notices his gaze. "What are you thinking about?"

"Uh—" The heat rises in his face. He does not want to lie to Her. "I was just admiring . . . your legs."

"I see." She doesn't miss a beat. "There is a desire deep within you. Do you long for my intimate touch?"

Peter's eyes widen. *Is She suggesting what I think She's suggesting?* He sits up, allowing the blanket to fall where it may. Struggling to catch his breath, he takes Her hand. "I do—I do long for your intimate touch."

"This evening, then."

"Oh, uh—evening? *This* evening?"

She nods, and he thinks his heart will pound out of his chest. He can't speak, so he wordlessly kisses Her hand.

She stands up. "In the meantime, there's nothing worse than an idle cleric on a Sunday morning. I am going to work on something here. You should take a walk."

"A walk? Can't I help you?" Peter has gotten used to the pattern of the last three days. *No morning lesson. Today will be different—in more ways than one, it would seem!*

"You will, later. For now, go for a walk in the wilderness and pray. And take a swimsuit."

"A swimsuit!?"

"I hear there's a swimming pool in the village only three or four kay from here. But please be back by around fourteen in the afternoon."

After a stop in the washroom, Peter eats a snack and accesses the village's coordinates. He puts a few things into his backpack, clips air cartridges onto his belt, bids farewell to Sophia, and walks out into the desert. It's not easy for Peter to pull himself away from Sophia, but he knows he could use some space to mull over everything he's feeling.

Her "intimate touch." This evening!

He takes a meandering path to kill time. The landscape offers few sights apart from cracked regolith and an occasional rock covered by the genengineered gray lichen the terraformers released into the wild. Peter has no reason to doubt Sophia's prediction that Meres will someday blossom into a magnificent "garden world." Presently, though, the plains south of Gordii Dorsum stand as a bleak monument to barren monotony.

About a kilometer from the village's coordinates, Peter begins crossing a ravine where steady winds have piled up long, rusty drifts of dust. As he wades into a drift, he finds himself sinking in past his knees. He imagines himself getting trapped in some Merian version of quicksand. *That sounds like the kind of fix I would get myself into. I've already gotten enough attention on Meres!* He can envision the netstory header: "Nun-Stopping Halibut Drowns in Turf." With this thought in mind, Peter retraces his steps to extricate himself from the drift and picks out a better path toward the village.

He checks the time. It's only half past eleven. Sophia will not expect him back for another few hours.

Sophia.

I'm so confused. Who am I to hope to have Her for myself? She's not just any feme. She's, well, She's . . . Who is She, really? Is it a sin for me to imagine being with Her—to want Her in this way?

He tries to put aside his desire and to reflect objectively on Dorcas's question about Sophia's identity. *Sophia is so filled with the wisdom of God— with the Holy Spirit. Is there any difference between Sophia being flesh filled with the Holy Spirit and Sophia being the Holy Spirit in the flesh?* That level of angels-dancing-on-heads-of-pins threatens to give Peter a headache. *Can there even be a "correct" theological answer to such a question?* Whatever the merits of Peter's studies in religion, they certainly did not prepare him to answer it.

Over the next rise in the land, Peter sees the promised village, a mul-tihued oasis in the boundless ocean of rusty Merian reds. On the eastern side of the village, a large holoprojection displays "SWIMMING POOL ENTRANCE HERE!" in both English and a script that looks like Indian Devanagari. Peter has no idea how many swimming pools exist on Meres, but plainly this one has the status of a local tourist attraction.

Some vehicles are parked out in front, but he sees no one else outside. He crunches through red dirt toward the entrance until he sees a mesh curtain. As soon as he walks through the curtain and loses his nanos, warm, humid air caresses his face, and his nose encounters a familiar smell. Unlike the pungent tropical scents of Eden, this smell leaps right out of Peter's own childhood. *Ah, the stuff they use to disinfect pools. It reminds me of going swimming during the summers when I was growing up.* Childish screams and peals of laughter reverberate through the hall. *They must keep the tempera-ture at twenty-six or twenty-seven degrees C in here—quite a difference from the negative twenty outside.*

Peter interacts with the automated teller in the building's entryway. As he finishes paying, a large, rambunctious family enters through the mesh behind him. Peter nods at the harried mother and enters the main hall. Glancing around, he guesses there are seventy or eighty people in and around the pool. The floor's blue tiling gives the hall the feel of an earthside swimming facility.

The similarity ends with the pool itself, which is completely ringed with transparent plexiglass walls. On each side, one can enter through a swinging door. To Peter, it looks more like a huge aquarium than the swimming pool where he played during his own childhood. A man jumps into the pool, and Peter realizes why the walls are there: droplets of water shoot up higher than Peter's eyes expect. *Of course—the weaker gravity. If there were no walls, everyone sitting around the pool would constantly get drenched.*

Peter locates a changing room and emerges minutes later wearing only a pair of faded athletic shorts, the closest thing to a swimsuit he has among the clothes he brought to Meres. Self-consciously, he walks toward the nearest entrance to the pool. He happens to glance to his left and notice a feme in a one-piece swimsuit walking away from him. For a split second, Peter thinks the feme is Sophia—maybe She wanted to surprise him?

But then the feme turns her head. She is not Her. He shakes his head and grins at himself.

He enters the pool area through one of the plexiglass doors and finds himself in a hurricane. Several children are having a splash war in that part of the pool, and water is flying everywhere. Fleeing the spray of water, Peter scuttles around the rim of the pool to find a drier spot.

People seem friendlier out in the country—several people nod at him in greeting. He manages to find a relatively calm corner, and he sits down, tentatively lowering his legs into the temperate water. The diving board at the other end of the pool looks frighteningly high. A teenager leaps from it and falls too slowly for Peter's Earther eyes.

Peter moves his calves back and forth in the water. *Well, what now? I have no idea why Sophia suggested I come to the swimming pool. Maybe I should spend some time in prayer.* He stills himself, bows his head, and begins to pray.

Almighty God, you—

(*No, that's just part of it.*)

Almighty, All-vulnerable, and All-embracing God . . .

(*Better.*)

. . . you are so good. Sophia has helped me to understand your goodness. When I ascribed anger and coldness and rigidity to you, I was painting you with the colors of my own brokenness! Your blessings upon me have been greater than I could ever—

A loud giggle in Peter's ear startles him, almost causing him to pitch forward into the pool. As his eyes snap open, the giggling stops. The dimpled face of a little girl hovers about ten centimeters from Peter's own face. Her huge brown eyes are open wide.

"You shouldn't sneak up on people like that!"

Unmoved by Peter's admonition, the girl smiles at him with no fear or hesitation.

Peter leans back and inspects the child. Her face looks like that of a three or four year-old, but she's taller than Peter would expect for that age. *Perhaps because she's grown up in the Merian g?* Her dark hair spills out in wild curls. Something in Peter's face must intrigue the child, because she continues to smile at him with undisguised delight.

We adults are hardly ever free enough to look at someone with such open innocence, he muses. The child's undefended openness begins to embarrass him.

"And, what's your name?"

She giggles. "Shakti."

"Nice to meet you."

I don't know what Sophia wanted me to see here, Peter muses. *But what teaching or idea could be more special, more of a miracle, than the reality of this precious child sitting before me?*

A tall woman walks over and addresses the girl: "Daughter, are you bothering this nice citizen?"

Shakti shakes her head, still staring at Peter.

The woman picks the girl up in her arms. "She can be overly friendly," she says to Peter as the girl giggles some more.

"She is friendly, indeed. What a sweet child."

"You're not from the village."

"No, I live in a nation in the western part of North America. My, my companion and I are camping a few kay south of here. She suggested I try the swimming pool."

Suave. I made it sound like She wanted to get rid of me. Well, I guess She did, actually.

"This is the only swimming pool between Kistrob and Bonaventura," the woman says, "so we get a lot of visitors. Anyway, welcome to Meres. I'm sure you will find it to be an interesting place."

Peter laughs out loud. "Daresay I already have."

The woman raises an eyebrow but refrains from asking for details. Shakti tugs on her arm and says, "Swim!" The woman gives Peter a polite smile, then she puts her daughter down and they jump in, creating a splash that raises goose bumps on Peter's bare chest.

He leans back and stretches his legs farther into the water. He remains at the pool's edge for a timeless interval, even as the pool area fills up with even more people. A deep contentment grows within him as he gazes out on the scene. The adults gab; the children splash; the toddlers toddle; the water laps against the side of the pool in chaotic little swells.

My God, Peter thinks. *This could be a scene anywhere there are humans. Whether you're big or small, dark or fair, born on Earth or Meres, so much is the same: childish joy, the energy of play, feminine and masculine beauty, love among families, dancing pulsating life!*

Something happens.

Oh! It's so beautiful. Sophia!

Peter's body shakes as he grabs onto the pool's lip.

It's 14:30 by the time he returns to the landhog—half an hour later than Sophia requested. She appears unconcerned, which momentarily disappoints him. He sits down with Her at the table and tries to explain what happened.

"... And as I sat there by the pool, what I had thought were individual people and actions and events I started to perceive as patterns—like it was all connected in one unified whole. It was as though the people were molecules in some great wave moving through time." He shrugs. "I mean, maybe the fact that I was looking at water made me think of that. But anyway, I just suddenly felt very strongly that—that—"

"Yes?"

"I felt very strongly that it was all part of *one life.* And it was so beautiful. I felt overwhelmed by love and joy. I felt a surge of energy almost like—almost like some sort of—"

"Of?"

"Well—just—well, it was like—like—" He sighs. "Well, it was like a full-body orgasm. I don't know how else to put it. It wasn't really sexual or—pelvic. But there was a release of energy into my whole body that overwhelmed me."

"This feeling is called an 'ecstatic experience.'"

"Oh. I've heard of that, but I've never, I've never—" He pauses. "Does that mean I had a 'revelation'?"

"An ecstatic experience may accompany a genuine insight into truth, but it does not guarantee that your insight is truthful. It says more about you than about the thoughts you were having."

"About me?"

"It's a sign that your yearning for the Eternal has engaged not only your mind but also something deeper, more embodied. We might call it 'the heart.'"

Peter stares at Her. Finally, he bursts out: "Sophia, *you've* engaged my heart!"

Her expression does not change, but She pats him on the hand. "Reflect on this profound unity you sensed. It is un-self-interested adoration which brings us into contact with such an intuition."

"Un-self-interested adoration?"

"Nearly all of the time, we judge what we encounter by our own needs. 'Is this person or thing useful to me or to the people I care about? Is it pleasant to us? What do I like about it? What don't I?' But when we can step back from our calculating minds, reserve judgment, and appreciate beauty for its own sake, then we may open ourselves to a fuller truth. We may find that we can look beyond the twists and turns of our own wandering path. In holding to the central unity, we can value and enjoy the varied, colorful life of the All."

Sophia's words trigger a memory for Peter: the two of them looking out at the world from the center of Grace Cathedral's outdoor labyrinth.

"Peter, early Christianity has frequently tried to place group loyalty or divine wrath at the center of reality. Driven by human fears and prejudices, you often portrayed God as angry and petty—as a bully who plays favorites. This painted God in an image of mortal brokenness instead of helping to shape mortal existence into an image of God's wholeness."

"Yes, yes." Peter nods as he thinks, *That's what I was praying about at the pool, when the little girl interrupted—*

"Hear me," Sophia commands. "You, Peter, have begun to step beyond the 'morning' of faith. It is time for the Christian church as a whole to do the same: to taste and see the truths of God's vast abundance, deep presence, and incarnate love. It is time for the Church to step fully into the 'afternoon,' where churches are not just clubs or clans or places that teach mere beliefs, but schools of love. Actually, it has been past time for a long, long while now."

He feels as if he's on the verge of tears. "I think I'm starting to understand now—about where the Church has been and where it can go. Thank you for showing me this. I have so much more to learn from you."

Sophia glances at the time. "We need to go. Time is running out."

Peter's joy abruptly turns to concern. "Wha—what do you mean?"

"I mean our time is short."

"Sophia—"

"Come, Peter."

The landhog takes them northward, targeting coordinates Sophia entered into the MGPS. She gently rebuffs Peter's questions. At a certain point in the journey, She says, "Would you mind giving me a few minutes of solitude?"

"Um, sure." Peter slides out of the driving compartment and goes to his bunk. *At least this will give me a chance to chew on Sophia's teachings some more.* In an attempt to summarize the most important points from Her lessons, he enters the following notes in his personal journal:

<u>3/11</u>

God's vast abundance (the "what" of God?), deep presence (the "how"??), and incarnate love (the "why"?) . . . maybe these are the broad standards for true, healthy religion I was looking for! She seems to be saying they're fundamental to the character of God (and thus reality), regardless what symbols and images one may use to visualize Him/Her.

Individually, each of these things seems like total "pie in the sky"— too good and too big to be true. But when I put them together, they begin to explain things I couldn't explain before, like why a good God would allow evil to exist. If our world had no potential for sin or suffering, it would be a different world (an "Angelic Magnificence" tree instead of a "Variety H. Sapiens" tree, so to speak). I'm starting to think the idea of "original sin" makes sense as a way of describing our "origin" in this particular (beloved but difficult) world—a world subject to scarcity, brokenness, and the brutality of natural selection. We live in a world that's deeply imperfect. But that's not some big mistake we could have avoided; our tree in the Apple Orchard was cultivated that way. It's also full of unique beauty and potential.

If what She has taught me is true—if, as I believe, She really can be trusted and isn't crazy or a grifter—well, then it changes everything, including the way humans relate to one another and to non-human creatures and the natural world. It provides an amazing way of seeing God, a way to breathe new life into the Gospel I have been trying, and failing, to teach.

But She still hasn't shed any light on the doctrine of the Holy Trinity (the "who" of God??) and how She might fit in. I hope She will soon.

Peter says a quick prayer and then continues.

About the Church: "Early" (!) Christianity has been largely in the morning: religion was often used for instrumental or authoritarian (even colonial!) purposes; "chronic compulsions" still dominated and sometimes even masked themselves as religion. It's well past time, says Sophia, to move into the afternoon: where the Church is really helping to teach people to fully participate in the joy and suffering around them (applying the teachings about vast abundance, deep presence, and incarnate love). Where churches are "schools of love."

*Speaking of love . . . I am in love with Her. Yes, I'm in love with
Sophia! I don't care if it makes sense.*

Peter rubs his eyes. He almost deletes the last paragraph. *I sound like a
teenager.* But it's the truth in his heart, so he leaves it.

Absorbed in his symbols, Peter doesn't see the signs. Nor does he
observe the fences or notice the moment when Sophia slows the landhog
and provides a code to open a heavy automatic gate topped with curls of
razor wire. Having missed it all, Peter stands up and pokes his head into the
driving compartment. The dusty, rusty road disappears steadily under the
landhog's tread.

"Mind if I come back in?"

"Please," She says. "Is everything all right back there?"

"I was just thinking about the lessons you've been teaching me."

"Ah. I could be very direct with you because you have already struggled
with these ideas and concerns. To reach others, you will usually have to use
more parables and stories."

"Like Jesus did."

"Indeed. Even his death was a parable." Sophia takes a deep breath and
points to the right. "There's a nice view from this stretch."

Peter looks out across the plain. "We've gained altitude. You've taken
us quite a ways across Gordii."

"Yes, we're almost to the spot I'm looking for."

"You've done a lot of planning for this trip."

She glances at him but does not reply.

Shortly thereafter, Sophia takes the landhog off-road and parks it
about forty meters to the west of a steep cliff. She shuts off the drive and sits
quietly. In the silence, Peter stares at Her until She meets his gaze.

"I need to go outside," She says.

"I'll come with you. I just need to step into the washroom first."

She nods and steps through the driver-side mesh curtain.

As Peter exits the washroom a couple of minutes later, he hears a soft
beeping. He walks over to the driving compartment and finds that a voice
message has just arrived for him.

It's from Uncle Jeff.

He scans the panorama beyond the landhog's front windows. Sophia
stands near the edge of the cliff, calmly gazing at the valley below. Peter cues
up the message:

*Peter, this is Jeff. Where are you now, exactly? I heard from Dorcas
Williams that that feme took you to some desert and has you there
alone.*

Look, you're a grownup, and I know it's not my place to meddle in your life. I know you want to believe that this feme, this Jasmine, is here to save your church, and I do understand why, I really do. I've never subscribed to metafiz, of course, but I can see how it might be beautiful. In my younger days, I was quite taken with the poetry of some of it. "The Way that can be told is not the eternal Way" and that sort of thing. Later, I could see how metafiz— "faith," I mean—animated your mother, how it helped make her the amazing person she was. And I know how much you loved her. I know you would do anything to protect her legacy.

But, Peter, there's something wrong *here. And I'm afraid you're in so deep you can't see it.*

Has it occurred to you that Jasmine made all these people in Sanef think she's some kind of deity and then just abandoned them without so much as a "see you later"? Have you thought for a nano-second about how they feel, waiting and wondering if you two are ever coming back from your outer-space honeymoon? How could any responsible, rational leader do something so sociopathic to her "disciples"? I mean, is this something G-Zeu—Jesus would have done?

Son, if a ro-feme is giving a ro-male sex, it can be hard for him to see that she might be unstable, that she might be manipulating him to achieve some hidden agend—

Peter angrily deletes the message. *You have no damn clue what you're trying to nose your way into. You could never understand the depths you're trivializing.* Out loud, Peter mutters, "For a genius, you sure can be an idiot sometimes."

He takes several deep breaths to collect his emotions, then he exits the landhog. Sophia is still standing near the edge of the cliff. Her back is turned to Peter. As he approaches, he sees that She is standing less than a meter from the edge. She's staring ahead and seems to be rocking forward. An alarm sounds in his mind.

He runs over to Her and grabs Her by the arm.

She starts. "What are you doing?"

"Why are you getting so close to the edge!?"

She stares at him blankly.

"You have no idea whether this cliff is stable!" He pulls Sophia farther from the edge—and closer to himself.

She looks at him curiously but does not pull away. They gaze out over the plain below in silence. Peter's arm tingles where it encircles Sophia's shoulders.

After several quiet minutes, She says, "Let's get comfortable and make a meal."

"It's a little early for dinner."

"I know, but it may be our last chance."

Before he can ask what She means, She takes his hand and says, "Follow me." She leads him back inside the landhog, then She steps into the washroom to change. When She emerges, he feels his breath catch in his throat. She's wearing the same button-up blouse he remembers from their first trip together to the redwoods.

He has never seen Her use cosmetics or anything he thinks of as feme beauty tricks, yet Sophia radiates feminine grace. He gazes at Her eyes, Her hair, Her lips. Even the scar on Her face somehow accentuates Her allure to Peter. He just wants to kiss Her, to touch Her. The force of his desire extinguishes the faint alarm still echoing at the back of his mind.

They sit down to a simple but enjoyable meal, and they talk about their friends in Sanef and various unimportant things. All the while, Peter mentally tracks the sun's agonizingly slow descent toward the horizon. Notwithstanding his impatience, Peter cannot remember anything ever tasting better than those simple rations as he basks in the heat of his longing to experience Her "intimate touch."

In later years, his memory will occasionally return to that final supper in the desert, and he'll shudder at his former self's naiveté—his failure to understand the truth of her.

20

Betrayal

They stand up to clear the dishes from the table. His heart pounds, and he's barely able to pull his eyes away from Her. He has become intensely aware of Her nearness, Her scent, their isolation together in the wilderness . . .

As they work side by side in the galley putting things away, his hand brushes against Her arm.

"Sophia," he whispers.

She sets down a plate. Her eyes meet his.

"I have to tell you how I feel," he says. "I love you."

"Oh, Peter." She wraps Her arms around him and pulls him into a tight hug. "And I love you more than you love yourself."

Huh?

Hearing the familiar phrase prompts him to pull back from Her embrace. He stammers, "Sophia, I am so. So confused. Is—is that a feme speaking to a male? Or is it meant to be God speaking to my soul? Or God—the Holy Spirit?—speaking to the Church?" Without intending it, Peter repeats Saint Francis's venerable prayer: "*Who are you, and who am I?*"

She touches his cheek. Slowly, She begins to whisper, "I am—"

"ATTENTION, TRESPASSERS," interrupts a man's voice, booming over the landhog's radio.

Peter flinches, and Sophia's eyes widen.

"YOU HAVE ONE MINUTE TO EXIT THE VEHICLE. COME OUT WITH YOUR HANDS RAISED AND NOTHING IN 'EM."

Sophia glances at the time as a worried expression creases Her face. Her eyes move to the security screen, and Peter's follow. It occurs to him that he doesn't know how to adjust the display. Fortunately, the landhog's external security cameras automatically track the owner of the voice blaring over the radio. The screen displays a lone man standing in front of a vehicle parked twenty or thirty meters from the landhog. He's holding a weapon in his hand.

"He's not supposed to be here now," Sophia whispers.

"THIRTY SECONDS."

The man appears to be wearing some sort of uniform, and Peter relaxes slightly. "I'm sure this is just a misunderstanding," he says, straightening. "I'll go out and talk to this officer and find out what the problem—"

Sophia grabs Peter's sleeve to hold him in place. The man on the screen is holding his weapon in his right hand, and he's slowly raising his left hand toward his temple.

The screen's sound and video blank out, displaying only the words "LOSS OF SIGNAL—HIGH SOLAR ACTIVITY." Peter tentatively taps the screen. After a few seconds, it snaps back on.

"FIFTEEN SECONDS."

Sophia abruptly turns toward Peter. "Listen to me. Do you trust me?" She doesn't wait for an answer. "Stay out of sight, no matter what. *No matter what.*" With that, She strides over to the living compartment's mesh curtain and steps out of the landhog onto the surface.

Confused by Her sudden exit, Peter whirls around to look at the screen, which has now automatically adjusted to display Sophia as well as the armed man. The man is holding his left hand near his temple, and he's still holding his weapon in his right hand, now pointed at Sophia's heart. She stands unmoving in the man's line of sight, completely defenseless. As everyone on Meres knows, nanomesh is decidedly not weapon-proof.

The screen blanks out again. In the silence, a sickening thought comes to Peter. *She's courting death. She thinks She needs to sacrifice Her life. Like Jesus.*

"My God!" he yells.

Time slows as he moves toward the mesh curtain to grab Her and pull Her back in. To stop whatever is about to happen. To save Her.

Then it happens. The screen image pops back on, and Sophia's voice wafts over the feed. "Hello." She speaks calmly, even breezily, and the hint of a Tennissippi lilt has crept into Her voice. "To what do I owe this visit?"

The very ordinariness of Sophia's words manages to bring Peter to a halt near the mesh curtain. Still hidden from view inside the landhog, he turns back toward the screen. Several seconds of silence pass. Then Sophia nods at the weapon. "Do you pull that thing out every time you meet a woman?" The man lowers his weapon, and Sophia takes a step toward him.

The screen cuts out once more. Peter taps it, harder this time. When nothing happens, he slams his palm against it, to no avail.

What's happening? What should I do? Why did Sophia tell me not to come out "no matter what"? What is She saying to that man?

Once again, Peter moves toward the living compartment's mesh curtain, but then he stops. He could try to look out the windows in the driving compartment, but that would place him directly in the man's line of sight. Peter sways back and forth with indecision until he finally returns to the screen and starts desperately looking for a setting that will fix what's wrong.

After further agonizing moments, the screen crackles back to life and shows the male and Sophia standing next to the male's vehicle, kissing. He's caressing Her, and She's not raising a hand to stop him. "Nanos gettin' in our way," Peter hears the male say.

The male leads Sophia through the mesh curtain near the back of his vehicle. She never looks back at the landhog.

Overcome by shock, jealousy, and a sense of betrayal, Peter slouches against a wall. He slides down to the floor and holds his head in his trembling hands.

Frank's hand is poised near his temple. He was about to open a channel to headquarters to call in the assault team, but the feme's emergence makes him hesitate. *What the falq do we have here?*

"Hello," she says. "To what do I owe this visit?"

Frank gapes at the lone feme, and it begins to dawn on him that he may have gotten very lucky. He holds his hands steady—both the one still poised near his temple and the one pointing his weapon at the feme's chest.

She nods at the weapon. "Do you pull that thing out every time you meet a woman?"

Frank looks down at his weapon, then at the feme, then back at his weapon. After some moments, he slowly lowers it to a forty-five-degree angle, ready to raise it again instantly.

The feme takes two steps toward him.

"You're on private property," Frank belts out in his sternest as-far-as-you-know-I'm-a-real-important-powerful-official-guy voice. "You're breaking the law. I could get you in big trouble." As he speaks, he lowers his hand from his temple and looks the feme's body up and down. He gives the scar on her jaw an appraising stare. Then he looks her body up and down again.

Sophia takes another step toward him, closing the distance between them to only two meters. "I don't want to get into trouble. I'm camping out here in this desert. It's a good place to get away from it all. Please forgive me if I'm not supposed to be here."

Nice tits. Overall about a seven, but she's a seven point five if I ignore the scar. More than a passing grade, no question. Aloud he says, "You're not from Amazonis, are ya?"

She shakes her head.

"Anybody else with you out here?" He unconsciously raises his left hand back toward his temple.

"It's just you and me out here." She opens her arms as if to take in the wide-open spaces surrounding them. Then she cocks her head and stares intently at Frank. "I am pleased that a man of integrity arrived to help me." She continues to give him a probing stare as if she's waiting for a particular response.

Frank smirks at the feme's babbling. *She's not even making sense.* He glances at the landhog. *Seems like a looney lost lowcontrib who I'd bet a thousand is running contraband in her vehicle.* He runs his eyes up and down her body again.

"I'm sure you'll understand I have to follow protocols. Your hands." He pulls a wrist restraint from his belt and gestures at her to turn around and extend her hands backward behind her. She hesitates for a moment and then complies, clenching and unclenching her fists. He binds her wrists behind her, glancing in several directions as he does. An erection now visibly tents the front of his pants.

He mutters into her ear from behind her back, gripping her restrained hands. "You're not lying to me about being alone out here, are ya, sweetheart? If I thought you were lying, I'd have to call in backup and search your vehicle. And I don't think you'd like that."

The feme takes a ragged breath. "You don't need to call anyone."

Frank stands still for several seconds, thinking hard. *She's not even trying to fight me off, so how could she say she didn't consent? Even if a falqing lawyer would disagree, I can't think of any way this wayward lowcontrib could get me in trouble—not for something that happens here on company property.*

Still holding her from behind, Frank leans in. Their nanos merge as he sniffs her hair—it smells good.

He makes his decision.

"Now I'll need to inspect your person," he says, jerking her close. "It'll have to be a very thorough inspection, I'm afraid."

He feels the feme shiver, and he pulls her over to his vancruiser. He pushes her against it, grabs her breasts, and presses his mouth against hers. "Nanos gettin' in our way," he says with a wink. He pulls her into the vancruiser's storage compartment.

Peter lies on his back on the landhog's floor and stares vacantly at the ceiling. Memories flash through his mind . . . the day she uncovered the labyrinth . . . the first time they went hiking in the redwoods . . . her sitting by his hospital bed in Kistrob. *Did any of it mean anything?*

Why was she kissing that male? Is this the real reason she brought me to Meres . . . to fund her trip so she could reunite with her lover? And she didn't want him to see she came with another male? What are they doing in there together? Has she played me for a fool this whole time? My God, was it all a lie?

Immobilized by uncertainty, he replays these thoughts over and over. Each fruitless iteration pushes him deeper into a green pit of despairing jealousy.

When Sophia finally steps back out of the vancruiser, she's clothed only in Frank's stained undershirt, which barely covers her. The nanos pull it close to her skin. Passing an air cartridge between her hands, she rubs her bare wrists and stares out at the long shadows.

The vancruiser begins to move. It maneuvers to the road and speeds off, kicking up a jagged wake of dust. When it is no longer in sight, she drops onto her hands and knees. Racking sobs seize her, and the nanos begin a delicate dance to transport the moisture from her face to the ground beneath her without causing decompression. Her tears flow down a small incline, reddening from the Merian dust until they pool into tiny crimson puddles.

The wind itself moans. For several minutes, Sophia cries there, alone, on her hands and knees. Then she sits back, wraps her arms around herself, and takes deep breaths.

His head jerks up anxiously when she steps back into the landhog. But when he sees her wearing only a male's undershirt, his blood burns hot in his ears and he feels his body shake. He doesn't get up off the floor.

Without speaking, she opens a storage bin and pulls some things out. She walks into the washroom and closes the door behind her. He hears the shower run.

After some time, she emerges with wet hair, dressed in a utilitarian khaki coverall that covers everything but her bare hands and feet. An air cartridge hangs from the coverall's waist. She pulls on socks and boots and approaches him. He's still slouched in misery on the landhog's floor.

Peter cannot bring himself to look at Jasmine.

"Peter, listen to me. You've misunderstood—"

"I've misunderstood? No, I understand!" Adrenaline courses through his veins. "How dare you lecture me! Don't you dare tell me anymore what I don't understand! Here's what I understand. You steal from us, you fool us into thinking that fixing some luminors is a miracle, and now this!"

Through gritted teeth, she says, "I can tell you, this was not what I planned—"

Peter leaps to his feet. "Well, it's sure as hell not what I planned either. *I planned* for you *not* to be a liar who dragged me here just so you could meet up with your lover. *I planned* for you *not* to be a demented con artist, fooling my friends and half of Sanef into thinking you were *so holy*, that you were Holiness itself. *I planned* that we—that we—" He stammers to a mortified halt, and a thick silence envelopes the landhog.

She breaks the silence. "I know you're confused and hurting. I very much wish . . ." Her lower lip quivers. ". . . that this hadn't happened, I can promise you that. But it did. And I have good reasons for the choice I made, if you can trust me enough to hear them."

Peter shakes his head back and forth. Red-faced, he's barely breathing.

She sighs. Reaching into a pocket, she pulls out a pair of metal keys and holds them out to him.

He stares at them blankly. He eventually recognizes them as the keys to the tabernacle at Grace, but he does not extend his hand. He doesn't want to touch her.

She carefully places the keys on the table. Then she glances at the time and walks over to her bunk. She sits down on it and bows her head.

The thought that Jasmine might be praying to God revolts Peter. He turns abruptly and climbs into the driving compartment, where he sits down stiffly in the driver's seat and stares at the vehicle's controls. *Everything is screwed up. Everything is broken.* A tear rolls down his cheek, and he practically slaps it away. *No way I'll let that lying psychopath see me cry.*

Peter attempts to focus on the controls, but his vision is blurred. He leans back and tries to breathe. *I've got to get away from her!* But that means he'll have to freedrive the landhog back to the trunk road. He momentarily considers just getting out and walking back to the village with the swimming pool. Surely, he could catch a ride to Kistrob from there?

Back to Kistrob—and then what? Back home to Sanef? What will Peter tell the Christians? What will he tell the catechumens? *Hi, I'm back. Your savior led me on and then screwed around with some guy, so I left her on another planet. But it's okay, because I'm pretty sure she was always just a fraud and a liar. Lemonade, anyone?*

Holy hell.

And then, after *that*? Could he ever go back to worshipping the God Jasmine had come to embody, however absurdly? What about her assurance that the Church would survive the threats against it? A lie? What about her lessons? What's Peter to do with them, now? What's Peter to do with *himself*? How could he ever again pretend to be "Bishop Peter"?

Who am I now?

He shakes his head and rubs moisture from his eyes. Then he sits up straight. *One step at a time. Get back to Kistrob and away from her. Then decide what to do from there.* The controls no longer swim in Peter's vision. He reaches out to activate the drive system.

The landhog's radio captures a signal, and a girl's panicked voice bursts in: "Help! Sophia! Help! Oh help, please help!"

21

Trinity

She darts into the driving compartment and slides into the passenger seat. Before Peter can react, she says "There!" and points out one of the front windows.

Peter's gaze grudgingly follows Jasmine's finger. He sees a figure in the distance, perhaps a hundred meters away. The unearthly curve of the Merian horizon still makes it hard to gauge the exact distance. The figure looks like an obese person.

"Come on," Jasmine says. In a flash, she passes through the passenger-side mesh curtain and out onto the surface.

Peter looks once more at the figure in the distance, then he stares at Jasmine rushing toward it. He sits there in silence for several heartbeats while megahurricanes of questions and emotions swirl through his mind. Then he takes a deep breath and makes his decision.

He runs into the living compartment, grabs an air cartridge, and follows Jasmine onto the surface.

The girl's voice comes again, fed into Peter's ears by the nanos. "I see you. I see you! Oh, is that you?"

"It's me. It's Sophia," Jasmine's voice replies.

"Thank good you came! Oh! Help!" The girl spits out panicked words between rapid breaths. "My brother is suffocating! My dad fell back behind us. He said to go on and get help, help for my brother."

Jasmine reaches the girl while Peter is still about thirty meters behind her. What from a distance looked like a large person is actually a scraggy teenage girl. She's wearing a bulky pressure suit and carrying a child who wears a somewhat smaller one.

Jasmine takes the child from the girl's arms, turns, and rushes back toward the landhog, bounding faster than Peter has seen anyone move in the Merian g. The nanos transmit her voice to Peter's ears. "The girl can get herself to the landhog. Look for her father."

Peter grunts. He gets his stride and heads in the direction from which the girl came. After just a minute, he reaches an outcropping. Behind it, he finds a man in a pressure suit struggling on his hands and knees.

"My name is Peter. I'm here to, to help you."

With an effort, the man nods at Peter, who lifts him in his arms. Thanks to the Merian g, Peter crosses the distance to the landhog rapidly despite carrying a full-grown man. Although weight is different on Meres, inertia is not—in his haste, Peter almost throws the man against the side of the landhog. Peter manages to stop their forward momentum with a boot to the vehicle. He enters through the living compartment's mesh curtain, which strips off the layer of nanos that protected him on the surface. The girl has already made it inside on her own power, joining Jasmine and the unconscious child.

Before Peter can even set the man down, he registers Jasmine yelling, "Peter, help! He's not breathing!" The boy lies face-up on the galley floor. Jasmine has removed his helmet, and his face has a bluish cast.

The man in Peter's arms grabs his shoulders. "Put me down!" Peter drops the man's legs, and the man stands uneasily, tightly gripping a handrail for support.

As the man begins pulling his helmet off, Peter kneels by the boy and starts working to free the boy from his pressure suit. "Unlatch that quick-release over there," Peter commands Jasmine. They hurriedly pull off the part of the clunky old suit covering the boy's torso. Peter begins performing CPR.

Pump. Pump. Pump. Pump . . .
Breathe. Breathe.
Pump. Pump. Pump. Pump . . .
Breathe. Breathe.
Pump. Pump. Pump. Pump . . .
Breathe!

Peter loses track of how long it's gone on. Maybe two minutes, maybe three, maybe longer. "Dammit, he's not responding," Peter mutters. Even with his renewed adrenaline rush, he can feel his arms tiring.

"Oh bubbie!" the girl cries. She babbles to Jasmine between gasps. "His suit. It started low on air. I guess they don't use the smallest one much. But we didn't have any choice! We had to go. Oh bubbie!"

Peter stops and feels for a pulse. *He's dead.* He looks up at them and shakes his head.

The sister wails loudly, and the father moans, "Russ, Russ, my boy! My Russ, my son, my only son!"

Peter puts a hand to his own cheek and discovers it's wet. He stands up and shakily holds onto a handrail while his ears ring with the suffering of the boy's father and sister. He sees Jasmine reach down and touch the corpse's face in a maternal gesture.

Just as Peter closes his eyes to try to regain some inner equilibrium, he hears a harsh gasp loud enough to be audible above the sounds of lamentation. He opens his eyes. The boy's mouth forms a wide "O," and his eyes look like they're going to pop out of their sockets. The boy takes another huge, rasping breath and then emits a keening, high-pitched whine.

"Son! Son!" the man yells. "Oh my good! Russ! Son!"

Russ breathes in-and-out, then in-and-out, then in-and-out a third time. His color starts to return to normal. Everyone—the father, the girl, Peter, Jasmine—everyone cries, but now they cry tears of relief.

It takes them a while to pull themselves together. Eventually, Peter looks around and asks himself who these people are and just what in the System they're doing there.

The boy is now breathing regularly. He says, "Daddy, I'm cold."

The father takes Russ into his arms and gently lays him on Jasmine's bunk. He removes the rest of Russ's pressure suit and pulls a blanket over him while Jasmine fetches him water.

"Spence," she says, "rest for a while, and I'll sit with Russ."

Spence nods and grabs her hand. He kisses it several times. "Thank you, thank you! You don't even know us. I can hardly believe you came for us."

She squeezes his arm and sits down on her bunk to tend to Russ.

A hard poke on the shoulder draws Peter's attention away from Jasmine, Spence, and Russ. He turns to find the girl facing him, a look of extreme impatience scrawled across her face. "Mister," she says, "we gotta get outta here. Like *fast.*"

"She's right," Jasmine says. "Kistrob, Concourse Six, left rear service garage." She glances at the girl. "Fast."

Peter climbs into the driving compartment and slides into the driver's seat. The girl sits down in the passenger seat and begins extricating herself from the rest of her pressure suit. He sets the MGPS to Kistrob, Concourse

Six, but they're beyond the autodrive zone. So he begins to freedrive them southward, worrying that he'll soon have to try to freedrive in the dark.

He shouts over his shoulder, "Soph—Jasmine, I mean—whoever you are, dammit!" He takes a breath. "You freedrove us up here. How long until we hit the autodrive zone?"

"I freedrove thirty kay!" she says, still sitting on her bunk comforting the boy. She calls out a code that will get them through the fences.

He grimaces and steers. *Until the autodrive indicator lights up, I'll just freedrive us down Gordii as fast as I safely can.* After one or two kilometers, Peter spares a glance at the girl. As gently as he can, he says, "I'm Peter. What's your name?"

"I'm Veronica."

"That's a nice name."

"I know what the name 'Peter' means."

"Do you?" His eyes remain fixed on the road. "That's super. What does it mean, then, Veronica?"

"It means *falqin' slow*, that's what it means! Let me falqin' drive!"

"Wha—young lady, who taught you to talk like that? You—"

"All right, dude, all right. Just let me drive!"

"Veronica!" scolds Spence. He pokes his head into the driving compartment. "Precious. Language."

Veronica crosses her arms and rolls her eyes.

Spence peers at Peter, who's steering stiffly. "Sir, she's a good freedriver. I taught her myself back home."

"I suppose you think I'm driving too slowly, too."

"We've gotta get away from here as fast as we can."

Spence and Veronica both stare at Peter.

"Fine," he mutters.

Veronica claps her hands in excitement as Peter climbs out of the compartment. She slides into the driver's seat, and the landhog immediately lurches with sudden acceleration. Peter and Spence both stumble backward and brace themselves against the table in the galley.

"This is a rental!" hollers Peter toward the driving compartment. "We have to pay for any dings, you know!"

A petite hand flashes a thumbs-up in the doorway and withdraws. Peter feels another lurch of acceleration. "Great," he mutters. He turns and catches Jasmine looking at him. Her eyes are puffy, but her lips reveal the hint of a smile. She quickly looks down at the boy and speaks to him in a low voice. Pressing her back against the end of the sleeping nook, she puts her hands on his legs to steady him.

Spence sits down at the table, holding onto its edges to brace himself against the bumping of the landhog. Peter remains standing in the galley, tightly gripping a handrail. As they race down the winding road, the setting sun's last pink rays lance through the driving compartment's windows and fall across Peter's frame.

Trying to calm himself, he takes several deep breaths: in-and-out, in-and-out. His eyes are drawn to Spence, who is rubbing his own temples.

We're rescuing these children of God, Peter thinks. *We're helping these people who, like me, are imperfect but beloved temples of God's deep presence.*

A memory flashes in his mind. All eyes in the chapel are turned toward Bishop Priscilla as she recites words from the old gospel codex with the shiny cross on its cover. ". . .Truly I tell you, just as you did it to one of the least of these who are members of my family, you did it to me." She nods at Peter.

Peter shakes his head and stares toward the front windows. *Is it true?*

No sooner does he ask himself this question than, for just a moment, something fills him. Fills him . . . or empties him. Or *opens* him:

A presence or a promise—an invitation, or
A silence that holds every sound, or
A piercing freshness—a throbbing beauty, or
A realm of possibility perpendicular to the horizon of day-to-
    day life, or
A lush, dark forest glade where one encounters one's beloved, or
A glimpse of an all-encompassing wholeness.

Words simply cannot describe the taste of that moment—more a feeling than an idea, but also more than just a feeling. But if Peter had to use words—

My soul, intimately touched.

Several minutes later, Peter carefully navigates himself to the bunk where Russ lies. The boy is quiet for the moment, but his eyes dart all around. Peter leans in toward him, gripping a handrail.

"Are you doing okay, Russ?"

The boy nods.

"I need to talk with your helper here. Is it okay if she comes with me for a minute?"

Russ nods again.

Peter turns to her and says, "If you don't mind."

She nods wordlessly.

Peter says to Spence, "We'll be in the washroom for a few minutes."

"Er, sure," Spence says. "I'll keep an eye on Russ. Be careful walking around back there." As he says this, the landhog hits another nasty bump—probably a billion-year-old rock now splintered into bits. Peter can tell that nothing is going to slow Veronica down.

He leads the way into the washroom and shuts the door behind them. He stares at the floor. Even with the landhog bumping around, it must be apparent to her that his hands are shaking on the handrails.

Before he can say anything, she says, "You must learn the truth, which I should have told you sooner. I'm sorry, I wanted you simply to experience what was happening today, rather than tell you all about it beforehand. But I obviously underestimated the practical difficulties . . . I misjudged some of the human choices to be made." She takes a ragged breath. "As you've already guessed, our new friends are refugees from the compound. Spence is Alma's brother."

"Alma? Alma the catechumen?"

"Yes."

He stares at her in silence.

"The pressure suits Spence and the children stole had just enough air for them to hike out to where we were, far enough away from the compound not to be detected." She shakes her head. "Or, at least, we weren't supposed to be. I didn't know Fr—the security guard was going to show up. He was supposed to be on a different route.

"If he had called in backup, an assault team would have shown up there." She inclines her head toward the front of the landhog. "Peter, all three of them would be dead. They would have let the whole family suffocate out on the surface. It's happened before."

Peter slowly shakes his head from side to side.

"At the place where we're going in Kistrob, there is an 'underground railroad' of sorts," she continues. "It's where I would have taken the Isnotist boy. Since he hadn't actually hurt anyone, I'm sure they would have agreed to help sort him out. Anyway, friends in this 'underground railroad' have forged movement credentials for Spence and his family so that they will be free to travel.

"I had hoped you might offer to take them back to Grace. Once they get off Meres, it should be safe for them to give public testimony about the abuse at the Gordii compound. I asked Alma to stay behind in Sanef to begin making arrangements."

He opens his mouth, but no words come out.

"I am sorry, dear Peter." A single tear rolls down her cheek. "Someday, you will understand why I had no choice but to—"

"*Stop! Just stop!*" he yells.

She falls silent and stares at his contorted face.

He squats all the way down—hardly a straightforward maneuver as they bump around the tiny washroom. Placing his hands on the floor for stability, he leans forward and kisses Sophia's feet, again and again.

"What are you doing?"

He continues several moments longer and then carefully lifts himself up. He cries, "Don't apologize to me! *Forgive* me!

"Forgive me for betraying you in your suffering. I was so selfish—so stupid! But I finally realized the truth of what you did, even before you told me the details. What you did and why you did it. My God, what it must have *cost* you."

Her lip quivers.

"I was standing there just now, and I felt as if an intimate touch caressed my soul. And I forgot my jealousy and pain. I forgot myself. I realized I had it all wrong.

"I didn't understand what you were offering me. I wanted to possess you, to hoard your love as if it were scarce. I'm so sorry." Peter reaches into a pocket and pulls out the metal keys. He places them in her palm.

Sophia sniffs and wipes moisture from her cheek. She slides one key off the antique keychain and carefully places it in the front pocket of Peter's jumpsuit, putting the other key in her own pocket. She then leans in toward Peter, puts her lips to his ear, and, as softly as the gentlest Merian breeze, whispers:

> *I Am*
> *the Ongoing Unfolding*
> *of the One Life.*

She pulls him close in a sudden, muscular hug. As they press into a corner of the shaking washroom for stability, Peter returns her hug with all his strength.

A minute passes, and he loosens his hold on her and takes a step back to see her face. "'The ongoing unfolding of the one life'? I'm not sure I understand. What does that mean, exactly? What—"

The landhog hits an enormous bump. Peter lifts several centimeters off the floor and collides with the washroom ceiling. A bright light explodes inside his forehead.

The wind is crisp and cold. It whips through Peter's hair. He's walking along a narrow, twisting path at a slow and steady pace. Back and forth. Inward toward the center, then outward toward the edge. A rabbit hops across his path and out of sight.

He stops.

Where am I?

He looks up from the stone path beneath his feet. The velvet black sky brims over with stars. They burn as brightly as they did when Peter viewed them from space. But Peter is in no spacecraft.

He rotates in a full circle, surveying his surroundings. He's standing on a mountain—on its summit, a flat expanse no more than a stone's throw across. On all sides, the ground falls away from him, descending steeply into the reds and pinks of the Merian landscape far below. He's surprised at how far he can see, perhaps hundreds of kilometers across the planet's stark plains. In the distance, pink sandstorms swirl below his feet.

I'm above the atmosphere. This summit is in space! He touches his cheek. *No suit. No mesh. How is it that I'm breathing?* He's not afraid, though. He's just longing for the center.

"Where am I?" he calls out. He can see nothing beyond his summit, the distant plains, and the brightness of the stars. Yet his voice echoes.

> *Where am I?*
>   *Where am I?*
>   *Where   am   I?*

He shrugs and continues walking the winding cruciform path beneath his feet.

A sonorous, masculine-sounding voice says:

> *Hear me, beloved. No one comes to the One Life*
> *except through me.*

Simultaneously, a familiar feminine-sounding voice says:

> *Hear me, beloved. No one dances within the One Life*
> *except with me.*

The words do not echo—they reveal themselves in crystalline clarity. They sound from every direction beyond Peter's ears and seemingly within them, too. What's more, he can see the words in his mind's eye as if they floated in front of him. As they form, the two voices resonate in sublime combination, their harmonies caressing in an interpenetrating rhythm. Just hearing the sound leaves a salty sweetness on Peter's tongue.

He stops for a moment and takes deep breaths of air that should not be there. He calls out again, this time asking, "Who are you?"

In harmony, the two voices reply:

> *I am who I am.*

Then the feminine-sounding voice says:

> *He is the Word, the Pattern and Shape of the One Life,*
> > *unblunting dagger sculpting reality,*
> > *carving verity out of illusion, freedom out of captivity.*
> *He reveals the universal blueprint of the divine flow,*
> > *of life's incarnation into time,*
> > *of incarnate life's magnificent creativity,*
> > *of its limits, suffering, and sacrifice,*
> > *of its resurrection into eternity.*
> *He is*
> > *the bush that burns but is not consumed,*
> > *unchanging truth you have heard,*
> > *deep roots to anchor a soul.*

Then the masculine-sounding voice says:

> *She is the Breath, the Ongoing Unfolding of the One Life,*
> > *who weaves worlds of being and communion,*
> > *quarrying the depths of what-may-be.*
> *She evades your grasp only to seize you in hers,*
> > *intimately touching your soul in inscrutable ways*
> > *from the hidden holy corners of your interior mansion*
> > *as she blossoms everywhere, dances, demands, and laughs,*
> > *again birthing the new, the unexpected, the unimaginable.*
> *She is*
> > *the flame ardently leaping from the bush,*
> > *evolving wisdom who offers you her kiss,*
> > *strong wings to give a soul flight.*

"And the One Life?" whispers Peter as he walks the pattern. "What is the One Life?" The edge of a fiery sphere peeks over the planet's distant horizon, and sunlight spills onto Peter's path.

In harmony, the two voices reply:

> *The One Life is, let's say, both ocean and drop, yet more,*
> > *is secret of secrets, presence to presence, grace for grace,*
> > *ever all-powerfully self-humbling in overspilling joy.*

> *The One Life loves more tenderly than a parent,*
> > *looms larger than the cosmos, throbs closer than your own*
> > *pulse, crying "I am!" in the most ordinary of creatures,*
> > *and cascades undammed by your concepts or agenda, as*
> > *your trash, invisibly to closed pupils, shimmers diamond.*
> *The One Life is wholeness, is*
> > *steady actuality in solidly dependable frolic—unsplit:*
> > *unsplit between time and eternity, between "you" and "I,"*
> > *between unchanging truth and evolving wisdom.*

Peter keeps walking. His breaths are coming rapidly, and he can no longer speak. He's so close to the labyrinth's center.

The feminine-sounding voice says:

> *You glorify the One Life when you root your soul in*
> *him:*
> *the Pattern and Shape of the One Life,*
> *called the Word or the Christ,*
> *whom you have beheld in Jesus.*

The masculine-sounding voice says:

> *You glorify the One Life when your soul takes flight with*
> *her:*
> *the Ongoing Unfolding of the One Life,*
> *called the Breath or the Holy Spirit,*
> *whom you have beheld in Sophia.*

Peter reaches the center, lifts his hands to the stars . . .
> . . . and wakes in her arms.

∽

A fleeting eternity later, Sophia and Peter step out of the washroom, their exhausted faces puffy from laughing and crying. The landhog now bumps noticeably less—Veronica has gotten them back to the trunk road in record time. A canvas of stars shimmers through the front windows.

Russ, for his part, is already back in action. He squats on Sophia's bunk and shoots backward with his fingers, slaying innumerable imaginary pursuers. Sound effects accompany each shot. "Pyew! Pyew!"

Spence squints at Peter's forehead. "Nasty bruise," he says over the sound of pretend weapons fire.

Peter smiles. "It's fine."

"All right," replies Spence. "Anyway, Veronica says a message came through to your vehicle while you were—er, back there." He raises an eyebrow. "Said it's from a prisoner at the Kistrob federal penitentiary. His, uh, name . . . ." He turns and hollers toward the driving compartment: "Precious! What was that guy's name?"

"Something like *Boo-vee*," she calls back.

"Something like Boo-vee," Spence repeats. "We don't know what it's about."

Peter glances at Sophia, and she gives him an encouraging nod.

"Thank you," Peter says as he moves toward the driving compartment. "It's from someone who needs to talk with a pastor."

"Pyew! Pyew! *Pyew!*"

"Russ, settle down," Spence says. "You need to rest."

"Pyew! *Zoom! Bang!*"

As Peter slides by, Spence raises his voice: "Lazarus Dale! Settle down."

"Huh? Uh, sorry, Daddy."

Peter does an about-face. "Your son's first name is *Lazarus*?"

"Yes," says Spence. "Russ is short for Lazarus. We named him after his grandfather."

Peter stares at Russ. "Spence, do you know where that name comes from?"

"I accessed once that it means *zombie*!" yells Veronica, listening from the driving compartment. "Bubbie's a little zombie!"

Ignoring her, Spence shakes his head and answers Peter's question. "No. Is it from a story?"

Peter and Sophia nod in unison. Little Lazarus is now listening closely. Spence looks into the eyes of his savior and says, "Please tell us the story."

~

Frank steps into his tiny, windowless quarters. Its walls vibrate almost imperceptibly with the distant throb of tovramium processing. He heaves himself onto his bed and stretches.

That slut was hot, oh man. He remembers telling himself she was a seven or a seven point five, but in his memory, she now feels more like a nine or a nine point five. He keeps trying to picture different parts of her body. Weirdly, nothing will stick in his head.

He sighs. *Definitely wasn't expecting to get real-world action today. It all happened so fast.* Frank peers at his belly. He has enough self-awareness to realize a feme like that would not have submitted to him if she hadn't been desperate. *She was up to something out there. Well, tit for tat, that's the way of the worlds. Or in this case, tit for tit.* He grins.

As much as Frank tries to focus on the memory of her body, it's her words that keep returning to him, unbidden. Without intending it, he spent most of the drive back to headquarters thinking about what she said to him. No one has ever spoken to him like that before.

He shakes his head. Kicking off his shoes, he gets comfortable and raises his hand to his temple to get back into *Olympia's Mount* where he left off that morning.

A "doop deep" and a bang on the door interrupt him.

"Frankie. Francophone! FRANKENSTEIN!"

Falq.

Frank pulls himself up and opens his door. His boss is standing there with his arm around the waist of his toy-of-the-week. She wears a skintite that barely covers anything. The boss is too busy staring down at the feme to look at Frank, so Frank has an opening to take a look, too.

She has a thin, nubile figure. *Well, all the refugees are thin.* Nice, long legs. A sweet young thing—but just a little scrap compared to Frank's sexy feme in the desert. Yet it's surprisingly easy to resist the urge to brag. *I'd be unbelievably falqed if anyone found out I didn't report a trespass.*

"Frankfurter, I need you on headcount duty at twenty-fifteen. You know, the division head's got to make sure we keep track of how many push through the mesh." He looks at Frank long enough to stick out his tongue as if he were suffocating. "I'd do it," he says, "but I've got a very special date." He winks at the feme and pinches her rear. She flinches and then smiles nervously.

"You bet, boss," Frank says.

His boss is already leading the feme toward his quarters. Frank steps out into the hallway and gazes at her. She looks back, and her gaze connects with Frank's. He finds himself staring into her sunken eyes,

her desperate
clever
vulnerable
living
eyes. Looking into his.

They are the eyes of the feme in the desert
as surely as if *she* stood in that gray hallway.

They are his *own* eyes
as if they stared back at him from a mirror.

Then Frank's boss pulls the feme into his room, and she's gone, leaving Frank standing in the hallway alone. He places a hand against a wall, trying to rid himself of his unprecedented feeling of vertigo. Shaken, he steps back into his room and closes the door.

He takes a ragged breath and sits back down on his bed. Unsure of himself, he says aloud, to no one, "I've got twenty minutes." He raises his hand to his temple to get back into his stim.

Then he stops. He lowers his hand and looks in the direction of the hallway. For the first time ever, he wonders how it would feel to be one of the refugees.

Epilogue

Russ just won't stop talking about the new play structure. "Doesn't it look like a big spiderweb?" he asks. He's hanging upside down from his knees.

"Eyew." Jean-Pierre Bouville shivers. "Quit saying that."

Russ giggles. "Sorry. It definitely does *not* look like a spiderweb at all, okay? Now, are you gonna climb on it or not?"

Jean-Pierre shakes his head. "I'm too old for that. And too heavy."

"Ppth. Aren't you pretty much Earth-adjusted now? You walked all the way to the Embarcadero the other day."

"With my body braces. I still feel heavy."

"That must make you miss home."

"No."

Russ continues to clamber around in the webbing while Jean-Pierre looks on in silence. Three adults walk the outdoor labyrinth while several others converse in the courtyard. Friendly laughter ricochets between the walls of the cathedral and the parish hall. Jean-Pierre occasionally cranes his neck to take a vertiginous look at the endlessly tall towers which dominate the alien city. The glare of reflected sunlight makes his eyes water.

Russ climbs down from the play structure and holds out a finger. "Look what I found."

Jean-Pierre jerks back. "What's your obsession with dangerous insects?"

"It's not dangerous!"

"It's bright orange. It's probably poisonous."

Russ sighs deeply and speaks as if instructing a five-year-old. "Spiders aren't insects, and ladybugs aren't poisonous." He touches his finger to Jean-Pierre's hand and, with some gentle prodding, transfers the ladybug onto it.

"So many crawly creatures on Earth," Jean-Pierre mumbles. He holds his hand away from his body and stares intently at the insect.

Spence emerges from the parish hall and squints in the sunlight. "Son," he calls. "It's almost time to go."

"Come say hi to Daddy," Russ tells Jean-Pierre.

Jean-Pierre follows Russ while distractedly studying the ladybug's energetic exploration of his hand. It never stops to rest. *Like Russ.* The feeling of an insect crawling across his skin makes him shiver again.

Spence surveys Jean-Pierre's face and asks, "How are you today?"

Jean-Pierre gently blows on the ladybug and watches it fly away. The distraction allows him to avoid looking Spence in the eye. "Fine," Jean-Pierre says. "Whatever else, every day I thank—well, God or whatever—that I didn't get my brains fried. I suppose I would have deserved it, but still, I'm glad it didn't happen that way."

Spence gingerly pats the teenager on the shoulder. "I know what it's like to be lost, disconnected—to want to hurt yourself or others. Sophia understands, too." Spence crosses himself. "That's why she worked so hard with Kistrob's underground railroad to get you here."

"And Bishop Peter." Saying his name brings a glimmer to Jean-Pierre's eyes. "He helped, too."

"Yes, and Bishop Peter, too." Spence turns to Russ. "We'd better get ready before Veronica starts hollering at us. The one today is gonna be a big one, so—"

Russ grins. "I know, I know. Look sad!"

"I'm not asking you to pretend. I just want you to remember how sad you really were at the compound. And remember the kids who are still trapped at places like that."

"I'm sorry. It really is so sad. And mean."

"Dorcas told me an important official from the Sanef government will be on the netcast with us. The publicity is making the politicians take notice. Some nations are saying they might sanction the ones who are mistreating refugees."

"I'll believe it when I see it," says Jean-Pierre without emotion. "We all know the cartels control the governments. And they don't care who's suffering."

Spence straightens. "I don't understand all the politics stuff. But Veronica and Russ and I will keep telling our story to anyone who'll listen. Sophia seems to think it will make a difference."

Jean-Pierre shrugs.

"Speaking of Sophia, she's gonna meet us in just a few minutes. Son, go on and get changed."

Russ nods at his father and waves goodbye to Jean-Pierre. Spence pats Jean-Pierre on the shoulder once more and follows Russ inside.

Jean-Pierre checks the time. He still has twenty minutes to kill before lunch with his counselor and Bishop Peter. He climbs the stairs up to the cathedral entrance and steps through the Ghiberti Doors. He hasn't spent much time in the church itself, but something, perhaps boredom, draws him in that day.

A wrinkled, gray-haired woman straightens cushions arrayed in a semicircle around the indoor labyrinth. Jean-Pierre guesses there are a hundred twenty, a hundred forty. The woman looks up when he walks in. "I'm afraid Sophia is scheduled to go on a netcast in a little while," she says. "Her lesson will be at fifteen today."

"I know. I mean, I didn't come for the lesson. I'm just, um, hanging out."

The woman's eyes narrow. "You're the young man from Kistrob."

He feels his cheeks grow warm. "They just—um—found me in Kistrob. I grew up in a mining village in north Amazonis. My name is Jean-Pierre."

"My name is Junia. I'm sorry I didn't remember yours, Jean-Pierre. We have so many new people in the church now." She stares at the sea of cushions. "I'm used to knowing everything that's happening with everyone, and now I'm having a hard time keeping up."

Jean-Pierre nods, but he isn't looking at Junia. His eyes lift from the cushions to the high altar.

"Don't mind me," Junia says. "If you want to go up there and pray, go ahead."

"Pray? Uh, sure. I'll just—do that. Thanks."

Jean-Pierre ambles toward the high altar. As he does, he peers at the riotously colorful stained glass windows all around him. He's seen them before, but this is the first time he gives them a careful examination. Names are conveniently etched into the glass next to many of the figures.

"Saint Mary Magdalene" has the best hair, he thinks, *but "Saint Martin of Tours" has the most kickass sword. I bet "Saint Francis of Assisi" wishes he could borrow the sword to shoo away all those stupid birds hanging around him.*

When Jean-Pierre reaches the stone railing that encircles the high altar, he stops and stares at it. After several seconds, he kneels down and leans against it.

Pray? Like, say words here, crouched down on my knees? Then what? Start pretending to drink blood!? The thought of blood threatens to bring up memories too painful to dwell on without inviting nausea.

Jean-Pierre glances over his shoulder and sees that the lady stepped out, leaving him all alone in the quiet cathedral. Soft snatches of birdsong drift in through the main entrance. He can feel, more than hear, the low throb of activity on the cathedral grounds and in the city around him. It's somehow soothing to abide in an oasis of stillness surrounded by a hum of liveliness. His own breathing creates the loudest sound in his ears.

In. Out. In. Out. In. Out.

To breathe. To want to breathe. To want to live!

He felt like he would suffocate the first time he tried to walk in the Earth g. It was as if every part of his body had weights strapped to it. Bishop Peter and Sophia held him up, one at each arm. Staggering beneath the too-hot, too-bright sun, he realized he had never before felt people bear him up like that. The physical sensation of being surrounded with support was as terrifyingly alien as Earth's pull. And wonderful.

To want to live. To want to be connected to others.

In. Out. In. Out. In. Out.

To want to be connected to others. To want to be a part of something lasting.

He lifts his eyes to the altar table. A row of three mottled-white granite plinths support a tabletop made from one long, heavy slab of polished redwood. On the table, tiny flames burn atop the long wax tubes the Christians like so much, their delicacy contrasting with the table's mass. For a moment, the steadfast slab of redwood feels like the most solid thing in the universe.

Jean-Pierre shakes his head and, for the first time in ages, smiles broadly. *What the hell. Maybe I'll drink the blood sometime.*

Appendix

Five Prayers

HOLY, LOVING, LOVELY GOD:
Let us glorify and adore you, great mystery.
Sublime father, mother, teacher, lover, friend, deepest self,
    you are ever present with us and in us.
If it is your will:
    grace us with another day,
    give us passionate gratitude for your abundance,
    heal our desperate brokenness,
    send us the humiliations that will grow our souls,
    open us to serve as conduits of your grace, and
    help us to see you in all;
So that we may incarnate your love.
Amen.

(Pages 93–94)

ALMIGHTY GOD OF VAST ABUNDANCE:
Tireless one, in freedom and joy
    you cultivate orchards of unimaginable variety.
Behold, you have said *yes* to every imperfect existing thing.
I give thanks that you chose even me, a soul-broken orphan.
Majesty beyond all glory! Artist of novelty!
We suckle at your breasts,
    your worlds without end.
Amen.

(Page 143)

ALL-VULNERABLE GOD OF DEEP PRESENCE:
In your merciful desire to redeem us from nothingness,
    you choose to sojourn within the limits of mortal existence.
Glory to you, consciousness within all beings, deepest me!
When I hate, I hate you; when I eat, I eat your flesh.
You have allowed yourself to be bound and beaten,
    cut and raped and broken—with me and in me.
Before Abraham was, I Am.
Amen.

                                                    (Page 160)

ALL-EMBRACING GOD OF INCARNATE LOVE:
You patiently purify our longing,
    toppling our idols of success and false certitude
    and gracing us lovingly with glimpses of your wholeness.
Help me to put away my infantile fears and appetites.
Strangle my blinding, grinding over-and-against-ness and
    my thirst to be separate and special and admired.
Entangle my most passionate desire with your own.
Amen.

                                                    (Page 169)

UNFATHOMABLE LIVING GOD:
Have mercy on the wretched who presume to write such things, on the fools
    who sweat to entomb your dynamic wisdom in a mausoleum of words.
Just when you appear secure, just when your epitaph is composed,
    the stone rolls away and you dance out of sight,
    because you mightily eclipse every thought and each grinding ax.
Beloved, give us to taste your reality beyond all words,
    so much as we can endure.
Amen.

Discussion Guide

This guide comprises twenty questions which may facilitate group discussion or individual reflection. It includes spoilers, so you should read it only after you have read the novel. The questions are divided among four interrelated themes: Church, Metaphysics and Theodicy, Theology, and Spiritual Growth. May they enrich your journey into the perennial wisdom at the heart of the Christian good news.

– J.F.A.

Church

1. In the novel's fictional future, the entire Christian religion has dwindled to less than a dozen members. Have you ever been part of a religion, denomination, or congregation that felt as if it were dying? If so, how has this affected your spirituality?

2. Peter inherits titles representing all major branches of the Christian church, including Orthodox, Catholic, Anglican, Protestant, Evangelical, and Pentecostal. (See pages 39–40.) Can you imagine a "Grand Reunification" of Christianity happening in real life? If it were possible, would it be desirable?

3. In Chapter 16, Peter ponders the fact that many diverse perspectives have been considered Christian. (See pages 153–154.) Given the many differing interpretations of Christianity (or any religion), what criteria can one use to differentiate between true, healthy religion and self-serving cultural myths?

4. Sophia tells Peter that it is past time for the Christian church as a whole to step into the "afternoon" of faith, where churches are "not just clubs

or clans or places that teach mere beliefs, but schools of love." (Page 188.) Is your church or spiritual community a "school of love"? How could it become more of one?

5. When Sophia and Peter visit the crypt in Chapter 4, she hands him several books to read (pages 38–39). Given Peter's struggles to lead the church at that time, what book(s) would *you* have handed him?

Metaphysics and Theodicy

6. Sophia's teachings delve into questions of metaphysics: the branch of philosophy concerned with the fundamental nature of reality, including aspects of reality that cannot be scientifically tested. In your view, what is the proper role of metaphysics in religion? Are there things which cannot be scientifically tested but which you nevertheless hold to be true?

7. The Denunciators (or "nuns") deny all "metafiz" and feel that existence has no meaning. Is the novel's depiction of the "nuns" fair? Has there ever been a time when you felt the way the "nuns" do?

8. While discussing God's "vast abundance," Sophia compares the universe (or multiverse) to a huge apple orchard. (Pages 143–145.) Might humanity be just one (precious, unique) branch in a vast orchard of God's abundant, eternally unfolding creation? How does this possibility make you feel?

9. Sophia teaches that God chooses to empty Godself into "deep presence," to "exult and suffer with and within us." (See pages 160–163.) Using the gendered language of his time, Thomas Merton expressed it this way: "The truth I must love in my brother is God Himself, living in him." Is it possible that every creature's own "I am" is the great I Am (see Exodus 3:14)? If so, how might such a truth affect your relationships with other living creatures?

10. If God is good and all-powerful, why does God allow evil and suffering? How, if at all, has the novel shaped your thinking about how to respond to this question?

Theology

11. In today's world, can Christians work effectively for healing and wholeness while continuing to visualize God in exclusively masculine terms? Why or why not?

12. Is God always the same, or does God's life unfold in some way? Explain your answer.

13. According to Sophia, Jesus' crucifixion reveals God's choice to participate vulnerably in suffering out of love for God's creatures. (See page 162.) Enacting an all-too-prevalent pattern of objectifying women, Frank's sexual exploitation of Sophia may feel to us like its own grotesque and disturbing kind of crucifixion. How do you respond to the choice Sophia made?

14. Sophia says (at page 171) that God was *not* "sitting up in heaven waiting for a debt to be paid in blood" by Jesus. (In other words, she rejects the "satisfaction theory of the Atonement" first promoted by Anselm of Canterbury eleven centuries after Christ.) What do you think about Sophia's alternative explanation for why Jesus came? If she is correct, what happens to the conceit that "only Christians can go to heaven"?

15. After moving through cycles of faith and doubt, Peter experiences a poetic vision of the Holy Trinity which weaves together several of the novel's themes and questions. Take some time to re-read pages 206–209 and meditate on this vision of God. How, if at all, does it speak to your heart and mind?

Spiritual Growth

16. Sophia speaks of "chronic compulsions." (See pages 136–137.) Is there a traditional Christian word that means essentially the same thing? (Hint: It has three letters.) Why do you think Sophia chooses the term she does?

17. Recall a time when you felt "the touch of a beauty beyond words." (Page 137.) What, if any, spiritual meaning did it have for you?

18. Peter's relationship with Sophia includes an erotic element. In real life, some saints and mystics, such as Mechthild of Magdeburg and John of the Cross, have described encountering God as a divine lover who seduced their souls. What is the healthy and proper role of erotic energy in the spiritual life?

19. Spiritual teaching sometimes makes use of ambiguity or seeming paradox—for example, when Sophia teaches that God can be *both* almighty *and* all-vulnerable. Indeed, the central doctrines of Christianity are built on the principle of "both/and." (The Holy Trinity is *both* three *and* one. Christ is *both* fully human *and* fully divine. We are *both* God's beloved children *and* in need of redemption. The list could go on.) What role, if any, does "both/and" thinking play in your spiritual life?

20. Sophia teaches that every person is "a precious child of God" no matter what has happened to them or what they have done. (Page 92.) Is Frank a precious child of God?